SYMPATHY FOR THE DEVIL

SYMPATHY FOR THE DEVIL

UNIVERSITY BOOK ONE

TERRENCE MCCAULEY

ROUGH
EDGES
PRESS

Sympathy for the Devil
Paperback Edition
© Copyright 2021 (As Revised) Terrence McCauley

Rough Edges Press
An Imprint of Wolfpack Publishing
5130 S. Fort Apache Rd. 215-380
Las Vegas, NV 89148

roughedgespress.com

eBook ISBN 978-1-68549-012-6
Paperback ISBN 978-1-68549-013-3

THE MAN who called himself James Hicks checked his watch when he reached the corner of Forty-second and Lexington. It was just past eleven in the morning. More than an hour before he was scheduled to ruin a man's life.

And plenty of time to smoke a cigar.

He braced himself against a sharp wind as he crossed Forty-second Street. A cold humidity had settled in over Manhattan and constant weather alerts on phones and weather apps had whipped New Yorkers into a frenzy over the coming storm. The fore-casters hawked it as 'The Big One' and 'Snowmaged-don'. A few had even trotted out the ever popular 'Snowpacalypse'. The experts were predicting over two feet of snow with high winds and freezing temperatures for the next few days. A single flake hadn't even fallen yet, so it was too early to call it the 'Storm of the Centu-ry', but Hicks knew the media was building up to it.

The coverage of the event was more predictable than the weather these days.

Based on the data that Hicks had been able to see via the University's OMNI satellite array, it looked like only about a foot of snow would hit the island; with wind and ice being more problematic than the snow itself.

He could remember a time not too long ago when New Yorkers would barely notice eight inches of snow, but panic was en vogue in the post-9/11 world where preparation was more important than execution.

Hicks understood why meteorologists exaggerated snowfall predictions. They were covering themselves in case they were wrong. If storm was a little worse than they had predicted, they would be close enough to claim accuracy. If the snowfall was a little less, then everyone was too relieved about dodging a catastrophe to blame the forecasters and the whole matter was quickly forgotten as everyone went back to their lives.

In some ways, Hicks was a forecaster in his own right. Though he didn't have the luxury of seeing an approaching storm on a radar map and waiting to see what happened. He was paid to stop the storm from forming in the first place. And when he did his job, the radar screens remained clear.

In his line of work, small mistakes were forgotten, and big mistakes got you killed. Such harsh, immutable constants brought a certain resignation to Hicks' life that he found almost peaceful. Danger could be something he could rely on– even use to his advantage – once he knew it was always there.

Hicks crossed Forty-second Street and headed for the concrete ashtrays standing in the alcove of the

Altria Building across from Grand Central Terminal. There were a few cigar stores in the area where he could smoke indoors in warm comfort. Maybe stir up some conversation with his fellow smokers on such a cold and blustery day.

But Hicks didn't want comfort and he certainly didn't want conversation. Conversations made you memorable and his business was all about blending in. He needed the cold air to keep him sharp, especially before he was about to roll up on a new Asset in an hour or so.

He stood out of the wind in the outdoor alcove of the Altria building and lit his cigar. It wasn't a cheap cigar, but far from the most expensive stick on the market. There was a time for savoring good tobacco and now wasn't it. The cigar was merely a tool to help him stay focused and calm while killing time before his appointment.

He took a deep puff on the cigar and watched the smoke filter out through his nose. It was an odd business he had chosen. The odd organization he worked for that had been created by an executive order during the Eisenhower Administration with one unique mission: to operate outside the Military Industrial Complex. To operate outside the official intelligence community to protect the United States and its interests at all costs. No federal oversight. No pesky laws to worry about. No federal funding, either, which meant the University had to find its own way to finance itself. That meant the organization raised funds in often unsavory ways, but at an obscene profit.

Hicks let out a long breath before taking another pull on his cigar. For although he had turned hundreds of regular civilians into Assets – a process the University called 'recruiting' -Hicks still believed that changing a person's life forever deserved some pause.

Assets were recruited because they could provide the University with information or options it required for a particular reason. Most of his colleagues didn't give much thought about the Assets they recruited into the University system. They focused their efforts on researching the right prospect to turn. They dug deep into the person's past for that one knife they could hold to their throat to make them comply.

Everyone had something to hide. Past offenses and indiscretions they didn't want to come to light. Current mistakes that could get them fired or ruin their marriage. Hicks found the threat of imprisonment worked best. Not everyone liked their spouse or their job and often saw ruination as a chance for a new beginning. But prison? Well, everyone was afraid of prison. Turning a criminal always made him feel a bit less guilty about the process, which was why this afternoon's efforts didn't bother him at all.

Hicks and his colleagues used OMNI's artificial intelligence technology to analyze every aspect of a potential Asset's personality to determine whether or not he or she could withstand the passive pressures of the University's constant influence in their lives.

If they passed, an Office Head like Hicks would approach the prospect, flip them, and put them to work for the University. An Asset didn't know what the University was and certainly didn't know they served its purposes. All they knew was that a stranger had entered their lives with the power to ruin it at any time.

If an Asset cracked and killed themselves or had to

be 'expelled' – the University term for eliminated, OMNI automatically changed its parameters to account for the shortcomings in the analysis model. A person's destruction was reduced to a series of ones and zeroes in the network's algorithm. It was all as simple – and inhumane – as that.

Hicks took another drag on his cigar as he pondered what a strange and wonderful invention OMNI had been. The Optimized Mechanical and Network Integration protocol. The name was a relic from the University's colorful history that began prior to the Second World War. The organization had been a quasi-Federal entity back then and one of the first of its kind to embrace computers after the war. That decision gave them a marked advantage over their other official and well- known counterparts that often sported three initials. In fact, OMNI had formed the basis of what ultimately became known as the internet.

OMNI's name might be outdated, but its reach and power only improved as technology grew in the decades since. The rise of the digital world expanded its power exponentially. When new staff members asked what OMNI could do, the simplest and most accurate reply was 'Everything'. Hicks didn't understand how it all worked himself but knew that any device online was subject to OMNI infiltration.

But as impressive a tool as OMNI might be, Hicks had been running Assets long enough to know human beings never fit neatly into a computer program. Turning an Asset was like bringing home a stray dog from an animal shelter. They found themselves in a strange, new environment that overlapped every aspect of their lives, which often went against their nature.

Their liberty was limited, and when Hicks called, they were expected to jump. Most accepted the leash. Some did not.

OMNI constantly scrutinized an Asset's digital footprint. Their work and personal devices, banking records and social networks. It listened to their conversations, emails, and texts. It saw what they posted online and what they read. It knew where they were at all times. It even knew how warm or cold it was in their house. The system did not have to hack into someone's life. It was invited and gladly.

An Asset's new friends and business associates were automatically scrutinized to see if they might also serve the University's mission or pose a threat to it.

If the Asset played along and did what was asked of them, they were rewarded with information OMNI provided to help them get rich. If they refused or got cute or threatened to go public, Hicks ruined the life they had spent so long building.

If the offense was serious enough, they were 'Expelled'. They weren't simply thrown out of the University system. They usually got a bullet to the brain.

From the shelter of the high alcove, Hicks checked the clock high above the stone façade of Grand Central Terminal across the street. The clock was flanked by the stone images of a strident Mercury, a sitting Minerva, and a lounging Hercules. The gods of Speed and Industry and Commerce all concerned about time. Just like everyone else. Hicks found it a refreshing scene. Not even the gods were free of mortal troubles.

And in about forty-five minutes, Hicks would

attempt to enroll a money man named Vincent Russo into the University system.

Hicks took a good draw on the cigar and let the smoke slowly escape through the corner of his mouth. The tangy aftertaste the cigar left on his tongue felt good. The frigid wind caught the smoke and blew it across Forty-second Street. The streets were empty thanks to the impending storm, so there was no one around to complain about the stray smoke.

Hicks wondered what Vincent Russo was doing just then. He could've pulled out his handheld device and used OMNI to hack the security cameras Russo had installed to watch his office, but there was no need. He had already studied the recruit and knew Russo was a creature of habit.

At this time of day, Russo was probably working away as diligently as he always did. He was verbally glad-handing clients over the phone about the status of their investments or convincing them that the fund he was investing their money in was a steal at the current price.

Hicks imagined he probably rolled his eyes when he looked at his calendar and saw his twelve o'clock appointment with a prospective client. The new one with the name he didn't recognize. He might even think about postponing it in favor of a longer lunch hour spent at the Algonquin with his mistress, but realized it was already too late for that. Then he'd remember the financial statement Hicks had sent him, the statement that proved he had inherited five million dollars from his mother and was looking to invest with Russo's firm. Greed would get the better of his lust as greed tended to do. The mistress could wait. He'd enjoy her much better after he'd secured five million dollars from a mamma's boy.

Hicks knew it was greed that had made Russo vulnerable to blackmail in the first place. And greed was going to be the reason why Hicks would success-fully enroll him in the University.

Hicks didn't feel sympathy for people like Russo or for any of the men and women he'd turned into Assets over the years. They'd all done things that had opened themselves to University pressure and blackmail. Any dirt he had on them was their own fault. He'd sooner have sympathy for the devil himself than for any of his potential recruits.

Still, becoming an Asset changed one's life and no matter how much they deserved it, the transition deserved at least some commemoration; hence the reason why Hicks was enjoying his cigar.

Hicks was about halfway through his smoke when a homeless man trudged into the alcove. He was pushing a creaky shopping cart as he escaped the wind of the coming storm.

Given the man's weathered appearance, Hicks couldn't tell how old the man was except to see he was a black man with a shaggy beard streaked with white and gray. His layers of tattered clothes looked liked they kept him warm, and his cart was overflowing with plastic bags filled with other people's garbage. They were the things people discarded, but this man found valuable. One man's garbage was another man's treasure.

Hicks could relate to such things. He decided he liked this man already.

He watched the man push the cart into the far

corner of the alcove. Hicks was ready to shake him off if he asked for money or a cigarette, but the man surprised him by saying, "Hey, mister. You trustworthy?"

Hicks hadn't been asked such a direct question in a long time. "As far as it goes, I guess. Why?"

"Because you look like a trustworthy man to me," the homeless man said. "The kind of man I could leave my things with and find them here when I get back."

Hicks looked back at the cart overflowing with garbage, then at the man. "Why? Late for a board meeting?"

"Nope," the man said. "Just got to find a bathroom is all and I need someone who can watch my stuff while I'm busy." He looked at Hicks' cigar. "Looks like you'll be here a while and I promise I'll be back way before you're done smoking that thing."

Hicks was curious. "Why so particular? I mean, why don't you just..."

"Just find a doorway somewhere to piss in?" The homeless man shook his head. "Because it's against the law and breaking the law just ain't my style, mister. I live on these streets and like to keep 'em clean. Besides, just because you're a certain way doesn't mean you have to act the way people expect."

Hicks liked the man's attitude and felt bad about the board meeting crack. "You take as long as you want, my friend. Just make sure you're back before noon. I've got an appointment."

"Funny, so do I," the homeless man laughed as he shuffled off. "Got that board meeting you was talkin' about. On Fifth Avenue, no less."

Hicks watched the man trudge back into the growing wind and head toward Grand Central

Terminal and the bathrooms in the lower level. He'd left Hicks alone with the pushcart filled with things only of value to him.

We were all like that, Hicks thought. *Pushing our own cart filled with shit we thought valuable through the world.*

Some valued love or comfort or money. Most wanted all three and thought money could lead to the other two. And if money didn't lead to it, then it certainly could buy it.

The formula varied, but Hicks knew everyone had at least one thing they valued most in this world. To that homeless man, it was his cart.

But most of the people Hicks dealt with had their valuables stashed in encrypted files on hard drives or in safe deposit boxes in banks no one was supposed to know about. They kept secrets buried deep within themselves and prayed that no one ever looked for them.

But someone always found out because part of every secret kept, was the yearning to be discovered. To get caught. To tell. To let someone in on it. To confess.

Hicks had been in the intelligence game for over twenty years. He'd seen damned near every aspect of the human condition, and yet it still managed to surprise him. No matter how many ops he'd run in any part of the world, he'd always learned something new from each one.

Even from a homeless man while he smoked his cigar on the street of a city bracing for Snowmageddon.

He flicked his cigar ash into the concrete ashtray next to him. Or maybe it wasn't that deep. Maybe all of it was just unrelated bullshit.

Hicks' cigar had burned down to a nub when the homeless man came toddling back for his cart, looking more refreshed than when he'd left. A cup of hot coffee piped steam through a plastic lid.

Hicks dug his hand into his pocket, fished out a twenty and held it out to the man.

He expected the homeless man to take it. Instead, he just looked at it. "What's that for?"

"Storm's coming," Hicks said. "I was thinking this could help you buy something to keep you warm."

But the homeless man backed away from the money, back toward his cart. "No thanks. I got all I need in this cart right here. Being prepared is what you might call a motto of mine."

Hicks put the twenty back in his pocket. "Mine too."

Hicks ground out his cigar in the ashtray. A light snow, barely a flurry, had begun to fall. The day was almost too pretty to ruin a man's life.

Almost, but not quite.

CHAPTER 2

VINCENT RUSSO's office suite was a modern space in the Helmsley Building that straddled Park Avenue on Forty-fifth Street.

Russo had gone with a chic minimalist décor: gray walls and glass desks; sleek telephones and computer screens. The paintings on the wall were equally chic, bland swirls that had just enough color to make them interesting.

The receptionist Russo had hired matched the décor: pretty, but inscrutable.

The reading material in the reception area had obviously been placed there for specific effect. Lifestyle magazines showing wealthy white people of a certain age with good hair and better teeth living the life they'd always imagined. Golfing. Yachting. Sitting on a beach. Biking through woods. Boarding a private jet with grandkids in tow.

Not a bald spot or a pot belly or a loud Hawaiian shirt in the whole bunch. Walmart had no place in the

SYMPATHY FOR THE DEVIL / 13

world Vincent Russo could provide to his customers. A great big dream there for the offering.

And since Hicks had been tracking every email into and out of Russo's firm for the past six months, he knew it was all one big lie. The office looked like it was trying too hard to be something it was not. Just like the man whose name was on the door.

Hicks looked up when he saw Vincent – never call him Vinny – Russo walking down the hall to greet him. From hacking into the firm's security cameras, Hicks knew that Russo normally sent his secretary out to bring prospective clients back to his office, but not this time. After all, not every client walked through the door with five million in cash.

Vincent Russo was a large, solid man a shade over six feet tall and just north of fifty years old. He moved like a man who was used to being given his way due to his size, which made it all that much easier for him to disarm you with his charm. He still had all his hair and most of it was black, combed straight back from his broad sloping forehead.

"Mr. Warren, I take it?" Russo asked as Hicks stood to greet him. "Vincent Russo. Happy to meet you, sir."

Russo went to shake Hicks' hand but stopped when he noticed Hicks was still wearing his black ski cap and black gloves.

Hicks acted embarrassed and mousey. "Bad bout of rosacea, I'm afraid. It hurts every time I touch something, so the gloves help minimize my discomfort. Mother always said prevention was the best cure."

Hicks could tell by Russo's grin that he already had 'Mr. Warren' pegged as a sucker. "Of course. Whatever makes you comfortable. Please, come back to my office where we can talk more privately."

Hicks made a show of looking flustered as he gathered up his nylon messenger bag and held it close to his chest. He let the larger man lead him back to his office, although Hicks already knew exactly where it was.

Russo provided a narrative of the dozens of people they passed along the way. The employees were all on the phone in cubicles with low walls.

"As you can see, we're a small but mighty shop here, Mr. Warren. And if you give me just a few moments of your time, I think I'll be able to prove to you that everyone in this firm is dedicated to giving each and every customer our undivided attention. As I'm sure you've heard, most of our customers have been quite happy with the results."

Hicks clutched his bag tighter and offered a simper that fit the character he was playing. "I've heard nothing but great things about your company, Mr. Russo. I'm sure mama's money couldn't be in better hands."

Russo ushered Hicks into his office and closed the door behind them. It was a corner office, with no windows out into the cubicle farm outside. There was no way anyone could see what was going on inside, either. The windows behind Russo's desk faced north onto Park Avenue. There was no way that anyone could see into the office from that angle, either.

Hicks sat in one of the chairs facing Russo's desk, which was as sparse as the rest of the office. No knick knacks on the walls. No mementos or awards. Just a slim computer monitor, a sleek phone and an old-fashioned metal stapler engraved as thanks for speaking to an accounting group three years before.

Other than that, there wasn't a sheet of paper or a family photo in sight. That would've told Hicks something about Russo if Hicks hadn't already known the whole story.

"Now, how might we help you today?" Russo asked when he was seated.

"Well, I was kinda hoping you could help me get rich."

Russo laughed. "That's always the ultimate goal here, of course. Given that you've told us that you have a substantial amount of money to invest, we have a variety of options available to us. If you could give me an overview of where you're currently invested, I can help chart a course for your future."

"Chart a course for my future." Hicks repeated the words and let them sink in. "I like the sound of that. Very nautical. Paints a nice picture."

He reached into his nylon messenger bag he had been holding and pulled out a thick file of papers bound by a precariously thin rubber band. He'd wanted Russo to be underwhelmed by the initial presentation. All the easier to overwhelm him at the right time.

"Mama held many of these investments for quite a long time," Hicks explained as he handed the bundle over to Russo, who reached to take it with both hands. "I didn't feel comfortable emailing or sending all of this stuff by courier. I've never been good with the computer and felt better giving it to you in person."

"That's understandable," Russo said as he laid the bundle on the desk. "But we should probably start with some preliminaries. For example, what kind of business are you in?"

Hicks nodded down at the pile. "You'll see. It's all right there."

Russo picked up the bundle again and gave an exaggerated grunt. "There's quite a bit here to review all in in one sitting." The thin rubber band snapped as he tried to remove it. "It might take me some time to go through it in order to get an accurate picture of your portfolio."

"That's okay." Hicks took off his black ski cap. Now that he was in the office, there was no need to continue the ruse. "Besides, I think you'll find much of it familiar."

Russo gave a good-natured shrug as he dug into the pile. "Well, let's see what we've got here."

But three pages into the pile, Russo began flipping through entire sections of the file. He began jumping from one page to another. "There must be some mistake here."

Hicks pulled his black gloves tighter and dropped the mousey act. "No Vinny. No mistake."

Russo rifled through the file now, finding one more familiar financial statement after another. Every dirty job and crooked transaction he'd pulled since he'd moved the firm to Manhattan five years before. Every name and account number of every cent he'd skimmed, thanks to the powerful reach of the OMNI network.

"Where the hell did you get all of this?" He looked at more sections before finally slamming the paper folder shut. "Just who the hell are you, anyhow?"

"A friend," Hicks said. "Or at least I can be if you're willing to listen to reason."

"Oh, I get it." Russo's friendly demeanor vanished as he pushed himself away from his desk. "This is some kind of blackmail, isn't it? Well, you picked the wrong guy, asshole. I've got this whole place wired for audio and video. One call to the cops and you'll be in Riker's before you know it."

"I've disabled the cameras and the audio," Hicks told him. "At least what you've got here in your private office, anyway."

"Impossible. All that's controlled remotely by..."

"By a security firm in Paramus, New Jersey, owned by a client of yours. They even gave you a break on the installation fees, but they're still over-charging you. Their network firewall is shit, by the way. A drunken monkey could hack their system."

Russo's eyes narrowed. "What is this, anyway? Who the hell are you?"

"Like I said, I'm a friend. I'm also the guy you need to listen to very carefully, because I'm only going to say this once."

But Russo was already beyond listening. He was in the first stage of grief. Denial. "Who are you? The Treasury? IRS?"

"If I was, you would've been greeted by a whole bunch of guys and girls in windbreakers as soon as you stepped out of your house this morning." Hicks grinned. "Those guys love a show, don't they?"

"Then I don't have to talk to you or listen to you or do anything except throw you out of my office."

"Calm down," Hicks warned. "This doesn't have to get nasty. And I'm not going anywhere."

But the finance man began to push himself out of his chair. Hicks reached over the desk and fired a straight right hand that nailed Russo in the center of the forehead, just above the bridge of his nose.

The bigger man dropped back into his chair like a sandbag. Hicks normally didn't like hitting a recruit, but Russo was different. He was an alpha male and used to being in charge. The sooner he accepted the new order of things, the better everyone would be.

Russo sat spread eagle in his chair, dazed. He blinked and shook his head to clear stars exploding in his brain.

"Keep your head still and breathe, Vinny," Hicks told him. "Just breathe. It'll pass quicker that way."

Russo cradled his head in both hands. "What did you hit me with?"

He saw no reason to tell him they were tactical gloves with hardened plastic coating the knuckles. "Just a straight right hand in the right place," Hicks said. "And I won't hit you again unless you make me. I know you think those Mixed Martial Arts classes have taught you a few moves, but you still ride a desk all day. I don't."

Russo seemed to forget how dizzy he was. "How the hell did you know about those classes? They're..."

"Off the books, I know. A favor from one of your friends in the Nassau County Police Department. His brother-in-law owns a dojo near your house, and he owed you a favor, so he set you up with a few free lessons for you. Not that you couldn't afford them, of course. It's the fact that they're free that's important to you, isn't it, Vinny? The principle of the thing. A sign of respect."

Russo sank even lower in his chair, legs spread even

wider. "If you're not a cop or a fed, how do you know so much about me?"

"Who I am isn't important. What I know about you isn't important. But the fact that I know a hell of a lot about you is of the utmost importance because that knowledge is going to be the basis of our relationship from here on in."

"Relationship?" Russo blinked. "What are you, a fag?"

Hicks grabbed the commemorative stapler from his desk and threw it at his balls. Russo stifled a scream as he shot forward to cradle his manhood.

"We don't do sarcasm here," Hicks told him. "Next crack like that gets your nose broken."

Russo's face red and his eyes watering. "If you know so goddamned much, then you know who I am. You know who I know. Shit, one phone call from me and you don't walk out of this building alive."

"Now you're embarrassing yourself," Hicks said. "The mobbed-up guinea act might play with the pensioners you reel in here, but I know better. You're a nice Italian boy from Ronkonkoma whose old man provided sound financial planning for cops and firemen and teachers until you took over the business and moved to the big city five years ago. You move money for some really nasty people, but you don't have enough juice with them to have anyone killed on your say so."

Russo forgot all about his sore balls. "How did…"

"Your father died from a bad heart almost seven years ago," Hicks went on, "but mom's still doing well. Works at the library three days a week and volunteers with the Don Bosco Society on weekends." Hicks smiled. "I wish I had her energy. You're about as mobbed up as I am Chinese and, in case you haven't noticed, I'm not Chinese."

"No," Russo went back to cradling his head in his hand. "You're just another asshole trying to put his hand in my pocket. Fine. Fuck you. Just tell me how much it'll take to make you go away."

"Vinny, Vinny, Vinny," Hicks shook his head. "There's more to life than money. I'm not here to blackmail you. I'm here to help you. Like I said, to be your friend."

"Great. Where have I heard that one before?" Vinny said. "You're just another bug looking to take a bite out of me. Just like every other parasite in my fucking life. My wife, my kids, my partners."

He lifted his head from his hands. His face was flush and pale in all the wrong places. The spot where he'd punched him was an angry red, and on its way to being a hell of a bruise. "But I've dealt with pieces of shit like you before in my time." He pushed the big file back toward Hicks. "What'll it take to make you and all of this mess just go away?"

"I just told you I'm not looking for money and I'm not looking to add to your troubles." He pushed the folder back toward Russo. "You're right about there being a price for keeping the material in that folder quiet. The price is you. Or, to put a finer point on it, your agreement to work for me."

"Why in the hell would I go to work for you? I don't even know who you are or what you want."

"I'm someone who can make your life very easy if you're smart enough to let me."

The damage to his ego brought the old Russo back to life. "I'm not interested in working for anyone. I've already got a boss and you're looking at him. I'm not just going to roll over for you or anyone just because they walk in here with a pile of paper."

Hicks ignored the bluster and laid it out as simply as he could. "From this day forward, you and I are going to help each other. My presence in your life and your business will be negligible, so long as you do exactly what you're told when I tell you to do it."

"That's what you think," Russo laughed. "Because if you know anything about me, you know I didn't get this far by taking orders."

"And you won't get any further if I send that file to Vladic."

Russo flinched.

Hicks went on. "You've ripped off a lot of people, my friend, but Vladic's the worst, isn't he? He might be an ignorant peasant who probably won't understand what that file means at first. To him, it's just a bunch of account numbers and transaction statements. Might as well be in Braille for all the good it would do that ignorant bastard. But when he passes it along to one of his money guys – and he will - they'll explain it to him. And when they do," Hicks shrugged a little, "well, I don't have to draw you a picture about what he'll do next."

Russo looked at him through his fingers. "You wouldn't do that. I'm not good to you if I'm dead."

"You're no good to me if you don't agree to work for me, so what do I care?"

Russo let out a heavy breath as he rocked back in his chair.

Hicks didn't see the point in pushing him any further. To do so would only lead to more posturing on

Russo's part and they'd already had enough of that. Hicks had made his point. Now all he could do was sit and wait for the seed to take root.

Hicks had learned long ago to let Assets take their time in making up their mind. Rush them and they'd say anything just to get away so they could take time to think of ways out of it. Hicks made sure they completely accepted the bit before he hooked them up to the plow. And Vincent Russo wasn't used to being a workhorse.

But he'd have to get used to it if he wanted to go on living.

Russo's chair slowly turned away from Hicks, toward his tenth-floor view of the northern half of Park Avenue. The snow was falling and had just begun to stick on the window ledges of the buildings in the area. "I don't even know your fucking name."

"You can call me Hicks."

Russo kept looking out at Park Avenue. "That's it? Just Hicks? No first name?"

"What difference does it make? It's not my real name anyway."

"Figures. Who do you work for?"

"I don't see as how that makes a difference, either."

"Sure, it does," Russo said to the window. "If you were connected to one of my clients, I'd be dead already. If you were a cop, I'd be in a cell. So that means you're either federal or some kind of intelligence guy." He lolled his head back against the headrest of his chair. "So, you CIA? NSA?"

"None of the above," Hicks said. "All you need to know is that I know everything about you. I've been tapped into every corner of your life and your family's life for months. I know everything there is to know about you, your company, your wife, your daughter who hates you and your son's nasty heroin problem. I know about the hundred grand you keep in your safe in your den, your whore on Fifty-third Street and about that nice Dominican girl you met at the Campbell Apartment last week. You should keep it up, by the way. Those selfies you texted her of your junior partner down there really impressed the hell out of her."

Russo closed his eyes and faced Park Avenue again. "Jesus."

Hicks went on. "I know about your accounts in the Caymans and Belize and in Cuba. I've got all your email accounts, your cell phones, your passwords, and every other secret you've kept from the world all these years. I know which clients you've stolen from, how much and when. There's nothing about you I don't know."

He leaned forward in his chair. "And none of that will matter as long as you do exactly what I tell you to do."

"Which is what?"

Hicks sat back in his seat. "Anything I know you can deliver."

Russo turned his chair to face him. "And what the hell is that supposed to mean?"

"Exactly what I said. It might involve you giving me information on one of your clients. Or moving money for me. I might need to borrow your boat or one of your cars or vacation houses. I'll never ask you to do anything you're not qualified to do. Whatever it is, whenever I ask for it isn't your concern. You do exactly what I tell you to do when I tell you to do it and your life goes on exactly as it has been until now."

"And if I don't," Russo said, "Vladic gets this file."

Hicks nodded. "So do all of the other clients you've scammed, but I think Vladic will get you first."

Russo drummed his fingers on the desk while he thought it over. "I know I'm no angel, but this is a damned dirty business you're in. Doing this to people trying to make a living."

"But it's fun. Especially when I get the chance to screw over a guy like you. But like you said earlier, you're used to being your own boss so let me give you a valuable piece of advice. Don't try to find a way out of our agreement."

Russo pointed at the file on his desk. "What can I do to you while you've got this?"

"You're thinking that now, but in a few hours after the dust settles, your ego will start eating at you. On the drive home, you'll hit the second stage of grief, and feel pain and guilt for what you've done. But by the time you pull into the driveway, the third stage will kick in. You'll be on familiar ground and you'll get angry. You'll start thinking you can actually do something about this. You might do something stupid, like having one of your friends at the P.D. investigate me. If you do, I'll know about it and there will be a penalty. If you tell anyone about our arrangement – your priest or your shrink or your girlfriend – I'll know about it and there will be a penalty. You try to run, I'll find you and drop you off on Vladic's doorstep with that file stapled to your chest. And if you kill yourself, that file goes to Vladic and your business partners. Your partners will bankrupt your family and we both know what Vladic will do to your wife and children, especially your daughter. What he lacks in brains he more than makes up for in cruelty."

Russo stopped looking out the window. "Don't threaten my family."

"I'm not threatening anyone, Ace. I'm just informing you of what penalties will occur if you try to break our contract. I suggest you skip all the remaining stages of grief and go right to acceptance. You're the one who you put yourself in this position by screwing around with other people's money, not me."

Russo sank even further back into his chair. He ran his hands back over his slicked back hair and let out a long, slow breath.

Hicks knew he was still looking for that exit; that escape hatch that would get him out from under all of this. The OMNI profile said he would. The profile also said Russo would accept the leash in time, but he'd buck before he did it. "When does this special relationship of ours start?"

"It started the moment I walked into this office. I'll let you know what I need and when I need it. It might be tonight. It might be never. I'll never ask you for anything you can't deliver, so don't waste time by making excuses if I call. If you play games, Vladic gets an email. And if I contact you, don't get smart by asking me any details about our discussion here today. I'll just assume you're trying to record me, or you have someone listening in. If that happens, Vladic gets an email. Understand?"

Russo closed his eyes and nodded.

"That's not an answer," Hicks said.

"Yes, goddamn you. Yes, I understand."

Hicks slipped his ski cap back on and slipped his

messenger bag on his shoulder as he stood up and went to the door. He didn't worry about fingerprints because he'd never taken off his gloves. He'd never handled the file he'd given Russo without wearing gloves, either.

He paused before he reached for the knob. "I know you're going to have some sleepless nights over this. But I've been doing this a long time and I know how to make this painless for all of us. Do as you're told, and you'll make a lot of money in the bargain. And you can take comfort in the fact that you really never had a choice." He finished it off with a smile. "I'll be in touch. And remember, I'll be watching."

When he reached the lobby, Hicks made sure he gave the receptionist a furtive wave as he went for the elevator. He was sure she didn't notice, but it was good to stay in character.

CHAPTER 3

As soon as Hicks got outside, the weather had taken a turn for the worse. Cold wind and heavy snow whipped around him as he crossed Forty-fifth Street toward the MetLife Building on his way to catch the subway at Grand Central. The storm was blowing in right on time, but Hicks didn't mind. The wind and the snow only made him feel more alive than he already did.

Hooking a new Asset always made his day. He imagined salespeople felt the same rush after closing a deal. Only this was much better. Because the thrill wasn't just over closing a deal on a house or selling merchandise. He had just bent a strong man to his will. This was more than a rush. It was a power trip. And even though he had not worn a uniform in twenty years, there was nothing like a successful mission.

As always, Hicks' happiness was tempered by reality. Despite all his threats, there was always a risk that an Asset might do something drastic like kill himself. Russo's OMNI profile showed a low likelihood of suicide, but not even the University's artificial intelligence was smart enough to predict what a desperate man might do.

Either way, Russo's ego would require some soothing. More carrot than stick to appeal to the same greed that had put him in a position to be blackmailed. Hicks made a note to let Russo move some of the University's New York Office funds in a day or so. Maybe three or four million to start. Let him make some coin off the commission and see the benefit his new partnership with Hicks could provide.

Hicks was riding down the escalator from the MetLife Building into Grand Central when he felt his handheld begin to vibrate in his pocket. He stepped out of the flow of pedestrian traffic and tapped the screen alive.

To anyone passing by, he looked like any other man checking his email on a smartphone. On the off chance the phone was lost or stolen, whoever found it would see a phone with a regular passcode screen. Even if they managed to crack the passcode, they'd find all the usual apps and features one would expect to find on such a device.

But Hicks' phone was unlike almost any other device in the world. It had been issued to him by the University and didn't operate on any cellular network available to the public. It only functioned on the University's secure OMNI network.

Hicks entered his four-digit passcode that unlocked the common features of the phone, then tapped on an ambiguous-looking icon that activated the device's camera. The camera scanned Hicks' facial features and retina to verify that he was, indeed, James Hicks.

Another passcode screen automatically opened and

asked for a longer twelve-digit password. Upon entering it, he was allowed access to the University's server.

A text message appeared, formatted in the University's usual spare style:

Student 1357 requests immediate interview.
20:00 HRS tonight. Location forthcoming.
Please advise as to availability.

Although the message was properly formatted and relatively short, Hicks still had to read it three more times to understand it. It didn't make any sense.

'Student 1357' was the official University designation for one of his deep cover operatives: Colin Rousseau. He had assigned Colin an undercover role as a driver at a Somali cab outfit in Long Island City, Queens. The owner, a man named Omar Farhan, and several drivers were on the University's terror watch list, which had a lower threshold than most national watch lists.

OMNI had been passively tracking their movements for over a year and Colin had been working at the cabstand for just over five months. Since Colin's family had originally come from Kenya, he knew enough of the language and customs to blend in without being an obvious plant.

It had been a sleepy assignment and Hicks was thinking of pulling the plug on it. But Colin had just hit the panic button. When an experienced agent requested an emergency meeting, there had to be a damned good reason.

Hicks wasn't surprised when his handheld showed

his Department Chair was calling him. Other professions had the option of allowing unwanted phone calls to go to voicemail. Hicks didn't have that luxury. He knew Jonathan would only keep calling until Hicks answered because, according to the University's structure, Jonathan was technically his boss.

Hicks tapped the icon to allow the call through and brought the handheld up to his ear. "This is Professor Warren." It was University code that he was safe and able to speak reasonably freely.

Jonathan always kept their phone conversations equally terse. "I see that you've read the message from your Field Assistant."

"I did. I wasn't expecting that."

"Neither was I," Jonathan said. "According to your activity log, you had your weekly guidance session with him yesterday." Guidance Sessions were University-speak for debriefings.

"I know. I wrote it, remember?"

"And I read it. I didn't see anything there that would suggest a sudden need to meet."

Jonathan's superior tone grated him until Hicks remembered the Dean of the University had chosen Jonathan because he wasn't field personnel. Jonathan was a planner and organizer. If it didn't fall into a cell on a spreadsheet, it held little relevance in Jonathan's world. Hicks remembered what the Dean had told him when he'd brought Jonathan on six months before: *Jonathan is only your superior on paper, James. He's merely your connection to us. Think of him as a link in the protective chain of command. That's all.*

That didn't make working with him any easier. "Field work isn't always predictable. Things like this happen from time to time. I won't know anything further until I actually talk to him."

"I find the sudden urgency of it disturbing. Will you require any assistance?" Jonathan asked. "Perhaps a Varsity team could be in the area to provide support."

"No thanks." The Varsity was the University's tactical unit, usually reserved for raids, security, clean up jobs following a hit, or an op gone wrong. Some of them were level-headed and some were cowboys. He didn't want them anywhere near this kind of meeting. "He's my student, my problem. I'll handle it my way."

"And if something goes wrong?"

"Like I said, I'll handle it."

"The Dean is confident that you will. I only wish I shared his confidence. The student should be sending through the location of the rendezvous in a moment, assuming he can still follow procedures. We'll decide then what precautions are best."

Jonathan killed the connection and Hicks' screen went dark. Jonathan always had been a last word freak.

The handheld vibrated again as the location for the meeting had come through. Despite the security of their network, the University had an elaborate, often cumbersome, security protocol for emergency circumstances. Since most University operatives were usually imbedded with sophisticated, careful terrorist groups, this protocol protected agent and handler alike. The agent called a central number, gave the handler's call sign and message. An operator then transmitted key parts of the messages to the handler. If the agent was in distress, there were subtle phrases to use that would alert the University that they were being forced to call in. Emergency Meeting locations were decided by the field agent, sent to the switchboard and relayed to the handler.

Colin's message had no such warning, so Hicks assumed he wasn't in immediate danger.

A map application opened on his device and showed the exact location where Colin wanted to meet.

Under a footbridge in Central Park at eight o'clock that night.

During the predicted height of the coming blizzard.

Hicks pocketed his handheld and headed down to the subway. There was no sense in questioning the message or looking at the map any more than he already had. He could ask himself all sorts of questions and speculate all he wanted, but he knew it wouldn't do any good. He wouldn't know what all of this was about until he spoke to Colin.

Until then, he had plenty of work to do.

CHAPTER 4

THE BLIZZARD HAD ALREADY DUMPED several inches of heavy snow on Manhattan by the time Hicks began his trek from Twenty-third Street up to Colin's meeting location in Central Park.

The streets were deserted except for the few people who were either drunk enough or crazy enough to be out in that kind of weather. The kind of people who always scrambled to get milk and bread whenever a snowstorm approached.

The streets and sidewalks were clogged with unplowed snow, so there were no cabs in sight. And since the MTA had shut down all bus and subway service because of the storm, walking was the only way he could get uptown.

Hicks didn't mind. He'd been in worse weather in worse parts of the world. At least no one was trying to kill him. Besides, he had a short barreled .454 Ruger in the pocket of his parka to help keep him warm. He usually preferred the compact feel of a .22, but given the blizzard, he went with a higher caliber.

Most people in his position would've gone for an automatic, but Hicks preferred revolvers. No worries about the damned thing jamming at the wrong time.

Hicks thought a lot about Colin and his message as he trudged through the snow. He'd spent the afternoon and early evening on OMNI analyzing Colin's phone and laptop activity.

He couldn't find anything suspicious except for the lack of activity in the past day or so. Colin was like most people in the twenty-first century: addicted to his phone. He used his burner phone to mostly visit sports sites and online Islamic bulletin boards to complete his cover. He scanned Al Jazeera and the New York Times. When no one was around, he watched SportsCenter clips online and porn sites. Hicks knew Colin had a weakness for Asian women and his surfing history proved it.

Since he was undercover, Colin wasn't allowed to have a University device. He went with an independent wireless carrier instead. Just because University devices couldn't be hacked didn't mean the Dean allowed their equipment to be put in harm's way.

Operatives were highly trained, but they were human, and humans made mistakes. They lost phones and left them at friends' houses. They got drunk and left them in bars. No need to tempt fate. Even terrorists got lucky. 9/11 had proved that, too.

Colin had been a rock since Hicks had taken over the University's New York office three years before.

Colin had joined the U.S. Army when he was eighteen and had shown a capacity for languages and an immigrant's love for country. He'd found a home in Army Intelligence and had been recruited to work for the University ten years before.

Hicks had worked with him in other parts of the world and was glad he'd been able to talk him into transferring to the New York Office. Colin was a rare breed who could work deep cover or handle the tactical aspects of the job seamlessly. He could imbed with the bad guys or run a raid on a cell with equal efficiency. And Hicks had every intention of nominating him for Office Head next time such an opening came up.

Hicks had expected Colin to balk at the cab assignment, but he didn't. Hicks had shown him the outfit's file and explained the cab stand owner was a Somali with some radical tendencies. He mostly hired Somali drivers with similar radical tendencies.

It was a job some University operatives would have classified as a cold assignment, but Hicks' gut said different. Too many rotten eggs in one basket always raised a stink and he wanted eyes on them for a while.

The cab stand vibed amateur, but it only took one strike to bring a cell into the pros. The digital surveillance Hicks had on their phones and computers led him to believe Omar and his boys would pull a job if someone gave them a chance – and enough money – to pull it off.

That's why Colin's sudden request for a meeting made Hicks wonder if something might be brewing. And he was glad he'd brought the Ruger to keep him company. Trust, but verify.

By the time Hicks finally reached Central Park, the sky glowed purple high above the barren trees. Central Park South was usually full of people and horse-drawn carriages lined up to take tourists on a ride inside the park. The blizzard had chased them all inside, except for the rare die-hard cabbie who rolled along the street looking for a fare.

The weather inside the park was even more severe than out on the street. Snow had been blown into knee-high drifts even on the paths. The wind blew the whole mess in a wild, circular motion.

The park was deserted, and Hicks hoped it stayed that way. He hated surprises and a snowbound park wasn't ideal for surprises. Footprints in the snow betrayed early arrivals. Tough going made it hard to sneak up unannounced. Harsh wind made bullet trajectory a crap shoot. Was that why Colin had picked it? He certainly hoped so.

The wind picked up steadily the further he got into the park. The snow had turned into a driving sleet just as he reached the footbridge. Hicks pulled back the sleeve of his parka and checked his watch. He was ten minutes early. He normally liked to arrive a half hour early but trudging through shin-deep snowdrifts had fouled up his ETA.

As he got closer to the footbridge, he saw Colin was already there. University protocol was clear: Operatives were never supposed to be on site until their Faculty Member cleared the site first. Colin knew University protocol better than anyone.

Red flag.

Hicks slowed as he scanned the area as well as he could through the blinding sleet and snow. There was no sign of fresh footprints in the snow leading to the site, meaning Colin must've entered through the west side of the park. It looked like he'd come alone, but Hicks wouldn't be able to tell for certain until he was under the shelter of the footbridge. By then, it would be too late to do anything but react.

University protocol was clear on this point, too: if an Operative fails to meet exact protocol, turn around and walk away.

Protocol had its place, but Colin was Hicks' man. He already knew something was off, but it was clear Colin needed his help. He couldn't walk away.

He gripped the handle of the Ruger in his pocket. Just in case.

The closer Hicks got, the less he liked what he saw. Colin was normally laid back to the point of appearing to be careless. Nothing appeared to bother him or upset him or make him happy. Hicks had never known him to betray any emotion other than what his cover required. He was an emotional blank slate, which had made him ideal for the kind of undercover work Hicks assigned him.

But now, beneath the footbridge, Colin was pacing back and forth like a caged animal. He was constantly blowing into his hands even though he was wearing gloves. His head was uncovered, and his eyes were wide. He looked nervous and twitchy like a junkie aching for a fix.

But Colin never drank or used drugs.

Hicks kept his hand on the Ruger in his pocket as he joined Colin under the footbridge. "What's going on?"

"Things, man. Things." Colin continued pacing

and muttering to himself. "Things you don't know, man. Things you can't see. Things you don't want to know and don't want to see, see?"

Hicks had only seen Colin the day before, but he looked like he'd aged ten years since. His eyes were red, and his pupils were pinpoints. He looked like he hadn't slept in days and Hicks wondered if he had.

He looked and acted high. Like coke or heroin high, which was a problem because Colin didn't do stimulants. He hated needles and alcohol gave him a headache. Even beer. He'd also been embedded with a group of pious Muslims who did not indulge in such things.

Red flag number two.

Hicks went to grab his arm, but Colin jumped back and slipped on the icy snow that had drifted under the footbridge. He fell back against the curved wall of the underpass and stared up at him with wild eyes. "You've gotta pull me out, boss. You gotta pull me out, now. I don't have time to explain, but it's bad, man. Real, real bad. These boys ain't playing and...and, oh, you've gotta pull me out and you've gotta pull me out right now!"

Hicks kept checking both ends of the tunnel. None of this felt right. Colin didn't do drugs. He didn't panic. And he didn't pace back and forth and babble like this. Hicks had seen panic and burnout in Operatives before. Panic was as a part of the life as breathing. People did odd things when they panicked. They were late or they were early, or they were hiding nearby or they ran to him when they saw him. But they never stayed in the open, pacing back and forth like Colin was doing now.

Pacing like a goat tied to a stake in the ground.

Hicks didn't try to help him up. He pulled the Ruger and kept it flat against his side as he kept an eye on the western approach to the underpass; backing up the way he'd come, glancing over his shoulder as he moved. "Let's get out of here. Let's go somewhere warm where we can talk. Just you and me."

Colin gripped at the stone wall with gloved hands as he crept away from Hicks. "Don't touch me, man! I don't need you touching me. I need you to get me out of here, that's all. I need you to get me the hell out of here and away from these people."

Hicks felt the Magnum flat against his leg as he backed up. He felt the snow and sleet begin to hit the back of his hood. "Then come with me, damn it. This way. Right now."

But Colin kept inching along the wall back toward the western entrance to the underpass. "Wait, man. Just...just wait a second, okay? We gotta talk, come up with a plan before we move, you know? Get this straight before we go anywhere so we can..."

Hicks brought up his Ruger when he saw a shadow move at the western end of the footbridge. Someone else might've dismissed it as a tree branch moving in front of a streetlight, but not Hicks. He'd spent his life in the shadows. He knew the difference.

Colin began to shriek as two black men in hooded sweatshirts spilled out onto the snowy footpath at the western entrance. The nearest man regained his footing first.

Hicks saw a cellphone in his hand. The son of a bitch must've been filming them the entire time.

The other man was further back, next to a snow-covered bush just off to the side of the path. Colin began to squeal as the man began to aim at him.

Hicks dropped to a crouch and fired twice just as the man's gun came around. Both rounds hit him in the middle of the chest. The shooter's gun fired once as he stumbled back into the blizzard.

The man with the cellphone slipped again as he turned to run away. He belly-flopped on the walkway but did not drop the phone.

He scrambled to his knees, trying to get his feet under him despite the thick snow. Hicks didn't wait for him to get to his balance and shot him in the temple. The side of his head became a red cloud of dust before he collapsed dead on the pathway. The cellphone tumbled into the snow.

A sharp wind picked up, blowing a thick stream of snow and sleet into the underpass. Hicks remained crouched and still. He didn't hear a sound, not even the echo of his gunfire.

Not even Colin's screaming.

Hicks found Colin slumped against the wall. He had a bullet hole in his neck. A red streak tracked the path as he fell against the wall. The gunman's errant shot had caught him in the throat, and he was steadily bleeding out into the snow.

Hicks knew calling for help was pointless. With that kind of a wound, he'd soon be dead if he wasn't already. Besides, despite everything they'd been through together, the son of a bitch had just set him up.

Hicks crept forward, listening as he swept the area outside the western approach with the Ruger in case anyone else was hiding in the shadows. All he found was a whole lot of snow and the two men he'd just killed.

The only footprints he saw showed three men approaching the site and the prints they'd made running away. Hicks lowered his Ruger and listened as the snow and sleet fell around him. Gunshots usually drove everyone away except for cops. And cops were the last thing he needed just then.

Hicks reverted to his training. He ignored the wind and the sleet and the snow and listened for sirens, a police radio, a barking dog, a stifled sneeze. Anything that would tell him if someone else was nearby.

But all he heard was the wind in his ears and the sleet hitting his skin. A quiet park on a snowy night. The scene would've been postcard perfect if it hadn't been for the three dead men at his feet.

Hicks took a knee and began patting down the dead men's pockets. He started with the gunman. He took in everything at once: the thick, hooded sweatshirt, the black ski mask, and the sneakers. He took a closer look at the footwear: cheap Air Jordan knockoffs. The cameraman was in a similar getup.

Why the light clothing and lousy footwear in the middle of a blizzard they'd been predicting for days? It didn't make any sense.

Hicks pulled off the gunman's ski mask so he could get a clear face shot of it with his handheld. The face was unfamiliar but common: thin and black, between twenty and forty and slack in death. He looked too thin to be American and, judging by where Colin had been working undercover, he was probably Somali. Hicks had never seen either of them in person or in in any of the surveillance images from the cab stand, either.

Whoever these men had been, they were new players to the game. A game they wouldn't be playing any longer.

Hicks took a picture of the gunman's face, then used his phone to scan his fingerprints. The man hadn't been wearing a glove on his gun hand.

Hicks went through the same procedure on the cameraman – also a young black man he had never seen before. He took a picture of his face and scanned his fingerprints, then uploaded the information to OMNI.

If their faces or fingerprints were on record with any government in the world, he'd know about it in less than an hour. If not, the network would automatically begin running image checks on every kind of camera available from that spot to see if it could find a match locating where they'd come from. ATM machines, security cameras, traffic cameras and even images posted on social media.

He patted down both men. No wallets. No car keys. Nothing that could help identify them. That meant they'd planned this, but if they'd planned it so well, why the light clothing and lousy footwear? They hadn't just hopped out of a car and shot at him on a whim. They hadn't tried to nail him with a drive-by either.

Colin had picked this location, specifically a secluded part of the park. Why do that if he was setting him up for a hit? Was he trying to warn Hicks somehow? If so, why not use one of the distress codes they'd agreed upon?

Hicks picked up the cellphone from the snow and held it against his handheld. His device immediately copied all of the phone's data to the OMNI network. The phone's camera was recording, but the snow wreaked havoc with normal cellphone signals. It wasn't broadcasting. It was the first break Hicks had caught. He simply turned it off and put it in one of the deep pockets of his parka.

Hicks searched Colin's body last. No keys, no wallet. No Metrocard, either. No weapon of any kind. Not even a knife. Nothing that explained his betrayal. Hicks knew he had a hell of a lot of work to do before he could make sense of any of this.

Hicks stood up and checked the scene one last time to see if he'd missed any relevant evidence. He hadn't.

He looked down at Colin last. The blood from his wound had finally stopped flowing. His eyes had taken on the passive gaze of death.

Why did you turn, my friend? How could you...

Hicks realized 'how' was the answer. Or rather, 'How' was the question.

How did you get here without money or a Metrocard? The subways and buses aren't running due to the blizzard. *How the hell did you get all the way to Central Park from a cab office in Long Island City in the middle of a blizzard?*

Colin's initial call to the Switchboard had come in around one o'clock in the afternoon. They'd begun shutting down the subways at two o'clock to beat the storm. Had they sat around the park for eight hours in the middle of blizzard just to set him up?

No. Someone had driven them there. That explained the attire. They didn't have far to travel, and they didn't plan on being there for long.

Just long enough to get a look at Hicks.

And Hicks wondered if that same someone who'd brought them there wasn't waiting to pick them up. Somewhere close by.

Hicks reloaded the Ruger and began following the footprints of the dead men in the snow. He re-traced their steps west, walking into the wind. At this rate, their footsteps would be obliterated in less than an hour, if they weren't already. But he wouldn't let that stop him. He'd tracked men in worse conditions than this.

The sleet and the wind picked up, causing the trees above to sway and creak. He scanned the snowy landscape for any signs of movement, but all he saw was the park's streetlamps struggling to provide light in the blizzard.

He bet that whoever was waiting for Colin and the others to return was probably in a car with the engine running. Nice and warm. The exhaust would make them easy to spot.

Hicks slowed when he reached the park entrance on Seventy-second Street; ducking his head into the wind more than he had to. It was just enough to hide his face, but not enough to block his view of the street.

He spotted a late model Toyota Corolla on the west corner of Seventy-second and Central Park West. Lights on, motor running.

Hicks couldn't see the driver clearly through the sleet but realized the driver must've seen him. He heard the gear creak as the driver took the car out of park and threw it into drive.

Hicks brought up his handheld and thumbed the camera feature alive. He aimed the camera at the car as it pulled away and waited for the crosshairs to lock in on the car's black box. Every car made since the mid-nineties had one. It was like waiting for a device to find a wireless network, only this search was much faster.

The phone found the black box transmitter and pinged it back to him. He tapped the University's tracking feature on his phone and sent the protocol to the University's OMNI system. Now the system and the Switchboard would track the car wherever it went.

Gottcha.

Hicks put his handheld in one pocket and the Ruger in the other. He saw no reason to go back to the footbridge. He decided to turn left and walk south along Central Park West. He typed in a five-digit code on his handheld and waited for someone at the Switchboard to answer.

"Switchboard," a male voice said. "How may I help you?"

He knew the operator already had his name and location on her screen. "This is Professor Warren," he said, using the pre-assigned codename that told the operator he was safe and not being forced to talk. "I need to schedule a pickup." A pickup was University-speak for a cleanup crew for dead bodies.

"For when?"

"As soon as possible."

"Understood, sir." He heard a few clicks of a keyboard. "And the pickup would be at your previous location?"

Hicks knew they had tracked him to the footbridge. His handheld always emitted a tracking signal, but Jonathan had probably flagged his signal for priority surveillance. He also probably had a Varsity team already staged nearby. "That's right. Three items."

"Very well, sir. We'll send someone out for it right away. Thank you for calling."

The line went dead, and Hicks put the phone away. He could've gone back into the park and waited until the Varsity's cleanup squad showed up, but he decided to keep trudging south through the snow. The more distance he put between himself and the three dead men, the better. Even though one of those dead men had been a friend.

He knew the Varsity crew would take the three bodies back to a University facility where full autopsies would be performed. The purpose wasn't so much for determining cause of death, but charting DNA and other biological statistics that might come in handy later on. The results would be run through OMNI and, in a few moments, their true identities would be known if they were on file with any agency in the world.

He also hoped the examination would explain why Colin had turned on him.

Despite the thickness of his parka, Hicks felt his handheld buzz again. He expected to see Jonathan was calling and was sorry to see he was right. A blizzard and a gunfight was not enough for one night. Now he had to deal with this son of a bitch.

Hicks answered the phone with the standard University all-clear protocol. "This is Professor Warren."

"Things got complicated. I handled it."

"We're processing the data now, but this is most disturbing, professor."

No shit. But Hicks stuck to protocol. "I gathered as much data as I could and we should know more soon. Until then, I don't have anything for you."

Jonathan let out a long breath into the phone. "We detected another device. Was it broadcasting?"

"No. There was no signal in the park due to the storm. I've already uploaded the phone to the system." Even mentioning OMNI over the phone was frowned upon.

"I know that. And the student?"

Hicks' voice caught. He blamed the weather for it. "He's no longer with the program thanks to one of his peers."

Jonathan was silent for a beat. "That was not anticipated."

"Nothing about this was anticipated," Hicks told him.

"Are you hurt?"

Hicks knew he wasn't hurt in any ways Jonathan would care about. "I'm fine. I'll talk more when I'm back home."

"Be safe. I've scheduled an in-person meeting tomorrow at nine o'clock sharp. The usual spot."

The line went dead before Hicks could argue. As if things weren't bad enough, now he had a meeting with Jonathan to look forward to.

Hicks slipped the handheld in his pocket and closed his eyes as he walked. The sleet had let up a bit, giving way once again to heavy snow. He could feel his frustration beginning to build, so he concentrated on being calm. He tried to control his breathing.

He'd just lost a good operative. He'd just shot two strangers dead. He'd retrieved good intel and OMNI was tracking a suspected transport vehicle. He had material and evidence to examine.

He'd made the best of a lousy situation, which was cold comfort on an even colder evening.

He pulled his hood a little tighter around his head and leaned into the wind as he headed back to the facility he called home and hoped OMNI had some answers for him by the time he got there.

CHAPTER 5

SINCE HE COULDN'T DO anything until he got back to the facility, Hicks kept his mind off what had just happened in the park. He thought about the facility itself as he trudged through the sleet and the snow.

After three years, the novelty of living in a bunker two stories beneath Manhattan had lost its appeal.

Before the Dean had put Hicks in charge, the University's New York Office had been a joke since the end of the Cold War. Not even 9/11 had done much to change that perception.

The University's Boston, Virginia and Los Angeles offices had done the lion's share of the University's intelligence work within the United States back then. Even Miami had generated better leads.

The New York Office had become a vanity posting. Window dressing at best. It likely would have been closed altogether if the U.N. hadn't been headquartered there.

The New York Office of that time bore little resemblance to the high-tech headquarters shown on television shows and movies. There was no command center with a wall of flat screen televisions tapped into live satellite feeds. No trim, young people in dark suits engaging in terse banter as they sifted through intelligence on the latest technological devices.

Back then, the University's New York Office had been a part-time operation run out of John Holloway's cluttered York Avenue apartment. Holloway had been the University's point man in the war against Communism and something of a mentor to the Dean of the University, so exceptions were made.

But time catches up to everyone eventually and spies were no exception. Holloway gradually became a doddering academic more interested in the dusty first editions of his library and attending policy conferences than doing actual intelligence work. The only information Holloway sent back to the Dean was the boozy gossip he'd cobbled together from minor diplomats he met at U.N. cocktail parties.

Holloway had never embraced the University's use of technology. He thought forwarding e-newsletters from the Council on Foreign Relations was a technological accomplishment akin to landing a man on the moon.

The Holloway Era came to an end one drizzly spring morning when a mailman found Holloway lying dead between two parked cars off First Avenue. His dog - a white Pomeranian named Publius – licking his face.

Hicks remembered the old man's untimely death had caused the University to activate its Moscow Protocols, which put the organization on a wartime footing. All activities and communications were suspended.

Everyone was required to be armed at all times in case their identities had been compromised.

But the University's autopsy report quickly ruled out foul play and blamed pate for Holloway's passing instead.The autopsy showed he had died of cardiac arrest due to clogged arteries from too many cocktail parties and not enough exercise.

The Dean had mourned the death of his mentor, but when he named Hicks the Head of the New York Office, it was with a clear mission: make the New York Office the flagship of the University.

The Dean had given him a healthy budget to establish a proper base of operations. He advised him to hide in plain sight. Rent an office or buy a large apartment and keep a low profile.

But Hicks knew such places were difficult to secure, making them more trouble than they were worth. Running the operation out of an apartment or condo was risky. Maintenance staff had pass keys. Neighbors were nosy. People remembered what they saw and heard every day. Not ideal circumstances for a clandestine operation.

Hicks needed something quiet and not easily found. Something without windows or other tenants. In New York, that was a tall order, but not impossible.

Because Hicks had a plan.

While working in Tel Aviv before coming to New York, Hicks had learned of a local developer looking to expand his family's Manhattan real estate portfolio. The young man had just acquired a row of dilapidated townhouses in the west Twenties. He came from a strong Israeli family who despised the Palestinians.

But the young developer had built a fortune of his

own by quietly accepting Saudi Arabian investments in his various projects around the world. The developer had done a good job of covering his tracks, but not well enough to fool OMNI.

Hicks showed the developer the evidence and made him an offer: give him the ground floor and basement of one of his new buildings and enough space for a sub-basement beneath all three buildings. No rent, no lease, no sale, no questions. Refuse and the family finds out you've been taking money from the enemy.

The developer gave Hicks what he wanted.

The result was the University's New York Office: a hidden concrete shelter buried beneath the base-ments of three townhouses on West Twenty-third Street. The University had arranged for defense contractors with security clearance to build the facility quietly and quickly. Some creative manipulation of the City's Building Department's records allowed the construction to occur without government interference.

As Hicks reached the brownstone, he opened the small gate and walked down the stairs beneath the stoop. He found his keys and unlocked the door, kicking off the snow that had accumulated in the treads of his boots.

The garden apartment he walked through now was just for show. It looked benign enough from the outside, with curtains on the barred windows, lights on timers. Furniture and a full bookcase completed the ruse. People on the upper floors paid fair market rent, too.

The stairs down to the basement from the garden apartment looked normal. The boiler served the two legal apartments above, but the washer and drier had never been used. The basement was merely a stop gap that led to the sub-basement facility below.

It was sealed by an ordinary looking wooden door with a large knob and lock. But there was no key to the lock and the knob didn't turn. Hicks gripped the door knob, which read the biometrics in his hand while a hidden sensor scanned his facial features and retina. When his identity was confirmed, the hatch hissed opened and slid inward.

The sub-basement was a large vault that ran beneath the basements of each of the three town houses above it. It was an entirely independent structure built with steel re-enforced concrete. The facility slowly bled power off the city's power grid and stored it in a series of massive batteries. This was masked by the electricity usage of the apartments in the brownstones above. The facility also had three backup generators as well as a diesel-fueled backup that could run for more than a week.

The HVAC unit had filters and sensors that could detect radiation and poisonous emissions.

Hicks took cold comfort in the knowledge that the entire island of Manhattan could get obliterated by a nuclear blast and Hicks would still be able to operate in the bunker for more than a month before he'd have to venture outside.

The entire facility, like his handheld device, was tied wirelessly to OMNI, with a redundant cable line piped directly to the mainframe. This feature was only activated in an extreme emergency.

Hicks slid the vault door shut behind him and fell back against it. The lock mechanism vibrated as the massive magnetic bolts slid home.

He hadn't felt this exhausted in a long time.

He didn't look like a strong man and that was the general idea. Every day, he undertook a vigorous workout routine. He did extensive cardio work and could lift weights far heavier than someone his size should. Yoga and stretching exercises followed.

But after an hour pushing through driving sleet and heavy snow, he barely had the strength to take off his parka. He knew it wasn't just physical exhaustion but didn't want to dwell on Colin or what had happened in the park. Not yet. He simply stood with the back of his head against the door and breathed. The cold steel of the vault door dulled his growing headache.

Hicks shrugged out of his parka and put on a pot of fresh coffee in the kitchen area. He brought the dead man's camera to his workstation and booted up his computer before he replaced his guns in the armory. The room was larger than some studio apartments in Manhattan. It was filled with more Kevlar vests, automatic weapons, explosives, and ammunition than most police precincts.

The facility was a designated fallback position for the University, meaning that if it ever needed to, Hicks' office could become a forward operations base. He couldn't envision a scenario when that would be necessary, but he hadn't imagined an attack like 9/11 either. He lived up to his motto. Semper Paratus. Always Ready.

Despite its status as an official University facility, he'd managed to keep its exact location secret from everyone except the Dean. Jonathan had spent the last six months trying to figure out where it was, but Hicks kept stonewalling him. It was more out of enjoying

Jonathan's frustration than anything else. The less that bureaucrat knew, the better.

Hicks secured the armory door and went back to his living area to change out of his clothes. His personal living area was in the furthest corner of the room from the workstation.

Although the bunker was also his home, he viewed it as primarily a workspace. He didn't have any posters or personal photos or knick knacks of any kind. He had no family worth remembering. Just the computer equipment, a bed, a treadmill, a weight-lifting bench, and a walk-in closet for his clothes and other gear. If the time came when he had to evacuate, he could grab his bugout bag and fry the electronics in the facility in three minutes. He liked it that way.

Hicks waited for the coffee to finish brewing and tried to keep his thoughts in check. Now that he was in an official setting, he allowed himself to think about signs of Colin's betrayal. Little things he could've missed. Hints Colin might've dropped during their meeting that something was wrong.

But Hicks knew he hadn't missed anything. Colin's debrief had gone smoothly and he had nothing new to report, aside from the general anti-American banter that went on at Omar's cab stand. Big talk and vitriolic rancor was nothing new. Men like Omar ran down America the way Yankees fans ran down the Red Sox.

Hicks and Colin had even begun to wonder if they should end the assignment and return to a more passive surveillance of Omar's cab stand. Tracing cell phone calls and emails as they came through the grid might suffice.

But the Colin he'd just seen under the footbridge

over an hour before was not the Colin he'd known. Whatever had terrified him must have occurred right after their meeting. The question was what and why. The answer had to be Omar. So that's where Hicks was going to begin his investigation.

Hicks logged into the system to see if OMNI had been able to make positive identifications of the two men he'd killed. The system had narrowed it down to twenty possibilities. They were all Somali nationals. They all had that same gaunt, haunted look of the other Somalis that Omar had hired at the cab stand.

Hicks knew Omar mostly hired men from Somalia. Omar believed men from other African nations were weak and susceptible to corruption from the West. Colin's cover had only been feasible since his parents had come from a region of Kenya on the Somalian border.

Colin had reported that most of Omar's drivers were peasants. Young men who'd gotten to America more out of desperation than Islamic ideology. If going along with Omar's ranting kept money in their pocket and a roof over their heads, they went along with it. According to Colin, Omar was the only hardcore radical at his stand.

That meant whatever had happened at the cab stand to turn Colin had happened since the debrief. Hicks intended on finding out what.

While OMNI kept narrowing its search on the dead men, Hicks scanned recent email and cell phone intercepts from Omar's cab company. Everyone who worked there was tracked. Many of them bought disposable phones – also called burn phones - believing that would make it harder for agencies to eavesdrop. In some cases, they were right, but most agencies didn't have the University's resources. Any phone activated near the garage was immediately tagged by OMNI and followed for the duration of the phone's life. Even the old Somali woman Omar had hired to clean the place once a week was tracked. Every conversation was transcribed, tracked, recorded and deciphered by OMNI and University analysts known as Research Fellows throughout the globe. OMNI software translated and deciphered all conversations and emails and texts, looking for key phrases and code words and patterns.

Most of what OMIN found was just mundane, everyday chatter, but every so often, something valuable turned up.

In reviewing the latest data from the garage and drivers in the past forty-eight hours, Hicks didn't find anything suspicious. Nothing out of the ordinary came up, but Hicks ordered OMNI to re-scrub the data to see if he could catch anything new about Colin.

Then Hicks took a look at the phone he'd taken from the dead man in the park. He connected it to his desktop and, within seconds, OMNI had found the code and opened the phone.

When he accessed the footage from the park, Hicks saw the dead man had begun filming as soon as Hicks walked into the underpass. The image shook and went out of focus as the man tried to keep Hicks in frame. Colin looked even more strung out and timid than Hicks had remembered.

The footage jerked wildly as the cameraman lost his footing and slipped from where he'd been standing just before Hicks began firing. The phone was still recording when the cameraman caught a bullet to the head and died.

The last image was of Hicks' face as he pulled the camera from the snow before he shut it off. OMNI scanned the rest of the device for any other information, but came up empty. The phone had been purchased and activated just before they'd come to the park. Tracking data showed it had been turned on in Long Island City and showed the route they took to Central Park West by car.

The footage didn't tell Hicks anything he didn't already know, but it told him something. Judging by the way the camera shook, the cameraman had been standing in the cold for a while.

It also confirmed that these men were amateurs. Pros would've had better equipment. They would've outfitted Colin with a small camera somewhere in his clothing. They would've picked a location where they could've seen Hicks without being spotted. They would've dressed warmer and had better clothes than cheap Jordan knockoffs. And they wouldn't have been waiting to shoot him with a gun in their bare hand in a blizzard.

The whole scene vibed improvisation. It vibed panic. It vibed intent with no thought given to execution. These men were underfunded and undermanned and inexperienced. Colin must've done something or saw something that scared them and now they were scrambling to protect whatever Colin had threatened.

Hicks straightened up when he saw OMNI's scan of the phone had picked up three deleted images. He had the computer begin to restore them.

While the system went to work, Hicks opened his

humidor, selected, cut, then lit a Churchill cigar. The humidor was his only personal aspect in the entire facility. The Churchill was a long smoke that would keep him focused and grounded while the technology did its job.

For even with all of OMNI's immense power and reach, human intelligence was still a waiting game. A patient man's game. Because intelligence involved human beings and, even in a high-tech world, human beings were unpredictable. They moved at their own pace. Technology was a tool, but human beings decided how to use it.

Hicks let out a long plume of bluish smoke and watched it drift up toward the air scrubber in the ceiling. The fan pulled the smoke from the room and the carbon filters kept the air clean. He wondered what Jonathan would say if he saw him smoking a cigar in a University facility. He'd probably fire off a terse memorandum reminding him that smoking was prohibited in all University facilities.

And Hicks would've politely reminded him this was technically not a University facility. After Holloway's death, Hicks declined the Dean's generous offer and had built the New York office from the ground up through his own means. Extortion, blackmail and good old-fashioned thievery were all fair when assembling an intelligence network behind enemy lines. He didn't just worry about terrorist networks. He had to worry about steering clear of the other intelligence agencies doing the same kind of work. The University had been created to remain independent and it often took a lot of fancy maneuvering to remain so.

Which was why Hicks funded his New York Office

the way he had set up other operations around the globe. He'd broken a lot of laws and even more bones to build the New York office into the flagship of the modern University's network. And although the Dean had given his approval, he'd given little else beside the hardware and remote access to OMNI to make it happen.

This independence gave him a certain degree of autonomy. Hicks liked it that way. He'd never wanted to be just a clock watcher, someone who scribbled down bits of information he overheard and entered them into a database while he calculated his pension every month.

Hicks had been trained to take the fight directly to the enemy. He couldn't do that from behind a computer screen. He'd crafted the New York Office to be the tip of the University's spear and he kept it sharp. Sharp enough to cut anyone who got in front of it.

And right now, that person was Omar.

Hicks' natural impulse was to order a Varsity squad to hit Omar's garage with as soon as possible. But that would only confirm whatever suspicions had led Omar to cast out Colin.

Hicks didn't know what Omar knew or what Omar suspected. Colin had been trained to lie under interrogation, but he'd died before Hicks could get anything out of him. Hicks decided to investigate Omar in other, more subtle ways.

Hicks took another long pull on his cigar when OMNI pinged that the deleted images had been restored. He clicked on the results and saw three ghost images. The first two were blurred shots of something that looked like a finger in front of the lens. It was as though someone had turned on the camera by accident.

But the third shot was solid gold.

It was a crooked but clear shot of a black man on a city street in front of what looked like a neighborhood cellphone store. He was lighter skinned than any of Omar's Somalis. He was clean shaven except for a pencil thin moustache. Hicks knew every driver Omar employed and had never seen this man before. At least the image was clear enough for OMNI to identify him. If his photo was in any database in the world, they'd find him.

Hicks selected the man's face, pasted it into the OMNI facial recognition software, linked it to the two previous searches of the dead men and let the system go to work. He took another long drag on his cigar and waited for the technology do its thing.

He had no idea who the man was or if he had anything to do with what had happened with Colin. He could've just been a guy who'd accidentally gotten his picture taken while the dead man was playing with the burner. He also could've been the reason why Colin was dead. That was the problem with intelligence work. A definite maybe was often the best one could hope for. But wars had been started over less.

Hicks brought up the OMNI tactical screen for New York City and selected the trace he'd put on the car that had sped away from him outside Central Park.

OMNI had tracked the Toyota as far north as an indoor parking garage just off Broadway up in Washington Heights. The program showed the car had driven straight there after leaving Central Park West and had reached the location in about thirty minutes. Pretty good time considering the streets hadn't been plowed yet.

He had OMNI check traffic cameras along the route for a clear shot of the driver. But the man had been wearing a face mask, making it impossible to identify him. The license plate was obscured by snow, but easily photographed by the cameras.

He clicked on the information icon and saw that the car was registered to Mr. Jacfar Abrar to an address in Long Island City, Queens.

The same part of Queens where Colin had been working undercover. According to immigration records, Abrar was also Somali. Just like Omar.

Hicks clicked on Abrar's file, which opened a window showing Abrar's Somali passport photo, age, height and resident alien status.

He didn't look like either of the men Hicks had killed in the park. Abrar didn't look familiar from any of the surveillance photos Colin had taken of cab company regulars, either.

Hicks knew that meant there were some new players in Omar's operation. The question was why them and why now.

He had OMNI run a full scan of Abrar's life. His screen filled with cell phone records, ATM and credit card accounts. Abrar's cellphone hadn't been turned on since noon the day before, but had last been located at the cab stand.

He had OMNI attempt to turn it on remotely, but the battery had either been removed or was dead. There'd been no cell signal coming from the vehicle while OMNI had been tracking it, so chances were, he didn't have a cellphone on him at the time.

And there'd been no sign of him anywhere since the

car had been parked in the garage in Washington Heights.

He had OMNI scan the satellite footage of the garage to see if any other cars had come out of the garage since his target's arrival, but none had. He looked for anyone who might've left the garage on foot, but saw nothing but snow.

Hicks doubted the man was still there. He had gotten away somehow. Like a man who knew he was being watched from above.

Smart.

Hicks flicked his cigar ash in the ashtray and decided he'd better write up a summary of what had happened in the park. Jonathan would want a thorough report, especially because Colin had been lost. Hicks already had enough on his mind without worrying about being berated by a bureaucrat.

He toggled away from his report when a window on his desktop appeared, telling him OMNI had identified the three men he had been looking for.

But when he clicked on the icon to retrieve the results, he saw the following message:

Please contact your Department Chair for more information.

Son of a bitch. Jonathan had blocked him from seeing the results. He was probably waiting until their meeting to tell him the results in person. The man loved his power.

Hicks felt his temper beginning to spiral, so he sat back in his chair and took a long drag on his cigar. An agent in the morgue, two dead hostiles and a third on the loose and Jonathan was playing parlor games with information. God, how he hated bureaucrats.

Hicks knew he'd better review every one of Colin's status reports for the last six months before his debrief with Jonathan. He poured himself another cup of coffee. He knew there was a damned good chance he'd need to make another pot.

CHAPTER 6

THE NEXT MORNING was like most New York mornings following a bad storm: brisk with blue skies almost too bright to look at. It was as if the city was trying to make up for the miserable weather.

The snow was still mostly white because the pollution and dogs hadn't gotten to it yet. Large chunks of the sidewalk still hadn't been shoveled and wouldn't be for some time, but there'd been enough foot traffic along Bleecker Street by then to have beaten down something of a path.

Hicks navigated through the snow and pedestrians while he balanced two coffee cups in the Styrofoam carrier.

One cup was a large black coffee for himself and a soy vanilla chai latte for Jonathan. Jonathan was a soy vanilla chai latte kind of guy.

Most of the cars on the street had been parked in the same spaces since before the storm had begun and were buried under several inches of drifted snow. But somehow, Jonathan had managed to park his black

Range Rover in the same spot where he always parked, midblock close to Sullivan Street. Maryland plates gave it away.

Hicks hadn't expected Jonathan to get out of his warm SUV to help him with the coffee and Jonathan didn't let him down. He simply watched Hicks go all the way to the corner and walk back in the street as cars crawled through the thickening slush. But he was kind enough to unlock the doors and take his latte from the carrier as Hicks climbed into the SUV.

"Thanks for the help." Hicks said as he pulled the door closed. The inside of the SUV was warm and spotless. He took special joy in grinding the snow and rock salt from his boot treads into the passenger side carpet.

"Thanks for making me drive up here in this shit." Jonathan took the lid off the cup and blew on it, even though Hicks knew it wasn't that hot. "Traffic into the city was a nightmare."

Hicks drank his coffee without removing the lid. "You're the one who decided to come up here, Ace. A video call would've saved us both a lot of trouble."

"That's not how I work and you know it. University protocol requires a field visit from your Department Chair when we lose an agent. And, as much as you might hate that fact, I am your Department Chair."

"And I already told you it's being handled."

"I find your definition of 'being handled' troubling to say the least. Do you call three dead men in Central Park 'handled'? Do you think allowing a suspected accomplice to escape 'handled'? Do you call having to bring in the Varsity to clean up your mess 'handled'? Looks like a Grade-A catastrophe to me."

Hicks looked at Jonathan for the first time since

getting in the car. He was as equally nondescript as Hicks, though his coloring was much fairer and his features more delicate. His penchant for J. Crew sweaters and Lindberg frames led people to believe he was a computer programmer or a high school swimming coach or an accountant. Anything but a spy runner. The Dean liked his people to appear innocuous and Jonathan succeeded. In Hicks' opinion, being forgettable was the only thing he was good at.

"It's tough to handle things when you block my access to the identities of the men I killed and their autopsy results. That was strictly a power play on your part, Ace, and don't tell me otherwise."

"Do you honestly expect me to allow you to see sensitive information less then an hour after what happened in Central Park? Without even being able to survey the situation or observe your status first hand? You must be out of your fucking mind."

Hicks smiled as he sipped his coffee. "Don't curse. It doesn't go well with the latte."

"You really think this is just one big joke, don't you? That you can handle everything with just a few keystrokes and a few emails."

"I think one of us has almost twenty years of field experience and it sure as hell ain't you. You've been on the job six months, and I don't know what you were doing before that, so forgive me if I don't take rebuke from a rookie."

"The Dean gave me this assignment for a reason."

"Yes he did," Hicks said, "just like he put me in charge of the New York Office for a reason. Know why? Because field operations aren't easy. They go to shit all the time and almost never go according to plan. Surprise is part of the job, even when a good man like Colin is involved. People snap. They make mistakes. Things go south and when they do, it's professionals like me who know how to handle it. And you holding back information from me makes all the bad shit that went down last night that much worse."

"I don't see how three dead men in the park could get any worse."

"Which is exactly why you're riding a desk," Hicks said. "You see three dead bodies. Colin was more than just someone who worked for me. He was a friend, but at least he didn't die in vain. I see two threats neutralized and a suspect pinged by OMNI as he escaped, not to mention the images we were able to pull off the dead man's phone."

Jonathan looked like he wanted to say more. He looked out the window instead. "You sound like a man doing his best to put a positive spin on a bad situation."

"Your job is about spin. My job is about taking effective action on the information we gather and I can't do my job if you block me from that information. You'd know that if you had any idea about how this works."

Jonathan slowly slid his latte into the beverage holder near the gear shift. Hicks knew he'd already pulled the chain of command as tight as he dared. He didn't care. He hoped Jonathan tried to hit him. He'd like a legitimate reason to break his arm.

Instead, Jonathan said, "You don't know the first thing about me or what I've done in my career, and I'll be damned if I'm going to justify my credentials to you. I'll release the identities of the men you killed when I'm convinced you're capable of running this operation according to University protocol. And right now, you haven't convinced me."

"Let me convince you of this. I've got a hot investigation that's getting colder each second I waste sitting here kissing your ass. Who gives a shit about protocols? All I care about is finding out what got Colin killed. So get out of my way and let me get to work."

Hicks watched Jonathan trace the inside of his mouth with his tongue. "And if I don't, you'll call the Dean directly, won't you? Go right over my head."

"No," Hicks admitted, "because he probably already knows what you're doing. You wouldn't have the balls to hold back those identities from me without his support. I know you've got his blessing for now, but for how long once I start leaning on him about you being a problem?"

Jonathan looked at the steering wheel; then back out the window. "The Dean knows I blocked your searches. He also knows why. I told him I think you were too close to Colin and have lost objectivity in this case. I think there's a good chance you missed something in your recent debriefing session and I'm not comfortable with your ability to see things clearly right now."

The idea he'd missed something in Colin's debriefing still haunted him. Hearing it from Jonathan only made it sting. "You've probably been through every report I've filed from Colin. I spent half the night going through them myself. Twice. And I know I didn't miss anything. You know it, too."

"We both know a report is only as thorough as the person who wrote it. I'd think a man with your extensive amount of field experience would know that. I think your objectivity here is clouded by your long friendship and working relationship with Colin. And I'm afraid that lack of objectivity will pose a serious hindrance in your ongoing pursuit of Omar. There's no room for revenge in our line of work, James. You've said so many times, according to your file."

"You read it in my file, but do you have any idea what it actually means?" Hicks realized he was grabbing the paper coffee cup tight enough to buckle it and slid it into the beverage holder instead. "When the Dean assigned me here, this office was one step above a glass-to-the-wall operation. Now it's the best network in the entire University system."

"No one's interested in listening to you narrate your own highlight reel, James. That was then. This is now."

"Then let's talk about now. Now, I've got an office with over a hundred sources and field personnel who turn over solid, actionable intelligence to me every single week. No other office in the System has that kind of output."

"Not every week," Jonathan said. "Let's not get ahead of ourselves."

"Then let's talk money. I've got a revenue stream that not only keeps the New York Office off the University's grid, but it keeps the University's bursar account fat and happy. That same money keeps your candy ass in Ranger Rovers and lattes and Izod shirts. You don't trust me?" Hicks laughed. "Ace, I don't give a shit because the Dean knows that if I go, the whole operation goes with me."

"Pride goes before the fall," Jonathan said. "We know more about what you do here than you think."

"You only know what I share with you. So, either

you release the identities of the three men or you and me are going to have a serious problem."

Jonathan slowly lifted his latte out of the cup holder. "I could be forgiven for taking that as a threat."

"I don't make threats. I just tell it like it is."

Jonathan sipped his latte as he watched New Yorkers of all ages toddling through the heavy snow. The city had closed the schools thanks to the blizzard and it seemed like every kid in the world was out on the street; letting themselves fall into the snow banks while their fathers or mothers or nannies told them to stop.

Hicks noticed the manicured nails on Jonathan's right hand and the wedding ring on his left. He wondered if the ring was real or just cover. He wondered if Jonathan had children and what kind of father he'd be. Was he an asshole in every aspect of his life or only with him?

Jonathan took another sip of his latte and licked his lips clean. "We don't have to like each other. We don't even have to respect each other, but we do have to work together. Under other circumstances, I'd probably ask the Dean for another posting because I don't enjoy working with people I despise and believe it or not, I despise you."

Hicks toasted him with his coffee. "Feeling's mutual."

"I despise you so much, that I'm not going to give you the satisfaction of transferring to another office. And I'm staying not just because I enjoy making your life miserable, but because I think you've lost your objectivity. I think you're putting the University – and the Dean – at risk and I owe him too much to let that happen."

"So making my life miserable is just a bonus for you?"

"Yes," Jonathan admitted. "Yes it is."

"Marvelous." Hicks was tired of arguing. "Are you going to release the search results on the three men or not?"

"I'll agree to give you the identities of the two men you killed, but not the image you retrieved from the camera."

Hicks knew he'd given in too easily. "Why not?"

"Because that image was embargoed by another government when OMNI ran the search."

"Embargoed?" Hicks hadn't heard that term in years. "By who?"

"We're working on figuring that out," Jonathan said. "It looks like one of our European cousins did it when OMNI searched Interpol's database. Their firewall slammed down like a hammer. Other networks came up empty, so Interpol is the only one who has the man's identity. OMNI could've punched through the firewall, of course, but not without raising a lot of red flags. The Dean is looking into it personally. He hopes to have some answers later today. This man is being protected and the Dean wants to find out why."

Hicks knew this was how it was in the Life. Two steps up and one step back. "Fine. Any word on Colin's autopsy?"

Jonathan referred to his handheld. "It came in a few minutes before you got here. Our doctors say his system was pumped full of a combination of heroin and cocaine. Chances are he probably would've died from cardiac arrest if Omar's man hadn't shot him. Given his known fear of needles and avoidance of alcohol and drugs, we surmise that he was drugged in a crude attempt to get him to talk. So, for all intents and purposes, he was already dead by the time you got there."

Jonathan frowned as he looked away. "I'm sorry about that. I didn't mean to be so...clinical about it. I know he was your friend. For what it's worth, the injection site on his arm was bruised, implying that he didn't let them stick him easily. As for what he may or may not have told them, that's anyone's guess. OMNI searched every digital signal within a couple of miles of the cab stand. Nothing appeared on passive surveillance, either. Whatever they did to him, they didn't have cellphones with them while it happened."

Hicks was glad Colin had put up a fight. "What about the two men in the park?"

"I'll see to it that the identities of the two men you killed are sent to your handheld as soon as we're done here. I'm afraid you'll find it pedestrian reading. No red flags and no known ties to extremists except that they're both Somali."

Hicks had figured as much. "I just checked our passive surveillance of the cab stand and the whole garage has been dark since yesterday. No sign of Omar, the drivers or any of the cars, either. It's seems they all scattered just before Colin went to meet me at the park."

Hicks didn't like where any of this was leading, but it only seemed to be leading one place. He had no choice but to state the obvious. "I think Omar's network is a hell of a lot bigger than we thought."

"Which makes Omar far more dangerous than we thought," Jonathan said. "Which means we're going to have to work closely on this from here on in. Our personal animosity aside, we need to help each other to keep a bad situation from getting even worse."

Hicks closed his eyes. "Why do I have a feeling I'm going to hate this next part?"

Once again, Jonathan did not disappoint him. "That means I need to be apprised of every new development. I need you to wait for my approval before you act on any intelligence. And before you accuse me of being on a power trip, remember the Interpol embargo of the image from the phone. Other agencies are involved here, probably more than just Interpol. We need to proceed cautiously lest we tip our hand. That's the reason for the tight leash, not ego. Are we absolutely clear on that?"

Hicks decided to quit while he was ahead. "We're clear. I'll keep you posted."

As Hicks opened the car door, Jonathan said, "Stay in touch. And stay safe."

Hicks smiled before he closed the door. "Gee, honey. I didn't know you cared."

CHAPTER 7

HICKS WAITED until he got back to Twenty-third Street to look at the files Jonathan had sent to him. And just as Jonathan had warned him, the background on the two Somalis he'd killed had been a dead end.

According to the file, the two men he'd killed were a couple of twenty-year-old orphans raised in a Christian mission in Somalia. That same orphanage sponsored them for student visas so they could come to the Land of Opportunity and bring their knowledge back home with them. Their passports had been stamped at JFK four months before and they'd fallen off the radar since then. They'd appeared to be model citizens until the moment Hicks had killed them.

They'd entered the country legally with legitimate passports and sponsors. That meant they'd probably gotten involved with Omar after they'd gotten into the country. And since OMNI had never tracked either of them to the cab stand or any of the drivers, it confirmed that Omar's operation was much bigger than he'd previously thought.

Somehow, Omar had managed to build up a network while being under the watchful eye of OMNI and Colin.

But Jonathan was wrong about the dead men being dead ends. They were rookies, not killers. They hadn't even been armed. That meant Colin probably hadn't told Omar much about the University despite being drugged. If he had, Omar would've sent pros or just flat out killed Colin and cut his losses. Omar had sent men to get information instead. To record and report back. That meant Omar was curious. The men were expendable. When they didn't return, he probably figured they'd been killed or grabbed up by Colin's handler. That meant they didn't know anything and couldn't lead anyone back to him. Omar had already scattered, so his operation was probably ongoing.

The bigger question remained. Why? What had Colin seen? What had he done to blow his cover? And how had Omar managed to keep such an operation secret from the finest intelligence array in the world?

Omar's operation was conspicuous by its absence. Whatever he was doing must be big. And whoever was behind it knew how to cover their tracks in the twenty-first century.

He toggled his screen to see the autopsy reports. The photo of Colin's corpse on a slab came up first. A white sheet draped over his body with gaps and sags where none would be if he had still been alive. Where the doctor had cut into him.

Hicks stared at the picture until he thought he could see each pixel of the image. *Why are you dead, my old friend? Why did you set me up?*

Omar had disappeared and the autopsies of the dead men came up with nothing out of the ordinary.

The only lead Hicks had left was the image of the man on the phone. An image a foreign government was protecting. And two dead men from an organization far larger than Hicks knew existed.

This was far above the skill set of an untrained Somali cab owner with bad intentions. This was something more.

Hicks almost jumped when his handheld began to buzz. The screen said it was the Dean himself.

The University prided itself on 'dynamic diversity'. There was no central office or campus, but hundreds of offices hiding in plain sight around the globe, all remotely connected through OMNI.

Hicks had worked for the Dean for almost twenty years, but had never met him. He had no idea where the Dean lived or where he was from. He didn't know his name or what he looked like. They'd always communicated over the OMNI network, but never in person. His image and voice were always digitally different and lifelike.

Hicks had spoken to the man hundreds of times and, based on the conversations they'd had and the decisions he'd made, Hicks pegged him for an old field man. A good one at that. The kind who knew when to step in, when to give advice and when to back out of the way. Skills Jonathan didn't have and probably never would.

When Hicks answered the phone as Professor Warren, the Dean said, "You're brooding, aren't you?"

The man's ability to read people had always impressed him. "How did you know?"

"Because you've been staring at the same screen for ten minutes after a night of furious activity. You've been staring at those pictures from Colin's autopsy for so long that I can practically feel it burning a hole right through you."

Hicks should've remembered that OMNI kept track of its users. No one else had access to that level of information except for the Dean. "I could've been in the bathroom."

"Not you. Not that long. Besides, I owed you a call to express my condolences over what happened to Colin. He was a good man. I hope you don't blame yourself for his death."

"I don't," Hicks said, almost believing it. "I just don't like how this seems to be much bigger than we know."

"All that means is that your instincts were right from the beginning," the Dean said. "You knew Omar was up to something and you stayed with it, despite all evidence to the contrary. That's the human element I'm always talking about, James. OMNI is an invaluable tool, but it still takes a human's instinct and training to wield her properly. This business with Omar proves me right."

"Speaking of humans," Hicks said, "did Jonathan debrief you on our meeting today?"

"He's promised me a full report by close of business today. All he said was that it was far more productive and went better than he expected it would. I know that working with him isn't always easy, but he really is quite brilliant in certain aspects of the job."

Hicks had never pulled punches with the Dean

before and he wouldn't start now. "He's nowhere near as smart as he thinks he is."

"He's smarter in aspects of the job you don't have to be," the Dean said, "but I know better than to waste time trying to change your mind. Jonathan is valuable if only because he's young and youth can always be exploited by more experienced men. Men like you and me."

Hicks heard the tinkle of ice and the sound of the Dean sipping something. Hicks always envisioned the Dean as a scotch man, sitting behind a large oak desk, sipping Laphroig or Johnnie Walker Blue Label. Neat, of course. He just as easily could've been sipping lemonade on a balcony in Dubai for all Hicks knew, but he preferred his vision of the man better to whatever the reality might be.

The Dean went on. "Besides, we should table the discussion of Jonathan's shortcomings as a Department Chair for another time. We have more important business to discuss. Your friend who drove the getaway vehicle is dead."

"Dead?" Hicks sat up straight. "How do you know?"

"There's a reason why we couldn't track him from the garage," the Dean explained. "I thought we'd simply lost him due to the angle of the satellite or the snow storm, so I took the liberty of having a Varsity member check the garage for the car. He found our friend shot and dumped in the trunk of the same car we were tracking. Whoever did it just walked away. I've had techs reviewing the footage of every camera in the area, but none of it bore fruit."

Hicks wasn't as surprised as he was troubled. "Sir,

the speed with which this situation is getting complicated is troubling to say the least."

"I'm more troubled about something else," the Dean said. "I was able to determine that the image you found was embargoed by British Intelligence."

That was a surprise. "Why?"

"I've made some calls to find out who the man is and why they're hiding him. But answers will take time, if we get them at all. In the meantime, tell me your next course of action regarding Omar."

Hicks hated what he was about to say, but didn't see that he had any choice. "We should probably grab Omar as soon as possible." He toggled over to Omar's OMNI screen, which showed zero hits in activity on any of his phones or emails or vehicles since the day before. "The system shows he's been quiet since before the incident in the park, but that's to be expected since he probably knows he's being watched. Taking out Omar is our best chance of stalling whatever Colin uncovered. At least for a little while."

"Assuming you can find him," the Dean said, "do you really think you can get him to talk?"

"I'll feed him to Roger," Hicks said. "He could get a mute to recite Shakespeare."

"Agreed," the Dean said. "Our friend's peccadillos make me glad he's on our side."

Roger Cobb's interrogation technique was brutally intricate and incredibly efficient. He wasn't afraid of gore, but gore wasn't the sole purpose of what he did. "He's a gifted interrogator, sir."

"Normally, I'd agree that picking pick up Omar and handing him over to Roger is the best course of action," the Dean said, "but I think there's another way to go about it. A cleaner way we can get this bastard to give us everything we want without typing him off and interrupting his plans."

Hicks knew the Dean wasn't a deliberate man. He never came at something head on. He also never simply thought out loud. Everything he said or wrote had a purpose, even when it was in the form of a question.

"What do you have in mind?"

"I've learned that Omar is in quite a panic," the Dean explained. "He's been on the phone since midnight calling every fundamentalist financier in the book, begging them to send him money."

Hicks was the one in a panic as he quickly scanned Omar's profile on OMNI to see if he had missed any of his calls. "How can that be? I don't have any record of him calling anyone."

"Calm down, James," the Dean told him. "You didn't overlook anything. He's using a different phone. OMNI's not tracking him. I've received this information from one of the financiers he contacted. Someone who owes me his life, not to mention his freedom. He's decided to deal with Omar on our behalf."

That made Hicks feel a bit better, but not much. "How could Omar even get their numbers, much less get them to take his call?"

"I don't know how he got their numbers," the Dean said, "but Omar has called several well-known patrons seeking financing of an imminent, major offensive he's prepared to launch against the West. Part of his pitch is that time is of the essence and he needs financing to pull it off. Unfortunately, he's not giving any details unless they agree to fund him."

"Did your source get a location on him?" Hicks asked.

"My source's people tell him he called from a strip mall parking lot in Hoboken. I already traced the number and it's dead. I doubt he uses any phone more than once. It's primitive but proven effective so far. The footage from the security camera in the area isn't working, but OMNI is expanding her search."

Hicks didn't like to question the Dean, but given the circumstances, he had no choice. "How reliable is your source, sir?"

"Quite reliable. As you know, such men pride themselves on anonymity and discretion. A stranger calling them out of the blue begging for money for a mysterious attack has caused them to circle the wagons. They're wondering how an unknown like Omar was able to reach them and they're not happy."

Hicks didn't mind that. The longer these old bastards kept their checkbooks in the drawer, the fewer people got killed. "Has Omar gotten anyone to finance him yet?"

"Everyone's turned him down except our friend, who has agreed to string Omar along until we tell him how we want to proceed."

"What's his name?"

"Compartmentalization, James. I'll tell you at the right time," the Dean said, "but now's not the time."

Hicks hated working blind, but he knew the Dean wasn't the kind of man you pushed. If he was holding something back, it was for a reason. "Did this source tell you what Omar needs to buy with these funds?"

"No. For a beggar, he's being very cagey about details. Omar isn't being greedy, either. He's only asking for a pledge before he agreed to tell them more, especially over the phone. Omar implied that he's being hunted by the Great Satan and in dire need of assistance. All he's saying is that he's working on a sacred plan that will strike deep into the heart of the infidels and leave a scar that will take generations to heal. His very words, according to my source."

It sounded like a lot of desperate bluster to Hicks. He knew Omar wasn't a trained terrorist, just a very enthusiastic amateur looking to make it into the big time. Colin must've discovered whatever Omar was working on. Whatever it was required an infusion of cash.

Hicks decided to focus on finding Omar instead of speculating. With the photo of the mystery man from the phone embargoed, Omar remained his best lead.

"We need your source to help us get close to Omar as quickly as possible. I think he's the weakest link in whatever's being planned here."

The Dean agreed. "We'll use his zeal and inexperience to draw him out and trip him up. "He's obviously very desperate and he doesn't have the slightest idea of how these kinds of operations are funded. We're going to use his naivety to our advantage by sending in someone to play savior for him. We're going to make sure an emissary from our Middle Eastern friend will arrive at just the right time with a bag of cash and the promise of more to follow; as soon as Omar reveals everything about his plan, of course."

Hicks liked the plan, in theory. But there was nothing theoretical about field work. A solid op took weeks, often months to plan properly, and they didn't have that kind of time. If Omar really was ready to hatch some kind of an attack, they'd need to move fast before he grew even more desperate.

"Unfortunately," the Dean went on, "I don't think you have anyone on staff who could serve as a convincing bag man on such short notice, do you?"

Hicks didn't and the Dean knew it. He had trained agents from every ethnic group. Dozens of men and women of all races, colors, creeds and backgrounds who could pass for damned near any nationality in the world if they had enough time to back away from their current assignments. As big as Omar's plot may be, the University still had dozens of important deep cover operations underway throughout the city.

Hicks wouldn't throw one of his own people into this without proper prep time. Hurry and haste usually got the wrong people killed. Colin had proven that. "I've got Enrollees and Assets who could do the job, but none are in New York right now. No men, anyway, and I know Omar will not accept a woman as an emissary."

"I know," the Dean said. "Which is why I've already got someone in mind."

Hicks figured he did. But he didn't like outsiders coming in on one of his operations, even one as flawed and rushed as this one was shaping up to be. Hicks' New York team was diverse and they'd all been hand-picked by him. He knew all their strengths and weaknesses. He knew how to use them and when. A new player in the mix could throw all that off. "I'm still confident one of my people can handle it, sir. I've got a man who was in deep cover in Tehran and another who..."

"Who has been working in J.P. Morgan for the past ten years and hasn't been undercover for almost fifteen years," the Dean said. "I'm familiar with all of the people at your disposal, James, but I'm afraid this decision isn't up for debate. Omar has already surprised us with his ability to evade surveillance and discover Colin's identity, at least in part. Besides, we don't know what Colin may have told Omar about our operations in New York, so we can't risk one of your men going in. We need to embed someone who is trained in this sort of operation very quickly before Omar gets desperate and does something wild. Amateurs are at their most dangerous when frightened."

Hicks knew he was right. The Dean was always right. That didn't mean he had to like it. "Of course, sir."

"I need you to alert all of your people about what happened to Colin and let them know they need to be on guard just in case Colin talked about them," the Dean said. "Send the alert via the liquor store spam email so they know it's a critical message."

Hicks didn't need to be reminded of protocol. "I'll send it out as soon as possible, but I'd like to talk more about the man you have in mind for the Omar mission."

"I've already got our people vetting several candidates I've deemed suitable. In the meantime, I need you to take an educated guess on how much money we should offer Omar to satisfy his immediate needs. If we give him too much, he's liable to think he's being set up by the CIA or one of our brother agencies. We give him too little, he'll only waste time bartering for more. You've been studying him for months, so your input is vital on this front."

Hicks had seen this scenario play out in other parts of the University before. An Office Head would let their superior run an operation and, gradually, the Dean's office pushes the Office Head out of the entire op. Hicks wasn't about to allow that to happen to him.

"Where is the money coming from, sir? I take it that our Middle Eastern friend won't agree to finance it."

"Not a chance," the Dean said. "He's an ally, but an irregular one at best. We can't compel him to pay for anything like this."

That was music to Hicks' ears because now he knew how he'd be able to control the entire operation. The oldest form of control there was. "An op like this will take at least a hundred grand for Omar to take our decoy seriously."

The Dean skipped a beat. "Did you say a hundred thousand dollars?"

"I did, sir. Omar probably doesn't know how much to ask for, so a hundred grand is a good way to buy our decoy a seat at the table. We don't offer it all to him at once, of course. Maybe half to start with as a good faith effort to get the conversation started."

Hicks could practically hear the calculations going on in the Dean's mind. The University bureaucracy was far more streamlined than the bureaucracy of any intelligence agency in the world, but it was still a bureaucracy. A hundred grand was more than he could approve through petty cash. And Hicks knew that.

"Are you sure you're not being too generous? That's an awful lot of money to offer a small-time operator like Omar. Maybe we offer ..."

Hicks cringed as he cut him off. "Omar has shown enough sophistication to detect Colin was spying on him. He's proven that he has enough resources to get the contact information of some very influential financiers in the Middle East. And he's confident enough in whatever he's planning to have risked getting himself killed by calling them out of the blue. A hundred grand is a nice round number. I'd rather have it and not need it than need it and not have it." He moved in for the kill. "Besides, I have that money on hand."

"I'm sure that won't be necessary," the Dean said. "The University has more than enough in the Bursar's account to finance it."

"I know, but it'll take a couple of days for you to get all the approvals to release that kind of money. We don't have that kind of time. Luckily, I've just closed a new Asset; a finance man who's cash heavy at the moment and is looking to stay in my good graces. Why finance it ourselves when we can use other people's money? Risk free, too."

"That's the Russo man, isn't it?" the Dean asked. "I still don't see why we need another finance man. We've almost got as many money men as lawyers enrolled as assets these days."

"This one is very good at moving large amounts of money very quietly," Hicks explained, "and we're going to need a lot of cash on hand to get Omar to trust us. If he checks and sees our man only has fifteen thousand, he might clam up and that defeats the purpose of what we're trying to do here. My man's got a hundred grand just sitting in his safe right now."

This time, the Dean skipped two beats. "Are you sure?"

"Positive, sir."

"I suppose you have a point, but are you sure you're that liquid?"

Between his dozens of extortion operations and other legitimate investments, Hicks' New York office brought in over three hundred grand a month to the University's Bursar's office. That didn't count for the operating capital he held back to independently finance the New York office, which was close to double that amount. "I'm plenty liquid, sir. And I know for a fact that Russo has that much cash on hand. He'll be happy to get it to us quickly and quietly."

"Not to mention that providing the money will give you a certain level of operational control." He heard the smile in the Dean's voice. "Well played, James. Well played indeed."

Hicks lied. "I'm only thinking about the success of the mission, sir."

The Dean laughed. "You've never thought of only one thing in your life. I think a hundred thousand is more than generous, but as they say, it's your money. How long would it take you to get it?"

"Within a matter of hours at most," Hicks said. He hoped Russo hadn't moved it from his home safe. "When do you think your operative will be selected and on the ground here in New York?"

"The process is already underway. I'll be in touch with the particulars." The line went dead.

Hicks tossed the handheld on the desk and slowly pushed himself away from the computer. Away from the phone and OMNI and anything to do with the University. Just for a little while, he needed quiet.

There was no other sound in the bunker, not even the pop and creak of his chair as he moved. Just the antiseptic hum of the florescent lights and the computer's drive.

Conversations with the Dean were often closer to sparring matches than knife fights, but still took their toll. The Dean never came straight out and said what he wanted, and he always held something back, even when he didn't have to. Secrecy was the hallmark of their business and details were a way of keeping score. In the University system, the truth was an arduous process and something to be avoided at all costs until absolutely necessary.

At least the Dean had allowed him to finance the operation. Hicks knew he hadn't talked him into anything or pulled the wool over his eyes.

Now all Hicks had to do was get the money.

Hicks checked the time on his computer monitor. It was going on six o'clock, so Russo should still be in his office.

Hicks called Russo's private line, but it went straight to voicemail. Then he called the main office number, but the receptionist said he was gone for the evening.

Hicks didn't like that. Russo going home early was a deviation from his schedule. And Hicks didn't like deviations.

He went back into OMNI and tried to track Russo's cellphone. The phone had been turned off, but his Cadillac was parked at Russo's house on Long Island.

He could've had OMNI send out a signal to turn Russo's phone back on, but Russo wasn't used to the yoke just yet. Turning on his phone might spook him into doing something stupid and Hicks needed him calm. He needed Russo alive; at least until he got the hundred grand he needed to finance the Dean's undercover operation.

Hicks directed OMNI to focus the University satellite on the two-story Tudor style house that the Russo family called home in Suffolk County. He selected the 'full scan' option and the image on Hicks' screen began to change.

The OMNI lens focused on a typical suburban home on a cul-de-sac, a bit larger than any of the others in the area. The Russo property's normally-manicured lawns were now covered in a thick layer of snow, as was the separate two car garage in the back. The whole scene appeared far more wholesome than it actually was.

Hicks selected the thermal option as the satellite began reading heat signatures in and around the property. It revealed two cars in the garage; one engine slowly cooling from red to orange in the brisk November night. Vinny's car. Judging by the heat signature of the engine, he'd just gotten home.

Hicks scanned over to the house. He saw a single heat signature in the living room; the size of the shape and its location on the couch read like Russo's wife, Marie. Another shape was in the den on the west wing of the house read it was Russo himself, sitting at his desk.

There were no other heat signatures in the rest of the house, except for the heat signature of a cat in the upstairs bathroom. And, from what Hicks could see, Tabby had gotten into the laundry.

Hicks could've called Russo or texted him but chose not to. Because some conversations were better in person.

He pulled his coat from the hook and went outside.

CHAPTER 8

THE DRIVE OUT TO Russo's home took just over an hour, which wasn't bad considering it was seven o'clock at night, the tail end of rush hour. A lot of companies had closed because of the blizzard, so rush hour traffic was much lighter than normal.

Russo's street looked like something out of a Norman Rockwell painting. The colors of the Christmas lights along the eaves and roofs gave the snow a multicolored glow. Someone had even made a snowman complete with a carrot nose and raisins for the eyes and mouth.

Hicks would've thought the scene was damned near wholesome if it hadn't been all so contrived. Because in the course of his research on Russo, he'd also done research on the people in his immediate circle. Neighbors, friends from church and people in the contacts folder of his phone. It paid to be thorough. After all, blackmailing a guy whose best friends were cops could make things more difficult than they needed to be without proper preparation.

That's why he resented the Rockwellian facade of Russo's street because it was just a facade. Russo's neighbors were tax cheats and embezzlers, adulterers and prescription pill addicts. Two had done time for vehicular manslaughter and one of them had been a coke dealer in college before she changed her name and moved to New York.

Some of them voted Republican but paid illegal aliens to shovel their driveways and mow their lawns. Some of them were vocal Democrats who drove Mercedes and gave nothing to charity. They celebrated holidays but left their religion at the front door of whatever church or synagogue they attended, if they attended at all.

Russo's street wasn't all that different than any of the other streets in the rest of the neighborhood or in the rest of the country for that matter. Human frailty was everywhere. Human frailty was Hicks' stock and trade. Frailty was the grease that made the wheels of the University turn. Frailty justified its existence and kept its coffers filled.

There was a part of Hicks that knew his choice of professions should make him regret what he'd done with his life. Living off other people's misery was less than admirable. But he didn't feel an ounce of regret for anything he'd done because what he did saved lives.

Hicks parked his brown Buick on the street a few houses away from Russo's house. He pulled up the OMNI scan of the house on his car's dashboard screen and saw that Russo hadn't moved from the den. In fact, it looked like he was more slumped at his desk than before. He looked well on his way to getting quietly drunk. Alone.

Hicks figured this was a result of their conversation. He'd seen this happen to new Assets before. Russo was no longer the head of the pack; the master of his own universe. None of his many secrets were his alone anymore. A stranger now had a knife to his throat and access into every unsavory aspect of his life.

Normally, Hicks could work up some sympathy for an Asset while he or she adjusted to the yoke, but not Russo. Not since the Madoff mess. Russo had gotten greedy and careless with the wrong people and would've gotten himself killed if Hicks hadn't stepped in when he did. Men like Vladic always found out when someone was stealing from them, and when they did, the thief and his family took a long time to die badly.

Hicks didn't have the time to accommodate Russo's acceptance of his new reality. He needed the hundred grand Russo had in his safe and he needed it fast.

Hicks walked up the shoveled brick path to the front door. He knew the Russos always entered the house through the garage, but he wasn't supposed to know that. He could've easily popped the lock and gone in that way, but with Mrs. Russo around, there was no need to cause a scene. He rang the front doorbell instead.

A string of gentle chimes rang somewhere deep within the house. The sound had just died away when Marie Russo answered the door.

According to Hicks' surveillance of her husband, Vinny complained to his mistress that his wife had begun to lose her looks. Hicks' file on her showed she'd certainly been prettier when she was younger - the years and children and a marriage to Vinny had certainly taken their toll – but she still looked pretty despite everything. Her eyes were sunken and harder than they'd been in their wedding photos. Her face thinner, but surprisingly free of wrinkles.

Judging by the emails Hicks knew she'd sent and the websites he knew she'd visited, Hicks knew she was overly conscious of the weight she'd been unable to lose after giving birth to her daughter twenty-three years before, but she carried it much better than most.

"May I help you?" she asked.

Hicks flashed his best weary smile and used a name he knew she'd heard – one of Vinny's employees - but had never met. "I'm Jerry Parsons from the office. Vince asked me to drop off something for him on my way home."

"Oh, of course," she said, remembering his name. She opened the door a bit more as she stepped back. "He's in the study just down the hall."

Hicks thanked her, but he already knew where it was. He'd already been in the house twice before when no one was home. Tapping into security cameras and reading emails and phone calls could only tell so much of the story. Technology couldn't completely replace seeing something with his own two eyes.

That's why he knew the door to the den didn't have a lock, so he walked right in without knocking.

Hicks found Russo sitting in the same position that he'd seen from the thermal image. He was at the desk with a glass of scotch in a rock glass in front of him. The TV was off and so was the radio. Even the computer screen on his desk was dark. Vincent Russo was a man in a wood-paneled man cave, with only his trouble and his booze to keep him company.

Russo didn't even bother to look up when he heard the door close. "Marie, how many times have I told you not to bother me when..."

And when he did look up, he saw Hicks standing on the other side of the desk. "Hello, Vince."

Russo's eyes went wide. "You? How did you...how did..."

"Marie let me in," Hicks explained. "She's not as run down as you tell people she is. You should do yourself a favor and compliment her more often. I know you've got Inez on the side, but you still live here, so..."

"What the hell do you think you're doing here?" He made a move for his desk drawer – the same drawer where Hicks knew he kept a nine-millimeter Glock.

That's why Hicks had his gun out first. He pointed the .454 Ruger at Russo's head more for effect than intent. "Leave the nine where it is, Vinny. No need to get killed over an empty gun."

Russo looked down at the drawer, then at Hicks. "How do you know it's not loaded?"

"Because I unloaded it when I did a final sweep last week and you haven't touched the drawer since."

Russo sank back into his chair and dropped his head in his hand. It was a similar pose to the one he had in his office, but much more resigned. "Yesterday, you punch me in the face and hit me in the balls. Today, you just stroll into my house and pull a gun on me. What'll you do to me tomorrow?"

"Nothing I don't have to." Hicks could see he already had Russo cowed, so he lowered the gun. "It's time to start being part of the team, Vinny. I need you to do something for me and I need you to do it tonight."

"So this is how it's going to be, isn't it? Never

knowing when you're going to call or show up with some request? From now until the day I die, I'll always have to worry about you buzzing in my ear like a gnat?"

"I already told you that you'll hardly even know I'm around as long as you do exactly what I tell you to do. I won't ask much and I won't ask often and I'll never ask you to deliver the impossible. And that's why I'm here now."

"I don't care why you're here," Russo said. "I don't care what you do to me or my family because I don't give a shit about anything anymore. Go ahead and shoot me. You'll be doing me a favor."

Hicks didn't like his tone. "What's wrong? What happened?"

"You're so plugged into my life, so why don't you tell me?" Russo pounded the desktop with the heel of his hand. "Do you honestly think I'm worried about some fucking lunatic four thousand miles away who *might* get around to killing me in a couple of days on the off chance him or any of the other fucking illiterate peasants who work for him can figure out that I skimmed from him? Why do you think they hired me? Because I'm their money guy. I'm the one who handles all the financials for them so they don't have to worry about it. He even said he expects me to steal, so long as I don't get crazy about it."

Hicks smiled. "A psychopath's sense of crazy changes from day to day."

"It would still take you a week to teach that ignorant bastard how to open his email and another week to explain what the spreadsheets mean. You want to send it? Be my guest. Because by the time he does get someone on a plane to come over here and whack me, I won't give a shit anymore."

Hicks realized there was more behind this than just bravado. "What happened?"

Russo rubbed the sore hand he'd just pounded on the desk. "What do you care?"

"When we were in your office, I told you that your problems are my problems, so if something's bothering you, I want to know what it is."

"My junkie son is what's bothering me. That's what you called him yesterday, isn't it?"

Hicks didn't bother apologizing because he knew it wouldn't do him any good. "What about him?"

"He's back to putting shit in his arm again. Or smoking it. Whatever the hell he's decided to do this time, the effects are still the same."

Hicks had been afraid of that. His son was Russo's one weakness. "What is it this time? Heroin?"

Russo nodded. "For the amount of money I've spent trying to get that kid clean, I could've bought a small island in the Caribbean. I came home last night after making your miserable acquaintance and he flat out hits me up for money. No explanation, just sticks out his hand and demands it. I was in no mood for his bullshit, so I told him to leave me alone. What does he do? He goes up to my room, steals a handful of my gold cuff-links and my Rolex before he tears ass out of here. I didn't know he'd taken anything until later that night and I haven't seen him since. He won't pick up his phone and he's not with any of the scum he usually hangs out with. None of the ones I know, anyway."

Hicks didn't want the answer to the next question but he had to ask. "How do you know?"

"You're not the only one with connections here. I have my ways."

Hicks didn't pretend to be impressed. "You've got an uncle who's retired NYPD and a few friends who are lieutenants on the local PD. Which one did you call?"

Russo shook his head. "Jesus, you really do know everything, don't you?"

Hicks didn't like Russo going outside the circle. He didn't like him asking people to look into his family problems. He might get the idea to tell them about Hicks and, if that happened, it could become a problem. Not an unsolvable problem, but messier than Hicks wanted. "Answer the question."

"My uncle worked Narcotics and still has some friends who work the streets. He called around but no one knows of anyone trading Rolexes for dope. Not in the last few days, anyway."

"You tell your uncle anything about me?"

"No, darling. No one knows about us."

"Keep it that way." In all of his surveillance of the Russo's family, Hicks hadn't really focused on the son, Vincent Russo, Junior. But with a little research, Hicks figured he could find him if he had to. Junkies were like rats, often taking the same paths to the same dens to get their fix. He hoped he wouldn't have to look too hard.

"I'll make a deal with you. I know you keep a hundred grand in cash in your safe. Don't bother lying about it because I know it's there. You hand it over and I'll see what I can do about finding your kid."

"No."

"That's not a word you get to say to me. Give me the money and I promise I'll help you find Junior."

"I said no. Want me to spell it out for you? N-O and here's why: I don't care what you do to me or how you've screwed over people like me in the past. Because you're not the only one here who can put things together. If you're coming in here unannounced like this, I'll bet it's because you need that money pretty damned quick. That's good, because I need my son back pretty damned quick, too."

Hicks was getting annoyed. "We can talk about that after you hand me the money."

"No, we'll talk about it now because he doesn't have that kind of time. This is the third time he's come out of rehab and if it doesn't take now, I don't know if it ever will. I don't even know if he'll survive the treatment and if he doesn't survive it, neither will I."

Talk like that was a bad thing for an Asset. "Don't say that."

"It's the truth. As God is my witness. You want to threaten my wife and daughter? Knock yourself out. They're two of the most ungrateful, greedy little bitches in the world. Neither of them has had any use for me for years and the second I die; I don't know who'd be the first to call the lawyer. Vladic can gut both of them as far as I'm concerned, if it would bring my son back."

Russo paled and sagged back in his chair. He looked at the bottle of scotch and his empty glass, but made no attempt to reach either. "He's a sweet kid when he's clean. Nice. Respectful. Creative as hell." His eyes began to water. "I know he can make something of himself if he can just kick this shit once and for all. He's only twenty years old, for Christ's sake. But he's my whole world and everything I've built is to give him some kind of chance, so if he's dead, I might as well be, too because I've got no reason to live."

When Russo looked up at him, Hicks saw no trace of hate or anger, just flat resentment in his eyes. "And in case you need help making up your mind, I got home early this afternoon and moved the money. I put it in one of the safe deposit boxes I've got all over the island. You say you know everything there is about me, so you know I'm right. I split the money up so none of it is all in one place and you don't know which banks I put it in because I stopped at all of them for exactly the same amount of time."

Hicks felt his temper beginning to spiral again. The Ruger was beginning to become a viable option. "Don't do this, Vinny. You're playing a dangerous game."

"You'll probably be able to pull whatever computer voodoo bullshit you do to get your way into some of the boxes," Russo went on, "but probably not all of them in time before you need the money. So here's what's going to happen. You're going to take the same resources you used to dig up shit on me and you're going to use them to find my son and bring him back home where he belongs. Dead or alive, I don't care. I just need him here with me so I know where he is, not lying dead in some crack den with the rats..."

He choked off his words and looked away. "And don't bother telling me you can't do it because I know people like you can do anything they want when the price is right and it's right now. I've worked with people like you before."

Hicks gripped the Ruger tighter. "You've never worked with anyone like me. So how about you open the safe, so I know you're not lying?"

"You know so damned much, how about you open it yourself?"

He snatched Russo by the hair and pulled him up out of the chair. He had good balance for a man so drunk and Hicks pushed him over to the picture that hid the wall safe. "Open it yourself and show me it's really empty."

Hicks stepped back as Russo slid the picture aside, revealing the gun-metal wall safe behind it. He spun the dial and pulled the safe door open. It was as empty as he'd said it was, except for the safe deposit keys.

"You don't lie to me and I don't lie to you," Russo said as he stumbled back to the chair behind his desk. "Get me back my son, and you get all hundred grand. You don't, I don't care what happens next."

Hicks stood there, staring into the gaping maw of the empty safe as if it was mocking him.

Only getting Junior back would get him the hundred grand he needed.

Hicks turned away from the safe. "Do you have any idea where I can find him?"

"No," Russo admitted. "I already told you he's not where he normally goes and I don't know where he could be. You've got fingers in so many pies, you can figure it out for yourself."

"You're about to cross a dangerous line here, Vinny," Hicks said. "You're sure you want to do this?"

"I don't care about you or your line. Just get my boy back."

Russo reached for the bottle of scotch, but Hicks snatched it from him before he reached it. "I'll find your son, but I need you sober. As soon as the banks open tomorrow, you get into those boxes and gather up the money. You'd better have it stacked and ready for me by noon when I pull in the driveway because, if you don't, I put a bullet in Junior's head before I put one in your belly."

"I'll have the money, don't worry about that," Russo sneered. "Let's just hope you're as good as you say you are."

Hicks tucked the Ruger back in his waistband before he decided to shoot this son of a bitch. He pulled Russo's glass toward him, poured himself three fingers of scotch and downed it. After the day he'd had, he needed it.

CHAPTER 9

ON THE DRIVE back to Manhattan, Hicks brought up Junior Russo's file on his dashboard screen, then had OMNI check Junior's police record. It read like a requiem for an addict. The kid had been in and out of the justice system a few times already and he was only twenty years old. All of them drug charges. Junkie beefs and juvie bounces. Nothing too violent or heavy.

According to his rap sheet, Junior had bounced back and forth between heroin and meth since he'd been fifteen years old. It was spoiled brat syndrome. A disease caused by too much money and not enough responsibility. It happened in every neighborhood in every country all over the world.

Junior's latest relapse had played into Hicks' reasoning about Russo making a good Asset. He figured Junior's struggles would make him easier prey and more willing to become an Asset. Hicks hadn't counted on Russo using it as leverage against him.

Getting Junior back wouldn't be impossible for Hicks, but it was an unscheduled pain in the ass. He could've blown off Russo's appeal for his son and easily gotten the hundred grand for the Omar meeting elsewhere. But Hicks could never afford to be that shortsighted. He played Assets for the long game. Russo could move a lot of money for the New York Office if he was in the right state of mind. Russo gave Hicks options. If getting his kid back made Russo more effective, then that's what Hicks would do.

Junior's record indicated that he tended to go on the nod in one area in Brooklyn. As junkies were creatures of habit, he decided known associates in that part of the city would be a good starting point.

If Hicks had the time, he would've farmed out the request to one of his NYPD Assets to track down Junior for him. Unfortunately, Hicks didn't have that kind of time, so he had to do it the hard way.

Hicks had OMNI open the folder he had on the tacit surveillance on the Russos. The system tracked all the phone calls, text messages, web browsing and online activity of all four members of the Russo family.

Hicks opened Junior's phone records and looked up the last time the phone had been used and where it was located. The last recorded position was heading west toward Manhattan from the Russo's house in Suffolk. It wasn't much to go on. There was an entire junkie wonderland between Suffolk County and The Big Apple. He could be anywhere.

Hicks checked the numbers Junior had called in the last day or so and found several calls to numbers that came up as either burner phones or to young women he'd called before. Hicks tapped on each of their numbers and accessed their records. Social media profile windows appeared on the right side of the screen as part of the search. It looked like Junior had a thing for brunettes. Hicks smiled. Maybe Junior was worth saving after all.

The only common thing about the phone calls was that they only lasted thirty seconds. That meant voicemails. None of the calls had been returned. Hicks knew why. Junior was junkie desperate. Pleas for cash or a place to crash. Daddy's cuff links and Rolex might help him get well for a while, but not for as long as he needed. There wasn't enough money or junk in the world to help him get well.

Hicks struck gold when OMNI hit Junior's text messages. He'd texted a number registered to yet another burn phone, only this one had been used more than once and paid for by a credit card belonging to one Devron Jackson.

According to his record, Devron was a twenty-six-year-old African American from Bensonhurst. Five feet, eight inches tall and weighed a buck forty soaking wet. Several convictions for possession and dealing and intent to distribute. An assault with a deadly weapon charge had been dropped, which told Hicks he'd ratted out someone bigger. Devron dealt heroin, Junior's poison of choice. Devron was sounding like a good way to start looking for Junior.

He brought up the location of Devron's phone, backtracking to where it had been answered when he and Junior traded texts. Only one location popped up for that number all day long. It was an abandoned railroad substation in the middle of Queens.

Hicks activated the OMNI satellite in orbit over Manhattan and typed in the address to get a live image of the drug den. Given that it was night, there wasn't much he could see under normal view, so he switched to the thermal view of the building. It revealed about a dozen or more red shapes milling around the ground floor of the substation. A few dull red blobs were on the floor. They looked unconscious judging by the amount of heat they threw off. Given the location, Hicks took them for junkies on the nod. He hoped Junior was one of them.

He paid attention to the two red shapes walking in between the people on the floor and Hicks pegged them to be watching over the customers, making sure none of them tripped too hard or choked to death on their own spit. Like the old saying goes: Dead men don't buy smack.

The thermal image also picked up two more men posted at the entrance and one in the back. Probably keeping watch to make sure no one robs the stash or the customers. Another heat signature at the corner was undoubtedly a lookout watching for cops.

The old building was a Grade-A shooting gallery. Protection was minimal, but present. Hicks would respect it, but didn't fear it. And it wasn't enough to keep Hicks from bringing Junior home quickly. Some people were going to have to die before that happened. But the way he saw it, everyone in the substation had already signed their own death warrant long ago.

Hicks tried to access Junior's phone. It was off, but there was still a signal. He tried to turn it on remotely, but the battery was drained.

Hicks had the satellite sweep the building for smartphones or tablets; anything that might have a wireless connection and a camera. He got hits on several phones belonging to some of the junkies passed out on the floor.

Hicks accessed each one in turn, but all phones were either in pockets or bags. None of them gave him any idea of what the room looked like. All he heard was muffled farts and snores while their owners tripped the light fantastic. Hicks closed his eyes. His was a charmed life.

But Hicks scored a hit on the second to last number he tried. The signal corresponded with a red thermal signature of a man who was walking among the images of junkies on the floor. Hicks activated the phone's camera and got a clear, but jerky picture of the inside of the building. It looked like the man had tucked his phone in a shirt pocket as he moved through the unconscious customers scattered on the floor.

Hicks had OMNI brighten the images and saw the cavernous old substation was lit by weak candlelight and whatever streetlight filtered in through the boarded windows.

The man's phone conversation appeared to have ended because the camera panned down to a view of his shoes. White sneakers. Laces pressed. Blue jeans cuffed just so. The phone came up on OMNI as a burner, but Hicks bet this was Devron, patrolling his domain like a boss.

Hicks didn't care about Devron's conversation, so he didn't bother listening to it. But he kept the camera feed active as he uploaded Junior's social media pictures to OMNI and asked it to match the image to anyone in the substation.

Hicks watched the system go to work as tiny hexagons flashed on faces Hicks couldn't see with the naked eye while the drug dealer moved among his customers.

The system quickly seized on one image of a figure slumped against a wall. OMNI froze the image and automatically enhanced it. The program lightened it and compared it to the images of Junior's face. A green status bar crawled across the screen from left to right as the program went to work. The original image was just a blurry profile shot of a kid passed out against the wall. OMNI came back with an eighty percent match to Junior's face. Not perfect, but close enough for him to go to work.

Hicks checked his watch. It was already going on ten o'clock and he figured Junior would be on the nod for a few hours. Plenty of time for him to pull together a quick raid of the den and pull Junior out of there. He selected Junior's heat signature and tagged his position. If Junior so much as scratched himself, OMNI would notify him.

He activated another of the satellite's lenses to scan the perimeter again. It looked like there were at least three guards. All of them probably armed. Hicks could shoot his way in there alone if he had to, but he didn't have to.

He could've had a Varsity crew go in and grab him. They would've cut through the guards, gotten Junior and disappeared in thirty seconds tops.

But using the Varsity would mean Jonathan and Hicks had answered enough awkward questions from him for one day.

Fortunately, Hicks knew the right man for the job. Except in this instance, the right man just happened to be a woman.

CHAPTER 10

IT WAS ALMOST eleven by the time Hicks got to the The Mark Hotel on Seventy-seventh and Madison. He'd stopped by Twenty-third Street first so he could change into a shirt and blazer before heading uptown. The Mark Bar wasn't the type of place you trudged into in a parka and gloves, even when the weather called for it. Not for the kind of role he'd be playing, anyway.

He had no problem spotting Tali as soon as he entered the bar. She was exactly where she'd texted she'd be; alone, nursing the same cocktail she always ordered, but rarely finished: Hendricks martini straight up with a twist of lemon.

She was wearing a classic black cocktail dress that could be found in almost any dress shop or department store in the world. She managed to make it look *couture*.

She had dark hair, light olive skin and high cheek-bones. She had green eyes one might not expect an Israeli girl to have. She was more striking than beauti-ful, but exotic enough to draw quick glances - both desirous and envious - from most of the men and women in the bar.

Yet, despite the empty stool next to her, no one sat near her. Despite her beauty, there was something about Tali that didn't invite company.

Despite appearances, Hicks knew Tali wasn't one of the pros who cruised the cocktail circuit of Upper East Side bars looking for a sugar daddy on a Thursday night. She wasn't looking for someone to buy her drinks or help with the rent or listen to her sob story about her sick kid at home.

Hicks knew Tali Saddon for who and what she really was – a highly trained operative from Israeli Military Intelligence, on an extended liaison mission to the University. And Hicks knew she was killing time while she waited for her latest assignment to meet her at the bar for a nightcap before heading back to her apartment for the evening.

Her current assignment happened to be a Texas real estate investor looking to buy his way into a couple of development projects in the Middle East. The man was long on cash but short on discretion, which made him a good source of information. Hicks doubted that Tali shared everything the man told her. She was Mossad first and foremost - but she passed along more than enough intel to keep Hicks funding her stay in New York.

Hicks and Tali had slept together once in London six years before. It was during a joint operation between their two organizations. The Mossad had always appreciated the University's efforts in Israel's earliest days and the two groups had a mutual respect for each other.

Hicks and Tali wound up stuck at The Savoy on a

rainy London evening. It hadn't been a casual fling, but it hadn't been a romance, either. Neither of them had mentioned it since, though Hicks often wondered if she'd given that night any thought. He didn't want to know the answer, so he never asked the question.

Tali played with her phone as Hicks sat one stool away from her, but knew she'd seen him. There were plenty of men now in their graves who thought they could sneak up on her.

He'd always admired her focus and discretion. There was no telling who might be watching either of them or why. And, in Hicks' experience, someone was always watching.

He caught the bartender's eye and ordered a Laphroaig on the rocks. Since that's what he'd had at Russo's house, he decided to stick with it.

The bartender served it to him with a glass of water on the side, then took his credit card and kept the tab open for him.

Knowing the bartender was probably listening, Hicks looked at Tali's glass and said, "That looks awfully dangerous."

Tali looked at his scotch and exaggerated her accent. "That doesn't look like buttermilk, either."

Hicks cued her by asking, "Your accent is familiar. What is that? Russian?"

She answered in Russian in a pleasant tone that didn't reflect what she said. "What the hell are you doing here? You know I'm working."

Hicks responded in Russian. "I wouldn't be here if it wasn't important."

She cocked an eyebrow as she looked back at her

martini. "Why are we speaking Russian anyway? Your accent is dreadful. Your French is better."

"But we're in a French hotel, my love. Why take chances on someone understanding us?"

"I'm not your 'love' and if you're so worried about taking chances, you're taking a big one by coming here tonight. That redneck pig will be here any minute and he won't like you being here when he walks in."

Hicks knew her assignment was six and a half feet, two-hundred and sixty pounds of pure Dallas bluster. He had a particularly mean, protective streak where Tali was involved. Hicks knew it was more about his pride than her honor. "Don't worry about me. I can handle myself."

"I'm not worried about you. I'm worried about you putting him in the hospital if he swings at you. He won't be much use to me if he's in a coma. I'm too close to getting him to tell us who he's working with and I can't risk you blowing that in a lousy bar brawl. Now, for the last time, why are you here?"

Hicks winced as he sipped at his scotch. "Because I need a favor. A big one that utilizes your unique skills."

He watched her stir the lemon rind in her martini with her pinky nail and found it surprisingly erotic. "I've told you before I'm not a whore. I do what I do for my country and that is all."

"I never said you were and I'm not asking you to be one now. I'm talking about your skills with a rifle."

She broke character and looked at him quicker than she should have. "Is this about the alert you sent out earlier?"

Since Hicks was asking for her help, he decided to tell her the truth. He only had a certain level of authority over her anyway and asking her to serve as a sniper was outside the mission parameters the University had agreed upon with her superiors.

"Colin got turned by the people I'd assigned him to watch. He set me up to take a bullet last night in Central Park and I don't know why."

It was the first time he'd ever seen Tali betray any kind of sincere emotion. "Are you hurt? Is Colin okay?"

"I'm fine, but Colin didn't make it. Neither are the two men he'd brought with him to kill me." Hicks took a sip of scotch to take a little of the sting out of the memory. "I've got a way of hooking the bastards who set us up, but I need your help to do it. The project is official, but what I need you to do isn't."

Tali went back to looking at her drink. "Is it at least tangential?"

"Of course it is, but it's complicated. I just need you to help me with a little housekeeping tomorrow morning."

'Housekeeping' was the University's code for an assassination. Even though they were speaking in Russian, certain protocols still had to be observed.

"What kind of housekeeping?" she asked.

"A little high dusting." It was code for a sniper assignment. "Nothing you haven't done before and in worse conditions. And with minimal risk to you."

Hicks would've been disappointed if she'd agreed to do it right away. "Tell me more about what happened with Colin. Did he compromise any of us? Are the rest of us in danger? I'm not just talking about me. I'm talking about the entire New York Office."

"Have you noticed anyone watching you?"

"Don't answer a question with a question." She

stabbed at the lemon peel with her pinky nail. "I hate it when you do that."

Hicks didn't dare annoy her any further. She wasn't the only sniper he had on staff in New York, but she was certainly the best shot. "My gut tells me he held his water, but, then again, I never thought Colin was at risk. I know you're working on a big assignment now and I know this is beyond our agreement, but I could really use your backup tomorrow morning."

Tali inched her cocktail glass away from her. "Is this against the people who hurt Colin?"

Hicks never lied to his people when he could avoid it. He decided he could avoid it now. "No, but it'll help me get closer to the people who did. It's difficult to explain in the time we have."

"Of course," Tali smirked. "There's never a straight line between Point A and Point B with you." Her Russian made her rebuke sound even harsher. "Where and when do you need me?"

"I'll send you a detailed mission package as soon as I leave here. I assume you still have your handheld."

"No, I pawned it to pay for the drinks. Of course I still have it. I just don't carry it all the time. I check it several times a day. How many subjects?"

Hicks shrugged. "Maybe four. It's an old railroad building that has become a shooting gallery for junkies."

She looked him up and down and surprised him by actually smiling for once. "You need backup for only four? You must be slipping in your old age."

Hicks felt himself smiling, too. "I'm not slipping. I'm just old enough to not push my luck when I don't have to. The layout's tricky and I'm going to have to extract one of the junkies. I'll feel a lot better with you watching my back while I do it."

Tali looked at her glass again. "High dusting, just like you said."

"With minimal risk to you," he reminded her. "Standard equipment should suffice."

"Of course," she said. "Just send me the details and I'll be in position before you get there."

"Thank you," he said. "It'll mean an early start, though. Your Texan won't like that."

Tali shrugged her slender shoulders. "I'll do what I always do. Give him his little blue pill and when he passes out, I'll him he was wonderful."

"Good girl." Hicks drained most of his scotch. The smoky burn felt good at the back of his throat. "Now, how do you want me to get out of here? If I just pay for my drink and leave, especially since we've been speaking Russian, the bartender might get suspicious. So you should act like I just..."

She quickly turned away from him and sat ramrod straight. She snapped her fingers at the bartender and said, "This man is bothering me. He is a rude and a common pig. I want him removed immediately."

The act drew enough attention from the other patrons to be convincing, but not enough to be unbelievable.

Hicks sold it by feigning drunkenness and threw up his hands. "I'm going, I'm going." He drained his scotch and signaled for the check, which the bartender quickly printed up and gave to him.

As he reviewed his bill, he said to the bartender, "Christ, this new crop of Russian whores sure are touchy, aren't they? There was a time when speaking

Russian got a guy special treatment from a Russian girl. Now? Nothing." He made like his mind drifted as he tipped the bartender thirty percent. He'd always had a soft spot for bartenders and wanted to make sure he could come back to the bar again if he had to. A generous tip was a good way of staying on a bartender's good side.

Tali didn't look at him as he walked out of the bar either, trailed by the murmurs of the well-heeled clientele of the Mark Bar. At least he'd given them a show.

CHAPTER 11

HICKS HAD ALREADY BEEN in position for over an hour by the time the sun began to rise. He was less than ten miles away from the stylish décor of the Mark Bar, but given his current surroundings, he might as well have been on the other side of the world.

The substation was set up in an ideal spot for a small incursion with minimal collateral damage. And, in clandestine work, minimal collateral damage meant minimal attention from any police patrols that happened to be rolling by.

The old substation was located in a seemingly forgotten industrial area that didn't see much traffic until later in the morning when workers showed up for their shifts. Across the street from the substation, an overgrown embankment led up to the deserted railway overgrown with trees and weeds. It afforded no cover whatsoever for anyone, including Devron's men.

In the light of a cold autumn dawn, the abandoned substation building looked even more run-down than it had on the OMNI satellite feed. Its red brick façade had been faded by time, scorched by fire and tagged with layers of graffiti. Every pane of glass had long since been broken and hastily boarded up, but not all. The roof had gone to seed and bore the remnants of dead shrubs and weeds that had sprouted up through the snow. Rusting corrugated metal gates and dirty windows and sagging power lines stretched between termite-ridden wooden poles. A wooly old junky adjusted himself as he shambled across the street, muttering to himself.

The building had once been part of a mighty transportation network that took goods and people out to and back from Long Island. Now it was a forgotten ruin from the near-past. A haven for junkies looking for a quiet place to shoot poison into their veins for a temporary glimpse at peace.

An apartment building across the street from the near side of the substation offered a perfect sniper's perch for Tali, assuming shooting would be necessary. And Hicks fully expected shooting to be necessary.

The convoluted absurdity of the entire situation wasn't lost on Hicks. He'd just arranged for an Israeli sniper to watch his back as he raided a drug den to retrieve the junkie son of a money manager who would give him a hundred grand to finance an operation against a suspected Somali terrorist who may or may not be planning some kind of attack on U.S. soil. One thing had led to another and none of it might lead anywhere except smack into a brick wall.

Hicks felt the enormity of all the possibilities and intricacies begin to build up inside him again, so he closed his eyes and focused on his breathing until he cleared his mind. Tali had been right. Nothing was ever a straight line in the intelligence game. The space between Point A and Point B was always crooked. Every single thing in the Life was just one serpentine path with the serpent frequently swallowing its own tail. None of the elaborate lingo or fancy tech could change that. If anything, it just made it worse.

Hicks had known all of that before he'd gotten into the intelligence game, but it still bothered him at times. He remembered what the Dean always said: compartmentalize. Focus on the immediate task at hand. Get Junior out of the shooting gallery and home to daddy and get that hundred grand.

When Hicks opened his eyes, the streetscape before him was still as bleak as it had been before. The OMNI viewpoint high overhead showed two men guarding the front door. One appeared to be a black man, the other appeared to be Latin. Both of them were wearing polar fleece with the sleeves cut off despite the temperature being just above freezing. The fashion statement revealed veined arms and bulging biceps. The Latin man was sporting some impressive ink: a tattoo of a grinning skeleton showing five playing cards over his bony shoulder: a red Queen, two black aces and two black eights. A Dead Man's Hand. The name 'Death Dealer' was written in calligraphy beneath it.

Hicks knew Tali would nail Death Dealer first. She kept kosher when she could and hated tattoos. His partner would die next, probably from the same bullet if she could get the angle right. She was nothing if not efficient.

The OMNI feed didn't reveal anyone else outside the building, so he flipped it back to thermal feed. He picked up the heat signatures of about a dozen people still inside. Junior hadn't moved from the spot where he'd been sprawled out for the past few hours. Only three other people appeared to be ambulatory, strolling around the prone figures on the floor.

Hicks didn't bother adjusting the satellite's camera to check if Tali was in position. It was easer just to ping her handheld directly. He texted her: *You in position?*

Her answer was immediate. A red dot appeared on his chest over his heart.

He texted: *Subtle. Real subtle.*

The red dot disappeared.

Hicks put his Ruger in his lap and slipped the Buick into gear. He opened a channel directly to her handheld and said, "Look sharp because here we go."

As SOON AS Hicks pulled up in front of the substation, Death Dealer and his friend puffed out their chests as they swaggered toward the car.

Death Dealer was the taller of the two and made a big show of bending to look into the car. Hicks didn't roll down the window.

Death Dealer yelled, "You best be moving that car, asshole, if you don't want to get hurt."

The .308 round from Tali's M24 rifle punched a hole the size of a fist in Death Dealer's chest. His partner was sprayed with a red mist but had less than a second to react before another round obliterated his skull. Both men were dead on the sidewalk before the faint echo of Tali's suppressed shots died away.

Hicks put his Buick in park and kept the motor running as he got out of the car. He kept his Ruger flat against his leg as he quickly walked toward the substation. He could see the doors were locked and was thinking about going back to pat down the corpses for a key when Tali fired again and blew the lock to pieces. Hicks kicked the doors in and walked inside.

Hicks recognized Devron from his mug shot. He was walking toward him; his phone still pressed to his ear. He lowered the phone when he heard the door bang open.

"What the fuck is goin' on out there, G-Dog. I already told you about keeping that..."

As Devron realized Hicks wasn't G-Dog; Hicks raised his Ruger and leveled him with a headshot at near point-blank range.

The Ruger was designed for impact, not stealth, and the shot boomed like a thunderclap in the cavernous substation. Every junkie anywhere near consciousness jumped to their feet and bolted for the door. The huge windows on the street side of the building had only been boarded up halfway to the top. Hicks knew that, from her vantage point across the street, Tali would be able to provide some cover inside if he needed it.

Hicks did his best to dodge the herd of staggering junkies as he tried to locate the two other men he'd seen on the thermal OMNI feed. They may have been guards. They may have already run away when they heard the gunfire. Either way, they were unaccounted for and most likely armed. Hicks kept an eye out for them as he made his way to Junior's location.

Hicks found the young man lying in the same position where he'd been for the past few hours. He was still unconscious and using a backpack as a pillow. A river of drool ran from the corner of his mouth. His arm was draped over a woman next to him, but there was nothing romantic about the gesture. The woman's eyes were open and vacant. Hicks figured she was either dead from opiate shock or was well on her way. Too far along for Hicks to try saving.

He saw Junior's chest rise and fall in ragged, shallow breaths and knew the little bastard was still alive. And Hicks was that much closer to a hundred grand.

He was about to pull Junior up off the floor when he caught movement near an old piece of machinery to his right. It wasn't the panicked movement of fleeing junkies, but the deliberate movement of someone moving into position.

Hicks hit the deck just as the man opened fire from behind an old turbine. The nine-millimeter rounds struck the brickwork of the wall behind him. Hicks rolled clear and came up ready to fire just as the gunman's empty pistol locked open.

Hicks had a clear shot and was about to fire when Tali's bullet punched a hole through the center of the gunman's chest; spinning him away from the machinery. Hicks held fire. No sense in wasting a bullet on a dead man.

In his ear, Tali said, "Get the boy and move. I'll cover you from here."

Hicks scrambled to his feet and went back to Junior. The young man was still too out of it to move on his own, so Hicks snatched him by the collar, jerked him to his feet and threw him onto his left shoulder. The effort was easier than it should've been for a kid his size.

Junior was only about a hundred pounds. Meth scrawny.

Anyone aware enough to get out of the building had already taken off by then. There was still a fair amount of people on the substation floor. They were too high to notice what was going on around them.

Just as Hicks carried Junior back to the entrance, a shot rang out before he reached the door. Hicks doubled back and laid Junior down behind an old turbine. He crouched low while he talked to Tali.

"You got an angle on him?"

"Negative," she said. "He ducked for cover just as you fell back. I don't have a shot. Leave the kid and search for the gunman on your own. I'll take him if I get the shot."

Hicks knew he could wait out the gunman, but that would take time and time wasn't on his side. Despite the early hour, someone had either heard the shots or seen the horde of junkies that had just hit the street and called the cops. He wanted to put as much space as possible between him and that substation, but turning his back on a man with a gun would be suicide, especially with Junior weighing him down.

To Tali, he said, "Fire a round at his last position. See if that makes him jump."

Tali began firing into the old machinery at the far end of the building, Hicks broke cover and ran at a crouch toward the row where he'd last seen the gunman. He found the man lying flat on the ground, hands covering his head.

As soon as Tali stopped firing, the man began to get to his feet, but turned when he saw Hicks walking toward him.

The man slowly raised his hands, but didn't make an effort to drop the gun. It wouldn't have mattered anyway. He wasn't one of the strung-out junkies. He was one of Devron's men and he'd gotten a good look at Hicks' face.

Hicks put him down with a single headshot.

"All clear," he said to Tali as he tucked away the Ruger and went back to grab Junior. "Keep an eye out. There may be one or two more hiding in here."

He threw Junior over his shoulder again and humped it outside. He opened the back door and dumped him in the back seat of the Buick before climbing in behind the wheel. He was glad he'd kept the motor running. He did a tight U-turn and headed back down the street toward Manhattan.

As he sped off down the street, he spoke to Tali: "We're clear. Any sign of survivors?"

"OMNI shows no active threats," Talia reported. "Just sleeping junkies and dead bad guys. You didn't need me at all."

"Couldn't have done it without you, Ace." Hicks saw the street ahead of him was clear, so he floored it. The V-12 engine he'd had the Varsity boys install in the old car came to life. "That was some real Oswald shit you pulled back there, young lady. I owe you one."

"Oswald was a joke," she said, "and you don't owe me anything. Colin was a friend. So are you. Stay safe."

Hicks didn't bother asking if she needed a ride. She'd probably just give him another smartass response and that would kill his growing good mood. Tali had gotten out of much worse situations than an industrial site in Queens. He knew she'd be long gone before the cops got there.

The cops would be a concern, but a minor one. Hicks figured they'd roll up on the scene and work it like a rival drug gang hit. The ballistics from Tali's rifle would probably throw them off a bit, but the ordinance was the same that American and European forces were using in Iraq and Afghanistan. The cops would figure a vet must be working with one of the gangs. They'd waste time running down all snipers with priors who'd just rotated back into the world. The cops would be extra cautious for a while until they began to forget all about the substation and think the sniper thing was just a fluke.

He doubted the NYPD would look too hard for whoever shot up the shooting gallery anyway. No citizens had been killed and no one would be calling out a manhunt to find the guys who'd killed half a dozen drug dealers. The event itself might make the eleven o'clock news, but it would be forgotten by tomorrow. The cops might even forget it before then.

And if they didn't, OMNI would let him know.

Hicks turned off the main avenue and hit the highway to take his hundred-thousand-dollar passenger back home. He stole a glance back at Junior and saw he was still passed out cold. Coasting from whatever poison he'd smoked or pumped into his veins.

Now that he could see Junior in the growing daylight, he noticed all the junkie signs clearly. The sunken eyes and pockmarked yellowed skin. The thinning hair that came from years of dedicated abuse. Junior was only twenty years old but looked like a hard fifty. His demons had him by the throat and whatever treatment his father had gotten for him hadn't done him much good so far.

All of that was going to change. Hicks was going to see to that. For Junior's sake. But more importantly, for the University's sake, as well.

AFTER TELLING Russo he'd rescued Junior, Hicks drove around killing time until the money man texted him he'd gathered the hundred grand.

It was just before ten in the morning by the time Hicks rolled into Russo's street. The cul-de-sac was buzzing with people going about their post-rush hour routine. People getting a late start into work and parents coming back from morning errands. Just a regular day in suburbia; a humdrum morning gradually blending into a humdrum lunchtime. Ham and Swiss on white - no crust - and a glass of soy milk. Carrot sticks for dessert. Gotta stay healthy. Life is so boring. Nothing ever happens in the suburbs. Woe is me.

It was all part of a sleepy, privileged existence they took for granted because they didn't understand what true lawlessness was like. They didn't know how easily their comfortable lives could be thrown into turmoil by just a few people with bad intentions at the right place and time.

OMNI confirmed the people on Russo's street complained about boredom. They had no idea of how hard men and women like Hicks and Tali worked to keep life that way. But Hicks knew because he'd made a career of doling out controlled doses of order and anarchy in order to keep everything in balance.

Hicks pulled up in front of Russo's house and got the money man on the phone. He wasn't surprised that he answered on the first ring. "Is that your car out front just now? Do you have him? Is he okay?"

"First things first, Vinny," Hicks said. "Do you have the hundred grand?"

"Yes. How's my boy?"

"You'll see for yourself in about thirty seconds," Hicks said. "You're going to bring the money out to the car, nice and slow, open the passenger's side door and get inside. You try anything stupid and I drive away. You'll never see your son again."

Hicks killed the connection before Russo could argue or waste more time asking a lot of damned fool questions.

Russo was out on his walkway less than ten seconds later. He was still wearing the same clothes from the night before and hadn't shaved, either. Hicks unlocked the doors and let Russo inside.

Russo dropped the bag on the seat and forgot to close the passenger door as he kneeled on the seat and reached for his son. "Junior," he said as tears ran from his eyes. "Junior, it's daddy. It's me. I'm here."

Hicks grabbed Russo by the collar and pulled him down into the seat. "Close the door and keep your mouth shut."

Tears streaked down Russo's face as he did as he was told. He pulled the door closed and craned his neck to look back at his son. "I'm grateful to you for this. So grateful. You'll see. I'll..."

"Open the bag and let me see the money."

Russo's hands trembled as he got hold of the bag – a regular laundry bag - and opened it. He pawed through it and, from what Hicks could see, it looked like all hundred thousand was there.

"You see? It's all right there, just like I told you it would be. Every penny. A hundred grand just like you wanted. And I promise, now that I have him back, I'll never let him do anything like this again. You've brought him back to me and I'm so grateful that..."

Hicks scanned the street for anyone who was looking at the car. But as busy as the street was with mommies and daddies and nannies, no one was at this end of the cul-du-sac. That was good.

"Put the bag in the back seat," Hicks told him, "and take a good look at your boy."

Russo did as he was told. He reached back and put a hand on his son's shoulder. "Wake up, son. Wake up and let's get well. Let's get you inside where you belong."

"The only one who's going home is you," Hicks said. "Junior's coming with me."

This time, Hicks didn't have to push Russo into the seat. He fell back on his own. "What...what are you talking about? You said...you promised that..."

Hicks drew the Ruger and jammed it into the side of Russo's neck; pushing him against the passenger side window. "I told you I'd get your boy back and that's exactly what I did. But I'm not going to let you have him because you don't know how to handle him. You said you haven't been able to get him clean, so I'm putting him in a facility where he won't have any choice but to straighten out. After ninety days, your boy will come back clean, sober and refocused."

"But you can't do this to me," Russo wept. "Why are you doing this?"

Hicks pressed the barrel of the Ruger harder against Russo's neck. "Because I need you focused on the things I need you to do and I can't have you worrying about this spoiled little bastard falling off the wagon again." He thumbed back the hammer. "So if you have any objection, tell me now and I'll kill you both right here because you're no good to me if you're worrying about him."

Russo nodded slowly as the tears began to fall again. "I do. I guess it's the right..."

Then, Hicks jammed the barrel of the Ruger against Russo's neck until the money man gagged. "And if you ever try to strong arm me or hold out on me again, I'm going to be really disappointed. So disappointed, in fact, I'm going to take it out on him. I'll even make you watch before I hurt you even worse. Do you understand me?"

Russo nodded as best he could before Hicks pushed him out of the car. He almost tumbled out into his driveway, but he somehow managed to keep his footing.

Hicks pulled the door shut and pulled away from the curb. As he drove away, he saw Russo in his rearview mirror. He looked lost in front of his own house while he watched a total stranger drive away with his son.

The same stranger he'd asked to rescue his son only a few hours before.

The same stranger who'd barged into his life and taken it over only a day before that.

The same stranger he'd allowed into his life by playing games with other people's money.

Hicks adjusted his mirror so he wouldn't have to see Russo standing there like a lost kid at a carnival.

He knew there was a chance Russo might be so distraught that he might go into his den and blow his brains out. The gun was empty and Hicks had already taken all the ammo from the house, but he could've bought more. Or he could OD on his wife's sleeping pills. Hicks didn't care if he did. He had the money now and that's what counted. If he got the kid straightened out, then it was a bonus.

He was halfway back to Manhattan when the dash-board screen showed an incoming call from Jonathan. He would've loved to ignore the call, but knew Jonathan was already tracking him on GPS. Ignoring him would only make a bad situation worse. He checked to make sure Junior was still out of it before he pushed the button on the steering wheel that allowed the call come through.

"This is Professor Wallace," he said, using the stan-dard code that he was safe, but not alone.

"I see you've been very busy," Jonathan said. "Using our assets for your own vendetta."

"No vendetta, Ace," Out of habit, he checked his mirrors to see if he was being followed. He wasn't. "Just doing what I've got to do to get the job done."

"Admirable," Jonathan said. "Who's that in the back seat anyway? OMNI can barely read his vitals."

Hicks didn't see the point in getting into the details. "He's not important."

"That's what you think. Do you have any idea how much you put us at risk? What if you'd been killed? What if the police had grabbed you? What if they grab you still?"

Hicks smiled. "I didn't know you cared."

"I couldn't care less about what happens to you," Jonathan admitted, "but there's the project to think about. The money from your Asset could've easily come from the Bursar's office."

"Which would've taken time we don't have," Hicks said. "Let's talk about something important, like my new Field Assistant. Have you narrowed down the search yet or are you still making up your mind?"

Jonathan hesitated. "Are you sure your guest is out of it?"

"You can read his vitals," Hicks told him. "Don't worry about him and answer my question."

"Our colleagues in Army Intelligence are bringing someone who should fit your requirements nicely. I'll send you a detailed profile on him in a few moments."

Hicks figured it could wait until after he dropped off Junior. "And what if I don't think he's qualified?"

"There's no doubt as to his qualifications," Jonathan said. "As for getting him to cooperate, I suppose we'll have to rely on your charming personality to win him over."

Great. They probably dug the guy out of the basement in Leavenworth. "When does he get to New York?"

"He's in transit," Jonathan said. "He should reach New York just before rush hour. I'll send you the coordinates on where to meet him when they get closer."

"They?" Hicks repeated. "Who's 'they'?"

"No need to worry about that now," Jonathan said. "Now it's my turn to ask a question. What about your friend in the back seat? What's to become of him?"

"Not your problem."

Hicks decided he'd be the first one to kill the connection for once. He fully expected the little bastard to call right back, angry that he'd been dismissed. Instead, the dashboard screen showed that Jonathan had sent the information package on the operative he'd promised.

Hicks didn't waste time wondering about what beauty they were sending him for the Omar operation. He'd handled countless bad asses in his day and always found a way to reach them.

Besides, he still had one more item to check off his list.

Hicks adjusted the rearview to get a better look at Junior. Still passed out cold. He hadn't moved since they'd left the substation. He probably didn't even know where he was.

In a way, Hicks envied him, but not what lay ahead of him.

CHAPTER 12

THERE WERE few things in the world that looked more ridiculous than a nightclub at ten o'clock in the morning. And despite its special clientele, Roger Cobb's nightclub was no different.

After parking the Buick in the fenced-in lot next door, Hicks let himself into the club through the service entrance. He didn't bother bringing Junior inside with him. The boy still had a couple of hours of flying time before he came back to life. Might as well let him keep sleeping.

The Jolly Roger Club was one of the more popular underground venues in the city. It had become a haven for the various types of vice that weren't exactly legal and therefore, the club was not open to the general public.

To call it a nightclub would've been vague, for the club never closed. To call it a sex club would've been limiting its customers' desires to the definable. It drew people from every level and strata of society with varying appetites of pleasure.

Anything beyond the pale was the norm at the Jolly Roger; 'a dish for every taste' as Roger liked to say, as long as they were willing to pay. The bar served top shelf booze and genuine absinthe, as well as liquid cocaine and other exotic opiates. All the usual drugs of choice were also on the menu.

The basement had a dungeon that would've make the Marquis De Sade blush. The sub-basement was an opium den deluxe. Private sex chambers and alcoves of depravity were tucked in every corner throughout the darkened club. The Jolly Roger catered to every fetish and passion and proclivity on the Kinsey Scale and some the good doctor had never even dreamed of.

Roger Cobb drew the line at pedophilia, bestiality and the slavery market. He loved children and animals and gladly honed his harshest questioning techniques for those who indulged in such appetites.

Everyone in the Jolly Roger was a consenting adult who had come there of their own free will. He saw no reason to entrap the unwilling when there were so many people willing to pay an insane amount of money to indulge their darkest fantasies.

Hicks had worked with Roger Cobb all over the world. He was regarded Roger as the best interrogator in the University system. He had mastered the delicate craft of using pain and fear to get the most out of a subject without killing them. He would break them or ruin their souls, but rarely killed them. He knew dead men couldn't say much.

When Roger told him he wanted to leave the rigors of fieldwork behind, Hicks jumped at the chance to bring him to New York. Hicks gave him the money to start The Jolly Roger and it had been one of the best investments he had ever made. It not only provided a source of steady revenue for the New York Office, but had proven to be an invaluable way to blackmail some very powerful people as they did some very lowbrow things deep in the darkened rooms of the club.

Hicks shook hands with the black-clad doorman and walked up the narrow stairway, through a maze of narrow hallways to get to Roger's apartment. He knew the door would be unlocked and didn't bother to knock before going inside. Roger had never been a modest man.

Roger's residence was more of a grand chamber than an apartment. Hicks wasn't surprised to see a young man, naked except for a leather mask, passed out in a sex sling suspended from a hook in the ceiling. Hicks didn't know when or how Roger had managed to rig the hook that high and didn't plan on finding out, either.

Other masked men and women in various stages of undress and unconsciousness were lounging in candle-light on couches and duvets and pillows throughout the large, windowless room. Roger's chamber had the sprawling dark majesty of a Medieval castle sans the tapestry.

Hicks found Roger propped up in the middle of an oversized bed that was twice the size of a normal king-sized bed. His reading glasses were perched on the end of his nose as he tapped through a tablet. He might've looked like a mild-mannered academic glancing over the New York Times on a sleepy morning if he hadn't been flanked by two naked men chained by their hands to the headboard. Their leather masks were the only allusion to modesty.

Roger looked up from his tablet when he heard Hicks clear his throat. "Ah, James. How good of you to drop by."

"Hope I'm not interrupting anything." Hicks motioned to the two nude men flanking Roger. "Looks like you had a hell of a night."

"This?" He waved it off. "Just another Wednesday." He set the tablet on the bare chest of the man to his left as if he was a nightstand. "You look tired. Want some coffee? I have just the thing. A client just sent me an entire sack of something I think you're going to love."

The idea of something as wholesome as morning coffee in a sex dungeon might have struck Hicks as odd. But in Roger Cobb's world, odd was a term that had no meaning. "Sure, but I'll make it if you're...busy."

"Nonsense!" Roger said as he swung out of bed. Hicks managed to look away before seeing more of his friend than he wanted to.

Roger ignored the bathrobe on the edge of the bed and walked naked to a small pantry in an alcove set into the side of the room. "What brings you here so early, anyway? It isn't like you to just drop by like this."

Hicks didn't like talking around strangers, especially when they were dozing on pillows or handcuffed to bedposts. "It's important and it's private. And speaking of private, I'd appreciate it if you'd cover up."

Roger turned and smiled ever so slightly. He was a pale man of forty with fair blond hair that was almost white. He had a runner's body, even though he didn't believe in exercise. He was lean and wiry and shorter than Hicks by an inch or two.

When clothed, Roger gave the impression of being slight; almost to the point of appearing gaunt. But like Hicks, he was far stronger than he looked.

"You jealous, old chum, or just embarrassed?" Roger looked him up and down. "Aroused, perhaps?"

Hicks tossed him the robe from the bed. "Just dangerously de-caffeinated. It's already been a long day and it's not even noon yet. I need at least a cup of coffee in me before I see your Jolly Roger flapping in the breeze."

Roger frowned as he shrugged into his robe. "You've become so Victorian since your ascendency to leadership. A wise man once told me that variety is the spice of life."

"If that's true, then your life is all peppers and hot sauce."

Roger grinned. "You have no idea."

He hit the grind button on the coffee machine. Hicks thought the noise would make at least some of Roger's guests react to the whirring blades, but none of them moved a muscle.

"We can speak freely around my friends here," Roger said over the sound of the machine. "Last night was my Sensory Depravation Workshop. Beneath their masks, their eyes are taped shut and their ears have been plugged. I allowed them to speak but I'm afraid their voices went hoarse a few hours ago."

Hicks tried not to think about exactly why they'd lost their voices and hoped Roger wouldn't tell him. Hicks' mind was already crowded enough without Roger's fetishes clamoring for space. "I'm sure everyone had fun, but I'll still wait until we're alone."

"Fun has very little to do with any of this," Roger

said as the coffee machine stopped grinding and began to heat the water. "Neither does sex, though it's got more to do with it than fun. It's about embracing one's true nature, James. One's entire *being*, not just the façade we present to the world. The light as well as the dark. The accepted as well as the taboo and everything in between. The pain and the pleasure and all that comes with it." He wrinkled his nose. "It's a real mind fuck when you start to really think about it."

He must've been able to see Hicks wasn't impressed, for he added, "Besides, that redhead in the corner has some very interesting friends in the cryptocurrency game. She's going to be a font of information after a couple of sessions."

Hicks just watched the coffee machine gurgle as the coffee began to filter into the carafe instead. He hoped the smell of fresh ground coffee would deaden the stench of sweat and stale sex that filled Roger's bed chamber.

"I think you'll like this particular type of coffee," Roger went on. "It's a civet bean; which is produced in a manner that men in our profession can appreciate."

Since Roger's asides always had a point, Hicks decided to play along with it. He was too tired to argue and still had a couple of minutes to kill while the coffee brewed. "Why?"

"Because civet beans come from Indonesia. The beans are first consumed by a civet; a creature that can easily be mistaken for a rodent both in appearance and action, but is actually a sort of mongoose. The animal first ingests the bean, digests it and excretes it."

Hicks hadn't gotten much sleep and knew his mind

might begin to drift, but thought he heard Roger correctly. "You're serving me cat shit coffee?"

"Don't be so crass, James. Yes, the bean is later collected from the dung of the mongoose, cleansed and roasted, thus giving it its unique flavor." Roger's smile returned. "Not unlike us. It's a process we can appreciate given all the shit we've been through and come out the other side better for it. I find the irony of the whole thing so...rich."

The idea of drinking coffee plucked from cat turds would've turned off most people, but Hicks had eaten worse things and would probably do so again before he was through.

They stood in silence while the coffee brewed.

Roger took the carafe once it was filled and led Hicks through a panel of sliding Chinese doors at the other end of the room. It was a small parlor with furniture that looked more suitable to Versailles than a sex club on the west side of Manhattan. Roger took two coffee cups and saucers down from a cupboard and set them on the table between them.

He poured Hicks a cup, then himself. The aroma was enough to give Hicks a jolt, but the taste even more so.

"That is good," Hicks admitted.

Roger agreed. "At over $150 a pound, it should be."

Hicks set his cup down on the saucer before he dropped it. "I know we make good money from this operation, but we're not making enough for you to be pissing away $150 on coffee."

"Don't be such a Republican. I get it as a gift from a client in Jakarta who has his own civet plantation. His tastes are a tad on the eccentric side whenever he comes to New York, so he always makes it a point to send me a couple of pounds when he can as an expression of gratitude for my discretion. If his family ever found out about his appetites, they'd behead him."

Hicks didn't want to think about the kind of sexual eccentricity warranted a free sack of coffee that cost one hundred and fifty dollars a pound.

Roger sat on a velvet-covered Ottoman and set his cup and saucer on the glass coffee table in front of him. "I got your email alert yesterday and it was disturbingly vague. What happened?"

He gave Roger a quick rundown on Colin and Omar and everything that had happened in the park.

"But Colin didn't use," Roger said. "He didn't even drink."

"I know," Hicks said. "The autopsy said they shot him up full of heroin to get him to talk. I don't know how much he told them, so it's best that everyone in the Office be on their guard."

"A wise policy." Roger looked at him, but not like he'd looked at him before. "I know you two were close. How are you dealing with it?"

Emotion was an expense Hicks couldn't afford yet. "By trying to find out Omar's game. Until a couple of days ago, I thought he was nothing more than an amateur, but he's a hell of a lot more organized than I thought."

"If he caught on to Colin, then I'd say you must've underestimated this Omar by quite a bit. What does our beloved Dean have to say about all this?"

Hicks gave him another quick summary on how everything had unfolded with Russo, Jonathan and the Dean.

"Ah, the serpentine path we tread to protect our great nation," Roger said when Hicks was finished. "Crafty move about the hundred-thousand-dollar buy in, though. You knew the Dean would rear up at the expense."

"He let me have my way," Hicks admitted. "I'm sure Jonathan lobbied hard to run the whole op himself, but all the trouble I went through to get the money was worth it to keep Jonathan out of our backyard. I'll be damned if I'll let that bureaucrat run an op in my own city."

"Our Jonathan does love his palace intrigue, doesn't he? The little shit." Roger sipped his coffee. "Is he married? Straight?"

"He'd have to be a human being first. I don't think they programmed him with a personality before they sent him to our planet."

"Interesting," Roger said over his coffee cup. "A week here with me might do him some good. Help him get in touch with the more intimate aspects of his nature. By the way, any idea about who they're sending up to work Omar? A familiar face, I trust."

"No. Jonathan just sent me the guy's profile while I was driving down here." Hicks saved the best for last. "I think he's a jailbird from Army Intelligence."

Roger laughed. "Doesn't Jonathan know the ones who stay out of jail are much better than the ones who get caught?"

"Either way, I'm stuck with him. Omar is panicked and I don't have anyone on staff right now who can play a convincing emissary in such a short amount of time." Hicks knew what he was about to say and stopped him. "And there's no guarantees that you'd be able to get Omar to talk in time if we grab him."

"Oh, I always get them to talk," Roger said with a glint in his eye. "But the open-ended time element is troubling. Trapping him with money is a wise tactic. Flush him out. Lower his guard and nail him."

Hicks began to grow aggravated again, so he took another sip of coffee. He'd spent the morning killing people. He wanted a drink. He wanted a cigar. But he wouldn't allow himself anything until the new Asset was in place. He needed to stay pure if his plan had any hope of succeeding.

"I need you to stay frosty until further notice, Roger. That means no booze, no nose candy until this is settled. If I call, I'll need you right away."

Roger threw open his hands. "Have I ever refused you anything?" When he saw the joke fell flat, he added, "Anything at any time. You know that."

Hicks knew what Roger could do when he put his mind to it. And it was a comfort to have him around. "In the meantime, I've got Russo's kid in my back seat and I need him to get the Treatment."

Roger frowned again. "Getting people sober isn't exactly my forte, but we have all the necessary accoutrements to do the job. What's the boy's poison?"

"Heroin. Meth. I don't know. I just need him straight because I need his father's head in the game and I can't afford to have him worrying about his son. I'd appreciate you taking a look at him while I review the package Jonathan sent me on our new Asset."

Roger drained the rest of his coffee and put it on the saucer on the table. "Then I'd best see what I can do for him. Enjoy the coffee while you wait. How old is he, by the way?"

"Twenty, I think."

Roger's eyebrows rose. "He cute? Corruptible?"

Hicks took out his handheld. "Good bye, Roger."

CHAPTER 13

JONATHAN TOLD him the military cops who were transporting his new Asset would be at the rendezvous point by two o'clock. Hicks was there by one thirty.

The meeting point was a small parking area near Chelsea Piers at Twenty-third Street along the Hudson River, just off the West Side Highway. Hicks chose it because it was a public area, outdoors and popular with joggers and dog walkers, even on a cold November afternoon with piles of snow still on the ground. It was the last place a spy book or movie would pick for such a meeting, which made it perfect for that kind of meeting.

People were easy to spot in abandoned or industrial areas. They stood out in deserted buildings, but not standing around a busy parking lot along the West Side Highway in the middle of the day.

Besides, after reading the Asset's personnel file, Hicks knew he had a lot more to worry about than being spotted by Omar's men. His new operative's name was Hasim Kamal of Detroit, who'd changed his name to Hank Kimmel before enlisting in the Army ten years before.

Now he was an ex-Army Intelligence operative; a Green Beret washout with a long rap sheet and a rotten attitude to match. According to his record, Kamal had breezed through the demanding Special Forces training regimen, but chaffed against the restraints of command. His personality tests showed that he had a natural resentment of authority but possessed a high level of self-motivation. That quality served him well running black bag operations in Afghanistan, but it had also landed him in prison when he decided to engage in other activities.

Men like Kamal had been trained to do much more than the Rambo guns and guts stuff they showed in the movies. His high level of intelligence led his superiors to send him to Wharton to learn how business worked. He breezed through the courses as easily as he had the demanding Special Forces program. Then Army Intel tasked him with setting up his own shop in Afghanistan to run guns and information to and from America's allies. He'd proven exceptionally good at espionage and living a double life.

He was so good that he'd managed to prevent his superiors from learning about the lucrative opium business he'd set up on the side. And the string of whorehouses for GIs in Karachi.

The fact that Kamal had branched out into the drug and flesh business didn't bother the brass as much as the fact that he'd kept all of the profits for himself.

During his court martial, he changed his name from Hank Kimmel back to his birth name of Hasim Kamal and claimed to be a pious Muslim persecuted by an infidel army. His sudden Islamic epiphany did little to endear him to the military tribunal and he was sentenced to twenty years' hard labor in Leavenworth.

This was the man Jonathan believed was the best chance at reaching Omar.

And Hicks had to admit that he was probably right.

Hicks needed a man who Omar would believe was representing a wealthy financier who might support whatever he was planning. On paper, Kamal had the skills to finesse Omar into believing the financier would fund it if it sufficiently glorified Allah.

Kamal sounded like he could project enough authority to command respect from Omar and his people, but not enough to scare Omar off. He needed to get Omar to spill his guts about whatever he was planning.

Hicks knew the trick would be to get Kamal to tell him everything that he saw because his new Asset was nothing if not enterprising.

When the black Explorer with Virginia plates pulled into the parking lot, Hicks watched the two plain-clothed MPs get out; one providing cover while the other opened the rear passenger door to help the prisoner climb out.

Kamal was in federal prison blue pants and a threadbare green Army parka that was too small for him. His hands and feet were shackled, and the MP discreetly unhooked him and let him loose. They pointed over to Hicks and watched their prisoner walk away. Both had their hands near their weapons. One deviation from the path and they'd probably put Kamal down.

Kamal was about a head taller than Hicks - about

six-two – and much broader. His mugshot from Leaven-worth showed he'd had a lean, trim physique once upon a time. A year's worth of prison chow had given him more of a sunken, fallow look.

His eyes were harder now and far more intense. That was good. Kamal's dark complexion and Islamic upbringing would help him fit in with Omar's crowd. It was human nature for people to be more inclined to trust people to whom they could relate. It would just help convince Omar that Kamal was the real deal. The man with the cash to make all his dreams of death and destruction come true.

In the latest pictures Hicks had seen of Kamal at trial, Kamal had a bald head and was clean shaven. The man who walked toward him now was still bald, but had a ragged beard streaked with gray. That was very good indeed, Hicks thought. That level of commitment would put him in solid with Omar's crowd. They liked their lunatics scruffy.

Hicks leaned back against the Buick as he watched Kamal approach. He didn't move to welcome his new charge or shake his hand. But given the drastic size difference between the two of them, he was glad he had the .454 Ruger on his hip.

When Kamal got close enough, Hicks let his coat fall open so he could see the grip of the gun on his hip. "You Hank Kimmel?"

"That was only the name I took to blend in with my oppressors. My given name is Hassam Kamal." He offered a hint of a bow. "As-salaam-Alaikum."

Hicks wasn't impressed. "Save the ceremony for the shitbirds in the prison yard, Ace. Last time I checked, pious Muslims don't run drug rings and whore houses. The Holy

Joe routine didn't cut you any slack with the tribunal and it cuts even less with me. Anybody tell you why you're here?"

"Broad strokes, but I guess you'll tell me more, right?" Kamal blew into his hands and rubbed his hands together. "Why couldn't we have met inside where it's warm?"

"Answer the question."

"All I know is that when I woke up this morning, a white man in a black suit told me I was being moved. He handed me off to two more white men who brought me here in chains."

Hicks looked back at the two MPs by the suburban. One looked Asian and the other was black. Neither of them had taken their eyes off Kamal. "Funny. They don't look white to me."

"White isn't just a matter of skin pigmentation. It's a mindset of oppression."

Hicks smiled. "Well, now you've got another white oppressor who is presenting you with two choices. The first choice is that you do a job for me and, if you follow orders and live, maybe earn yourself some good will from your Uncle Sam."

"I already got that part in my cell," Kamal said. "How about you tell me what's behind Door Number Two?"

"I let those two nice MPs back there take you back to that cell you keep talking about. Twenty years of hard time in a military stockade. I don't care which one you choose so long as you choose right here and right now. Just know whatever you decide, it's final."

"I need to know more before I make up my mind."

Hicks shook his head. "You know that's not how

this works. You come on board, you're in, and then you get briefed. You say no, your oppressors back there take your ass to jail."

Kamal smiled. "Is it dangerous?"

"We didn't bring you here to sell Girl Scout cookies. Last chance."

Kamal looked around him. There wasn't much of a view of the Hudson from where they were standing, but the sky was high and blue overhead. Cars sped by them in both directions on the West Side Highway. It wasn't ideal, but it was life and it was more of life than Kamal had seen since being in jail. Hicks knew it was a beautiful day to make a choice between bad and worse decisions.

"What about when it's all over?" Kamal asked. "Do I have to go back to jail?"

"That depends entirely on you," Hicks said. "You get results, you go free. Maybe even have a chance at a better life for yourself. But if you fail or lie to me or defy me at any time, even once, you go straight back and do every minute of your sentence."

Kamal shook his head. "Sounds like some real Dirty Dozen shit if you ask me."

Hicks tapped his wristwatch. "What's it going to be?"

Kamal looked up to the cloudless sky and closed his eyes. "I choose freedom."

Hicks gave a thumbs-up to the MPs and watched them climb back in the Explorer.

Kamal turned and watched the men drive away. "Just like that, huh? You got that kind of pull?"

Hicks opened the back door of the Buick. "Get in.

We've got a hell of a lot of work to do and not a lot of time to do it."

Kamal clapped his hands and let out a whoop as he began to get in the back seat. "Free at last, free at last. Thank God almighty I'm free at last."

Hicks knife-edged his left hand hard into Kamal's throat. The move caught the bigger man off guard and at a bad angle. He dropped to the asphalt, dead weight, gagging. All of the advanced training in the world couldn't prepare you for a quick punch in the throat.

Hicks put a knee into the small of Kamal's back and his .454 Ruger Alaskan against his head. "Get this straight right here and now, asshole. This isn't a vacation and you're not free. Those men were the last chance you had to back out and stay alive. From here on in, I own your miserable ass. One false move, one mistake?" Hicks pressed the barrel of the gun against Kamal's left ear. "You catch two rounds right there and get dumped in the river. Understand me?"

Hicks didn't know what he expected Kamal to do once he got his breath, but he sure as hell didn't expect him to laugh. And that's just what Kamal did. A deep belly laugh from the soul. "You crack me up. You think this is the first time I've had gun at my head?"

"No." Hicks thumbed back the hammer. "But it'll be the last unless you do exactly as I say. The second you think you're indispensable; I'll show you just how wrong you are."

"Killing me in a parking lot ain't very subtle for the CIA."

"A dead black man in a parking lot ain't exactly breaking news. And I'm not CIA." He moved the Ruger away from Kamal's ear. "We good?"

Kamal winced as he tried to get up, but couldn't. "Can't get any work done by lying here, now can we?"

———

HICKS DROVE, taking intermittent glances in the rearview mirror to watch Kamal rubbing his throat.

"You slammed my head good when you took me down back there," Kamal said. "I might have a concussion."

Hicks focused on the thickening crosstown traffic. "I thought you Green Berets were supposed to be tough."

"We're as tough as there is," Kamal told him. "You move pretty good for a smaller man, but next time will be different. Fool me once shame on you. Fool me twice, it's your ass."

Hicks laughed. "Yeah, I'll have to keep that in mind."

"Hey, what's that gun you pulled on me anyhow? Looks like a .38 but felt a whole lot heavier."

Hicks saw no reason not to tell him. "That's because it's a .454 Ruger Alaskan. Range isn't great, but up close, it'll core a charging grizzly bear."

"What's that supposed to mean?"

"You ever core an apple? Same thing. Except a hunter did that to a charging grizzly a few years ago with this gun. Put a hole in him from crown to *culo* and stopped him cold in the middle of a hard charge."

Kamal blinked his eyes clear as he looked out the window at the growing midtown traffic. Hicks saw him mouth the words 'core a grizzly bear' and knew he'd made his point.

Given the traffic, the drive out to the apartment he'd set up for Kamal in Queens would take time, so Hicks decided to strike up some conversation. Maybe get to know him a bit before he started briefing him. "I read your file and it looks like you were a pretty good soldier. How'd you go from being G.I. Joe to the Birdman of Alcatraz?"

"You don't know how it is, man," Kamal said. "They train you to serve and they train you to kill, but they don't train you how to live with it afterwards. To handle all the shit you see and keep it from eating you up inside. It's hard to maintain, man. It's damned hard."

Hicks took a sip of the civet coffee from the coffee tumbler Roger had given him for the road. It was an hour cold, but still flavorful. "Wow," Hicks said without emotion. "Sounds rough. Poor baby."

"Man, you don't know the half of the shit I've seen."

Hicks decided to play along. "Let me get this straight. You volunteered for the Army, then volunteered again to become a Green Beret, then volunteered yet again for Army Intelligence. You knew all of these things you were volunteering for were forward units bound to see action. You see said action, then decide to use that as an excuse to run drugs and whores." Hicks laughed again. "Don't bullshit a bullshitter, Ace. You saw your chance to get well and you took it. Don't make it about more than that."

"Alright, white man. Let's follow your lead and cut the bullshit. If you're not CIA, what are you? NSA? FBI? Some other black bag outfit?"

Hicks wouldn't tell him any more than he had to, but he had to tell him something. He needed him focused on Omar's men, not who Hicks worked for.

"I'm not part of the alphabet soup you're used to dealing with, so don't waste time guessing. All you need to know is that we had the juice to get you out of jail without the paperwork. That ought to tell you everything you need to know about me and who I'm with."

Kamal threw up his hands. "No problems here, boss man. I've always been more of an entrepreneur than a detective, so it doesn't make a damned bit of difference to me who's signing the checks. Just tell me who to salute and who to kill."

"If everything works out the way it's supposed to," Hicks said, "you won't be doing much of either. You're going to be playing the money man for a financier from the Middle East. Where exactly isn't important. I don't know, so don't ask. The man you're supposed to be fronting for doesn't know you, either, but will vouch for you when the time comes. Just stick to the mission package I give you and you've got a great chance at living."

"What's this money paying for?"

"We don't know and that's the problem," Hicks told him. "We need you to give this clown Omar the money, get him talking, and then tell us whatever you learn. He's supposed to be planning something big, but those are all the details we have. The money you give him will help us find out a hell of a lot more. And don't waste time thinking I'm holding out on you because I'm not. I'll give you a complete file on Omar when we get to where we're going."

"Omar," Kamal repeated as if he was trying the name on for size. "What kind of player is this Omar trying to be?"

"A big one from the sound of it," Hicks said.

"What put you on to him?"

Hicks was impressed by the level of questions Kamal was asking. It meant he was taking this seriously. "Omar's travel pattern tipped us off at first. Yemen, Pakistan, Egypt and Syria, but never back home to Somalia. That was strange. He also made some large cash transfers while he was over there; the last one for thirty grand to an electronics store in Aleppo, Syria."

"I know where Aleppo is, man," Kamal said.

"Good for you," Hicks said. "We've never been able to get to trace where Omar's donations went or what they paid for, but it was large enough to catch our attention."

Hicks decided not to tell Kamal about Colin or the cab stand or what had happened in the park. The Dean's financier didn't know that much, so Kamal didn't need to know about it, either. Besides, he didn't want Kamal trying to cut a side deal with Omar once he got in the room with him. Cellphones would probably be kept outside wherever the money exchange happened, limiting OMNI's ability to listen in. Hicks might have to rely on Kamal's honesty more than he wanted to. The less background he knew, the better the op would be.

"Where's this Omar now?" Kamal asked.

"Off the grid," Hicks said. "He's using burner phones, so we can't track him that way. At least not in time. The only way we can flush him out is with the money you give him. Find out everything you can about what he's planning, then report back to me and we move on from there. A day's work, maybe a day and a half and you're home free. All you have to do is follow your training and you get your freedom."

"If it was that easy," Kamal said, "I'd still be in a cell and you'd have some other fool doing this. How the hell did a cab driver from Queens get contacts like that? And all that money for the store in Aleppo?"

"That's something I hope you'll ask Omar," Hicks said. "You're the man with the money he needs, so you're entitled to ask all the questions you want. I've already put a list of questions I want you to ask. You'll have plenty of time to memorize it before I put you with Omar."

"Whole thing sounds a little too simple for my taste."

"And simple's the way it's going to stay, unless you complicate it. If I had someone on staff with your combination of skills and background, I'd be briefing them right now instead of you. But you know Omar's religion and you understand his customs. You literally speak their language. We've even worked out a cover that's close to the one you had in Afghanistan. Your cover's still good as far as the locals are concerned in case they make any calls. Your pals in Afghanistan think you ripped them off and ran back to the states. No one knows you were Army Intelligence."

Kamal enjoyed that. "Man, I was good, wasn't I? How much of a bankroll are you sending me in with, anyway?"

"A hundred thousand. You'll give them ten at the initial meet. More later after you and I debrief. You'll have the entire hundred in your room at all times in case they demand to see the money."

Kamal let out a long, low whistle. "That's an awful lot of money to give a convicted felon like me."

"I'm not crazy about it," Hicks admitted, "but

you're a stranger to them and they have no reason to trust you right off the bat. We never told them how much the financier would send them, but a hundred grand in cash should make them believe you're serious. Tell them you can get more if that's what it takes."

"A man like me could have a lot of fun in this town with a hundred grand."

Hicks looked at him in the rearview. "A man like you will catch a bullet in the eye if you take that bag from your room without my say so."

"Are you really always this uptight or is this just for my benefit?"

"This isn't the Tonight Show and I'm not exactly in a joking mood. You take these guys lightly, you're liable to wind up dead."

Kamal threw up his hands. "Fine. Jesus. How many people are we working with?"

"I don't know how many Omar will have with him."

"No, I mean our team. Us. You and me, Kemosabe. How many others working with us?"

"Enough to get the job done." Hicks never shared operational detail with an unknown operative. He talked about the setup instead. "I've set you up at a small apartment in Astoria. It's simple and plain because Omar and his people like simple and plain."

"How plain?"

"You'll have a bed, a laptop and a burner phone at your disposal. You'll be able to read all about your cover story on the laptop once I give you the password, but you won't be able to email any friends or reach out to anyone while you're under. Our mission files are encrypted, so even if they do look at your computer, all they'll see is spreadsheets and travel itineraries. Your file says you're good with computers, but you're not better than me. If you try to email anyone, I'll know and there will be consequences."

"I figured that," Kamal said. "Now how about answering my question about backup?"

Hicks was encouraged. At least he was paying attention. "You'll be under constant surveillance," was all Hicks said. "Anything happens, we'll know about it. Keep your phone on you at all times, even if they make you take out the battery."

"What good is it if it doesn't have the battery?"

"Don't worry about that," was all Hicks told him. He checked the rear and side view mirrors to see if they were being followed, but didn't see anything. "Just keep the phone on you if you can."

"You got it, chief," Kamal said. "By the way, I'm going to need a gun."

Hicks had been wondering when that would come up. "No way."

"Then you might as well turn this thing around and take me back to the joint because there ain't no way I'm going in there unarmed."

"You're not muscle," Hicks explained. "You're the money man and money men don't need to carry guns. You're a boss. You're Santa Claus, the Easter Bunny and whatever Muslim equivalent there is all rolled up in one package for these guys."

"I ain't bulletproof neither," Kamal said. "If these boys throw down, I'll need to be able to defend myself."

"You're a Green Beret," Hicks said. "You are a weapon. Besides, if they pat you down and find a weapon, they'll get suspicious. We need them calm and talkative. No one's going to throw down anything but information. All you have to do is pump them for details, pass it along to me and you're a free man. And I'll be there to back you up the entire time."

Hicks took another look at him in the rearview mirror. He watched Kamal pull at his prison shirt. "I'm gonna need some walking around money. Get me some new clothes, at least. The shit I've got on are stockade threads. I can't roll up on them dressed like this. I need to make an impression."

"I've got the kind of clothes Omar will expect you to wear at the apartment. The studio is already stocked with food, too. After I drop you off, you're not allowed to leave the apartment until you meet Omar. No walking around money. No getting beers or getting drunk because pious Muslims don't drink beer or get drunk, remember? After we get you settled in and debriefed, you'll call Omar and set up a meeting for tomorrow. Everything you need to know about your cover is already on that laptop. We won't call them until you're comfortable with your cover."

"As long as I'm comfortable with it by tomorrow, right?"

"Like I said before: you're a Green Beret. You can handle it."

"I'm glad one of us thinks so," Kamal said. "So what do I call you, anyway?"

"Whatever you want, Ace. It makes no difference to me."

"How does Power-Tripping Cracker sound to you?"

"I've been called worse." He looked at Kamal in the rearview. "Don't be nervous, honey. This isn't your first dance. You'll do fine and all the boys will love you. Just stick to the plan and you'll come out of this better than you were going in."

Kamal folded his arms across his chest and went back to staring out the window. "I don't like you."

Hicks steered the Buick into the passing lane. "Then you're in good company."

CHAPTER 14

HICKS DROVE across the Fifty-ninth Street Bridge to Manhattan after he got Kamal set up in the apartment.

When Kamal had heard he'd be acting as a financier's representative, he'd expected to change his jail cell for a penthouse suite at the Standard Hotel. Champagne and caviar and women just a snap of his fingers away.

He'd been disappointed when Hicks led him to the top floor of a four story walk up in Astoria. Kamal complained about everything. The furniture was run down. The TV wasn't a flatscreen. His clothes were old and uncomfortable and bland. The food in the fridge was lousy. Why couldn't he at least have a beer?

Kamal even complained about the large Islamic wall calendar Hicks had tacked to the wall next to the door. It was a picture of the Dome of the Rock on a cloudy day. He said it was depressing as hell.

"If you wanted bright colors," Hicks told him, "you should've become a Hindu. Instead, you're supposed to be a pious Muslim who works for another pious Muslim, not some drug dealer. Act accordingly."

When Hicks left, he reminded Kamal he had to contact the number Omar had given the financier to initiate contact. Hicks left the time of the outreach to Kamal's discretion. Hicks found it paid to give a field operative some degree of latitude in making certain key decisions. Deference built confidence and confidence was often the difference between life and death in the field.

Hicks didn't tell Kamal that the cellphone, the laptop and even the ancient TV were all hooked into OMNI. Everything he did was being watched, measured and recorded without Kamal's knowledge. He must have known that he was under some kind of surveillance, but he didn't know the extent of it. If he grabbed the hundred grand and tried to escape, Hicks would know about it before he reached the street. What Kamal didn't know couldn't hurt Hicks.

But Hicks had seen how tired his newest Field Assistant was. He figured Kamal would take a couple of hours and get himself acclimated to his newfound freedom. Maybe take a shower or grab some sleep in the first real bed he'd seen in over a year. He was a free man now and he wouldn't be going back to prison no matter what happened with Omar.

If he followed orders, Hicks would give him a position within the University system. If he failed, Hicks would put a bullet in his brain. Either way, Hasim Kamal had spent his last day behind bars.

Hicks was halfway across the bridge when an alert flashed on the Buick's dashboard screen that Kamal was

making a call from the burner phone he'd given Kamal.
It was the number Omar had given the Middle Eastern
financier so his emissary could reach him when he had
reached New York with the money.

Hicks didn't know whether to be pleased or
disturbed by Kamal's enthusiasm. Hicks had given him
access to Omar's file only twenty minutes before. There
was no way he could have become familiar with it in
such a short amount of time.

Hicks listened to the phone ring as the traffic on the
bridge slowed to a crawl. It was just after six o'clock and
rush hour was in full swing. But for once, Hicks didn't
mind the traffic. It allowed him to concentrate on
Kamal's conversation with Omar.

The second the call connected, and someone
answered in Arabic, OMNI went to work. It tracked
the number to a phone located in Connecticut, then
Rhode Island, then Massachusetts. Someone was using
a scrambler as well as inscription. OMNI would hunt
down the location in a matter of seconds, but he
doubted the call would last that long.

As Kamal and the man who answered it began to
exchange vague greetings in Arabic, OMNI's translator
program immediately threw up captions on the dashboard screen.

KAMAL: I have been sent here with greetings
and respect from a mutual friend.

OMNI was still trying to identify the other man's

voice, so it called him SUBJECT 1: We are grateful for his generosity. Please remain close by. Our brother will call you soon.

The connection ended and so did OMNI's translation. The system still worked on hunting down the location and on identifying the man's voice by comparing it to known hostiles in databases all over the world.

Ten seconds later, as traffic continued to stall, OMNI generated two pop up windows. One told him the location of the call could not be traced. And the man's voice could not be identified.

Hicks knew the scrambled call had not lasted long enough for OMNI to narrow it down, but the lack of a voice identification troubled him. The system had been able to give a partial identification list of up to eighty percent accuracy on conversations shorter than Subject One's. He began to wonder if this man wasn't in the system because, like the dead men he'd left in Central Park, they were new to this game.

The more he learned about Omar's people, the less he liked it. If all of his men were new recruits to the cause, it would make him that much tougher to stop.

He knew Jonathan - and probably the Dean - were watching this remotely. They would have the same concerns.

The two alert windows faded from his screen and were quickly replaced by a new window announcing an incoming call to Kamal's phone. OMNI was already tracing the call when Kamal answered.

The translator window showed more standard greetings before Kamal got down to business. The translator kept track, but Hicks didn't need to wait for

OMNI to identify the voice on the other end of the phone. It was Omar.

KAMAL: Our mutual friend has sent me to offer you gifts and praise, my brother.

OMAR: And we are honored by his faith in us. We would like to show our appreciation by welcoming you properly to this city of the infidels.

KAMAL: I appreciate your kindness and look forward meeting such a dedicated servant of Allah.

OMAR: May I send someone to meet you tomorrow morning at ten o'clock so we can begin our joyous celebration? We are most anxious to meet you, brother.

Kamal gave them an intersection near the Astoria apartment.

OMAR: We will send a van to meet you and bring you to us. We have much to discuss.

The conversation concluded with the usual praises of Allah and the bidding of peace before the connection ended.

Hicks punched the steering wheel in victory. For the first time since this whole mess began, the University was finally on offense.

Hicks waited for Kamal to call him, just as they'd discussed. He expected Kamal to be like most field agents and need some kind of reassurance that he'd done well.

But Kamal didn't call. Hicks toggled the screen to the cameras on the cellphone, the laptop, and the television. The laptop was closed, and the phone gave him a perfect view of the ceiling. Hicks tapped on the feed from the television camera and saw the entirety of the small room.

He saw Kamal turn off the lamp next to the bed, plunging the studio apartment into darkness. The camera switched to infrared mode and Hicks watched his agent fluff his pillow, pull a blanket over himself, and go to sleep. He started snoring a few moments later.

Hicks tapped the window closed. OMNI would continue to monitor the scene and alert him if Kamal moved from the couch or made another call. If he so much as went to the bathroom, much less left the apartment, Hicks would be notified.

Kamal was obviously one cool customer. True, he hadn't called like Hicks had told him to, but he was experienced enough to know the call was already being monitored. Hicks was beginning to think that Jonathan might have sent him the right man for the job.

As if on cue, a text message from Jonathan appeared on his dashboard screen:

An encouraging beginning. Where are you going now?

Hicks decided not to respond. A little bit of Jonathan went a long way and he'd been dealing with the insufferable bastard for a few days now.

Everything that could be done had been done. OMNI was on top of it all. Now, he needed a drink.

CHAPTER 15

HICKS LUCKED out and found a parking spot on the street a block from the Hotel Alsace-Lorraine.

There was nothing more he could do for Kamal or about Omar. He was already as prepared as possible. He couldn't do much until tomorrow's meeting with Omar except watch Kamal sleep and OMNI already had that well in hand.

Which is why he left the events of the day and the chilly New York evening behind him as he pushed through the revolving doors of The Jack Bull Club. It was after seven o'clock by then and the after-work crowd had thinned out a bit. The pre-dinner folks had already gone, but the restaurant was still busy.

Hicks had always preferred the lobby bars of New York's grand hotels as opposed to the Irish bars, cocktail lounges and other types of watering holes throughout the city.

He liked the mix of locals and visitors. He liked how the crowd was almost different every night. Change made patterns harder to form and patterns lead to predictability. Predictability meant death for people in his line of work, so the fewer who knew his habits, the better.

The Jack Bull Club wasn't an actual club, but it was a tourist's dream. Its clean lines and smooth Art Deco décor made people feel like they had stepped back in time. They half expected to see William Powell and Myrna Loy clink martini glasses at the next table over.

The circular wooden bar was inviting and the way the light made the bottles glow only added to the sense of elegance. The bartenders were efficient and friendly, but never too chatty.

The bar that evening was a nice mix of well-heeled travelers and jaded New Yorkers who sometimes dropped in for a couple of drinks before catching the train back to suburbia. Occasionally, some wide-eyed tourist wandered in to nurse a beer, only to be shocked at how much it cost. Elegance didn't come cheap, especially in New York.

Others gawked at the drapes and the large bronze bulldog in a top hat behind the bar. Said bulldog was even rumored to have spoken to more than one pie-eyed patron in the club's long history.

Mostly people went there so they could tell the folks back home that they had drinks one night at the Hotel Alsace-Loraine, as if overpaying for booze made them cosmopolitan.

The crowd around the oval bar all had the same vibe. Men and women who either had nowhere they had to be or were on their way to being too drunk to go anywhere else except up to their rooms. Business travelers, mostly.

That made it easier for Hicks to spot the woman

who was sitting alone at the right side of the bar; near the stairs that led back up to the rest of the hotel. She was tapping away furiously on her phone and didn't look happy about it.

He decided she was north of forty, but not by much. She wore a gray business suit that revealed a thin, but not skinny frame. Her short blonde hair might've looked severe on another woman, but she wore it well. Her pearl earrings were just feminine enough to soften her look without trying too hard. She the fingers of a pianist – long and elegant – that busily pecked out that email or text on her phone with great urgency. She wasn't wearing a wedding ring, either, but a lot of people didn't these days.

He decided there was something different about her. It was more than just her solitude or possible avail-ability. He sensed strength. An intent sense of purpose and poise. In his experience, most women either consciously or subconsciously put some amount of thought into how they looked. If that was the case, and Hicks believed it was, then he was certain he would like the way her mind worked.

The half-drunk glass of white wine at her elbow didn't look like it had been touched in a while. The lack of lipstick on the glass told him she'd been too consumed with work for a touch up. She wasn't here to impress. She was here to kill time. Perhaps unwind. Whatever she was typing, it was demanding her concentration. And judging by the stern look on her face, he was glad it wouldn't be appearing in his inbox.

He sat down two stools to her right on the other side of the curve. It gave him a good view of most of the bar and restaurant. He could see who came in off the avenue and who walked down the stairs from the hotel. He wasn't expecting any trouble, but in Hicks' world, trouble was never that far away.

The bartender – a brunette he remembered as Gayle – recognized him from the last time he'd been there about a month before. She knew him enough to be polite, but not enough to be overly friendly and certainly not enough to remember his name.

"Long time, no see." She laid a paper napkin on the bar. "What can I get for you?"

"I'll have a Laphroig, double and neat. Water on the side, please."

He'd hoped ordering a strange-sounding drink might divert the businesswoman's attention from her phone but didn't. He'd often found the name of the scotch to be a good icebreaker. And if that didn't work, the smoky aroma usually did the trick.

But the woman kept tapping away at her keypad, paying no attention to him at all. Just like Tali. But he saw her expression soften just a bit as Gayle placed the double Laphroig on the napkin as the bartender took his card. Hicks told her to keep the tab open.

The woman finally lowered her phone and looked at his drink. "It smells like an ashtray."

Hicks tried his best grin. "That's part of its charm."

"Which scotch is that?"

He noticed her eyes were an unpleasant shade of blue. "It's called Laphroig. It's got a real smoky flavor."

She went back to her phone. "Cool name. Still smells like an ashtray."

"Beauty is in the palate of the drinker. And on a cold night like this, there's nothing better."

"Not for me." She resumed tapping away at her phone. "I'll stick with my wine."

Hicks knew he had to strike the right balance if he wanted to get her talking. It would be good practice for him. Keep his field skills sharp. He needed to be charming without being suave. Suave tended to put women on the defensive so early in the dialogue and he was far too intrigued by her to let her pull up the draw-bridge just yet.

"*In vino veritas,*" he quoted. "And judging by the way you're pounding away at your phone, someone's about to get a hell of a lot of truth from you."

"That's one way of putting it." Her eyebrows flicked up as she kept typing. "Don't you just hate it when people tell you how to do your job?"

"Happens all the time. What kind of work do you do?"

"I'm a consultant," she said as she typed. "Organizational Psychology. Sounds like a lot of nonsense unless you're familiar with what it is. But it's important, believe me."

"I'm sure it is." Hicks sipped his scotch and felt warm as the smoky booze hit home. The temporary relief alcohol gave him was the only real emotion he allowed himself to feel. It was a safe emotion because it was easy to control. It came out of a bottle and could be kept there until he decided to indulge it. "You don't strike me as the kind of woman who enjoys wasting her time."

She continued typing. "Really? How so?"

Hicks gave it some thought. "You look like someone who had a long day and wasn't expecting to respond to emails. I think you'd prefer to be enjoying your wine right now instead of dealing with whoever is bothering you after hours right now."

"So, you're saying I look like hell. You sure know how to charm a lady."

"You look fine and know it," he said. "You just look annoyed and for good reason."

"Very perceptive of you." She tapped her phone one last time, turned it off and tucked it in the right-hand pocket of her suit jacket. He noticed she didn't put it on the bar or in her bag, which was on the bar next to her. Strange because he was sure she was a lefty. Her wine was on her left side, but Hicks was sitting to her right.

She let out a long breath and signaled Gayle to pour her another glass. "What did we do before cellphones anyway?"

"We had conversations," Hicks offered. "Real relationships and real lives, not all the virtual reality of tablets and smartphones. I remember when you had to go to the store if you wanted to chat online." He lifted his scotch and smiled. "Back when dinosaurs roamed the earth."

She smiled, too. "I think we've gotten dumber as the phones have gotten smarter." He watched her reach for her wine with her left hand. "What about you? What do you do for a living?"

Hicks was in a playful mood. "Take a guess."

Her eyes narrowed as she gave him an appraising look. "Given what you've said so far, I'd say you're probably a philosopher. Or a professor of some kind. I don't think you're in town on business. You're too relaxed for that. I'd say you live here."

"Now look who's perceptive. As for what I do, let's

just split the difference and say I'm a philosophy professor." Hicks laughed. "I wish I had it so good. I'd have tenure by now. Unfortunately, I don't." He went with his standard line. "I'm actually in sales."

She wasn't impressed, but he hadn't meant her to be. "Sales can be interesting, depending on what you sell."

"I sell technology solutions to businesses. My clients tell me what they need, and I help them find a way to meet their needs." It wasn't a total lie, and it was close enough to the truth so it was easy to remember after a couple of drinks.

"It's not as sexy as Organizational Psychology." He flicked his finger against his glass, "but it pays well enough to keep me in Laphroig."

"Sounds like you help people solve problems they didn't know they had."

"That's the general idea, in theory. When everything works out the way it's supposed to, which it almost never does."

"If things always worked out the way they were supposed to, most people would be out of jobs," she said. "All day long, all I hear are problems and that's after everything has fallen apart. I just sift through the pieces; make recommendations and they pay me for my time. I'm never around long enough to see the good I've done, if any. There's always another contract to fill and another company that needs help. Just once I'd like to be there for the finish. To get a pat on the back when it goes well."

She caught herself and rolled her eyes. "Listen to me grumbling. I can't really complain, though." Gayle refilled her glass and she picked it up in her left hand. "It pays well enough to keep me in white wine."

Hicks drank as she sipped. He decided to let the silence between them grow. He knew they'd reached a critical moment. The conversation had either run its natural course and they'd go their separate ways or she'd find a way to keep the conversation going. He had a feeling she'd find a way to keep it going. He was nothing if not a tolerable distraction from her phone.

He took a casual look around the bar. A few new people had drifted in and out since he'd sat down, but no one had come in alone. No one was paying much attention to anything other than the glass in front of them or the person sitting next to them.

She asked, "You're very observant, aren't you?"

He was glad she'd decided to keep the conversation going. "People watching is my favorite hobby. Everyone has a story, and everyone has a reason for being here, even if it's no reason at all."

"You really *are* a philosopher, aren't you? And what's your reason for being here?"

He shrugged. "Good conversation. Good scotch. Good company. Yours?"

"Work," she sighed. "And maybe some good conversation as well."

Just the kind of answer Hicks had been expecting. "Where's home?"

She hesitated for an instant before saying, "Virginia. Alexandria, actually. Nice town, but it's not New York."

"Well, if it was, it wouldn't be Alexandria. Where'd you go to University?"

This time, the hitch wasn't as subtle, but she

rebounded better this time around. "That's a European way of asking a question. Most Americans ask what school you went to."

Hicks feigned embarrassment. "Occupational hazard. I work with a lot of Europeans, so I guess they've rubbed off on me. I can rephrase the question if it'll make you feel any better."

She shook her head. "I never had the grades for a university. It was Dallas Community College for me and proud of it. First in my family to ever get that far in school, by the way. Communications major. Never thought I'd wind up in Organizational Psychology, but here I am."

"Life is like that. Who would've thought a philosophy major would end up selling computer solutions?" He tried another track just for fun. "How long have you been working in education?"

This time, there was no hitch. No pause at all, just correction. "Well, it's not really education. It's Organizational Psychology, which is kind of related, but not really."

"It's all psychology, I guess." Hicks took a drink and put his glass back on the napkin. "After all, if you weren't really a psychologist, you wouldn't have been sent here to analyze me. Would you?"

She tilted her head just enough. The very picture of confusion. "I'm sorry?"

"Jonathan's craftier than I thought," Hicks explained. "They used to only send men to analyze men and women to analyze women in the field. The whole opposite gender thing risks skewing the results. Attractions, turn-offs, factors like that."

She appeared flustered. "I'm not sure what you're

talking about, and I don't even know anyone named Jonathan."

"Maybe not," Hicks said, "but we definitely have the same boss. I'm just surprised they didn't send a trained Field Assistant to look me over. I'm curious. Why did they send you?"

He watched her take her phone out of her suit pocket and put it in her bag as if she were getting ready to leave. "I don't know how much you had to drink before you got here, but I think you're past your limit already. You're not making much sense at all."

Hicks looked at his glass of scotch and focused on the facts. "The first mistake you made was asking what kind of scotch I was drinking. I asked for Laphroig, which could be bourbon or rye or even whiskey. But you already knew I only drink scotch because you read my file. Then you put your phone in your pocket instead of your bag. Most women put their phone on the bar or in their bag if it's near by. You didn't do either. You put it in your right-hand pocket because it was closer to me even though you're left-handed."

"No, I'm not."

"Your bag and your wine are on the left side of you and you drink with your left hand. That's not much to go on normally, but remember, I'm trained to see those things. You put it in the pocket closest to me because you thought it would hear our conversation better." He smiled. "That thing can practically pick up a single conversation in a stadium full of people, so there was no need to do that. That's why I know you're not a Field Assistant because you didn't know that. You're not familiar with the device, either. I could tell that by the way you were pounding the damned thing when I got here. Clearing the screen is tricky if you don't have the knack for it." He leaned in close and lowered his voice. "You didn't need to turn on the recorder. That thing's always listening. And you shouldn't have opened it in a public place like this. Protocols and all."

"I don't know what..."

But Hicks wasn't done. "Your other mistake was that you hitched when I asked you where you lived. You were going to say something else, probably Maryland, but forced yourself to say Alexandria. I'd wager you live in Maryland. Virginia's close enough, though, but I wondered why you'd lie about where you're from? That's why I asked where you went to University. You paused for just a second and said Dallas. But you don't have a Texas accent and you would've had one if you'd spent enough time in Dallas to go to a community college, even if you had lessons to tamp it down. And you wouldn't have lost it by living in Virginia. Softened it, maybe, but you'd still have it."

She folded her arms. "Are you a writer? Because this is some good material you're coming up with."

Hicks went on. "And perhaps the most damning mistake of all, you never asked my name because you already knew it."

She blinked. Twice.

"Now, if I'm wrong, I'll pay for your drink and walk out the door. But if you leave, I'm going to give the Dean a full report on how you screwed up and, my guess is your equipment will be terminated before you reach the corner and Jonathan will be in a hell of a lot of trouble for wasting resources like this."

Hicks paused to look at her. "How'd I do?"

She didn't react. She didn't even blink. She simply

sat still with her arms folded across her chest. She looked around at various people at the bar and then back at her glass. "This...this isn't..." Her hand quivered as she reached for her wine.

Hicks subtly slid it away from her. "Calm down. You're not in trouble and I'm not going to burn you with the Department, either, if you do exactly what I tell you. I already scanned the room and no one is shadowing us so it's just you and me."

She looked at her hands. "But the hotel cameras and our handhelds. They already know I screwed up."

"I checked them a long time ago. The cameras in here face the street and the cash registers, not the patrons." He had another question on his mind. "As for the handhelds, that's going to depend on who sent you."

"You already said his name."

He was glad she hadn't forgotten everything they had taught her about field work. "Let me see your handheld."

She dug it out of her bag and handed it to him. "It's not my normal device. They gave it to me today before they sent me up here. There's an icon I had to select to start recording, but..."

Hicks found it and toggled it off. "That's what you were banging away at it when I got in here, wasn't it?"

She nodded. "It didn't seem to have a signal."

He handed it back to her. "That's because it doesn't. These old concrete buildings make it tough for our friends to track us. Why do you think I come in here? It's nice to drop off the grid occasionally."

She dumped her handheld back in her bag like it was on fire. "They'll still know we met, right?"

"They'll know we were in the same bar together,

but since you're not recording, that's all they'll know. That is, except for whatever report you submit on me."

She reached for her glass of wine again and, this time, Hicks let her take it. "You were wrong about one thing. I don't work in Behavioral Analysis. I work in the Field Analysis Department in Maryland." She took a sip and shook her head. "Christ, you picked up on that fast. Your file said you were highly observant, but I didn't know you were that good."

"Skip the flattery and tell me why our friend sent you."

"I don't know," she admitted. "The order came in through the system yesterday morning with an information package on you with an assessment date starting today. I only got off the train a little more than an hour ago."

Hicks knew she wasn't lying. "What did they want you to find out about me?"

"General appearances and impressions," she told him. "Your state of mind. Your mood. How you conduct yourself in social situations. Are you chatty where alcohol is involved? Do you say too much or too little? Your superiors seem to be concerned that you might be showing signs of field rust and are in need of a sabbatical. I've read your record and God knows you could use it. Moscow. Tehran. Guatemala. Tel Aviv."

Hicks wasn't interested in going down Memory Lane with a total stranger. "How did you know I'd be here? Not just where I was, but where I'd go. Hell, I didn't even know where I was going until I got over the bridge."

She set her glass of wine on the bar. She closed her eyes as she decided whether or not to tell him the truth.

"The system predicted there was a high degree of probability you'd need to wind down tonight. I don't know why but that's what it said. There was a more than eighty percent likelihood that you'd come here, based on your previous patterns."

Hicks sat back on his stool. He'd heard rumblings about OMNI's A.I. expanding into field analysis for a while, but he had no idea it had already been implemented. He hated being predictable, even when a supercomputer was doing the predicting. "Jesus. They don't even trust their own people anymore."

"We're not in a trusting business, James." She took her glass of wine and finished it. "Guess that's why people like me have a job." She set her glass on the bar and looked at him. "You too, I guess."

Hicks motioned for Gayle to come back over. "Another one for me and another wine for the lady."

"No," she said. "I'll have what he's having."

The bartender cleared their glasses and went to pour their drinks.

Hicks looked at her. "You sure? You said it smelled like an ashtray."

"It does, but I really hate wine. I prefer tequila. Your file said you preferred elegant blondes and, since I don't like cocktails either, white wine was the best I could come up with."

"Is that really in my profile? That I like elegant blondes?"

"It is, along with a lot of other things. But your real name has been redacted. It's the only file I've ever seen where an Office Head's entire background was missing. All it lists is your current cover name."

"Adds to the mystery," he said. "You haven't told me your real name, either."

Gayle laid the scotches in front of them and slipped away.

The woman took the glass of scotch. "Do we really need names at this point?"

Hicks clinked glasses with her. "Touché, madam. Speaking of mysteries, are you really a blonde?"

She drank the scotch and didn't even flinch at the taste. Maybe she really was a tequila woman. "That's smoother than I thought it would be."

Hicks drank too. "The booze or my line?"

"Both. And just like with the Laphroig, there's only one way to find out. By trying it for yourself."

THE UNIVERSITY HAD ALLOWED her to book a room in the Alsace-Lorraine for the rest of the week. The mystery was solved after a short elevator ride to her room on the eleventh floor.

She was different than Hicks had expected her to be, even after she'd lowered her guard. Her body was lean and toned, yet soft. Their lovemaking was more sexual than sensual and kissing hadn't entered much into the equation. She squeezed his neck when she climaxed, but no nails across the back or moans of ecstasy.

When he climbed off her, he thought she'd be distant and avoid being close. She surprised him by laying her head on his chest.

"Well, I would've lost that bet," he admitted.

"What? That I'm not the stuck-up bitch you thought I was?"

"No. That you really are a natural blonde after all."

She ran her hand over his chest. "That's one mystery solved." He felt her tense. "You know this wasn't part of the assignment. This was about you and me, not work. Not your evaluation, either."

Hicks had run honey trap operations for a good portion of his life and knew this wasn't one of them. "I know, but I thank you for telling me anyway."

"Yes, of course you knew." She settled back down. "Stupid me."

Hicks held her closer. "You're married, aren't you?"

"Was it that obvious?"

"No, just a feeling I got."

"I suppose you have to live off your feelings, don't you? Your impressions of people."

"I do. They're usually right for the most part, the way my impression of you was right about you working in the same place as me." He dared not say the University. Even now, after what they had shared, it was better not to talk about some things openly.

But some things had to be said. "So, what's your verdict of me, doc? What are you going to tell Jonathan about crazy Hicks?"

She pinched his side which made him jump. "You're not crazy. No one thinks that. Your reputation is stellar, and you've got the highest ratings of anyone at your level."

"But?" he prodded.

"But I think you're tired," she told him. "Not in a dangerous way or in an unfit way, but tired in your heart. And who could blame you? Your file is woefully short on personal details. The only hobby they have listed for you is that you like blondes and drink scotch."

Hicks was glad. That's all he wanted them to know about him. "There are worse pursuits. Some might call them virtues."

"But other members have many hobbies listed. Painting or art or travel. Things like that. Nothing like that is listed for you and I have a feeling I know why."

She picked her head off his chest and looked at him. "You don't have anything else besides this, do you? All of you have is this job, this life. And you don't want anything else. That makes me sad because I can tell you're capable of so much more."

Hicks liked the way she looked now. Not as hard as she had looked downstairs at the bar, but her eyes were still just as cold. He'd never been big on self-analysis, mostly because the subject bored him. And a one-night stand wouldn't change that.

"I can see why they sent you to kick my tires. You're very perceptive."

She laid her head on the pillow and slowly ran her finger over his chin. "Deflection. You're a master at deflection, aren't you?"

"No." Hicks said as he gently pulled her closer. "I just have my mind on other things at the moment."

CHAPTER 16

AFTER HICKS LEFT her early the next morning, he stopped by the facility to shower, change clothes and gear up for the day ahead. He'd checked his handheld throughout the night and saw that Kamal had not moved from the couch. Hicks was glad because he'd be needing his sleep.

Hicks knew he'd be spending most of his time in the car trailing Kamal, so he wouldn't need the parka. He opted for a lighter winter coat with a Kevlar lining. He wasn't expecting things to get hot, but he took extra speed loaders for the Ruger and six extra clips for the Glock backup. *Semper Paratus.*

Hicks had been parked around the corner from Kamal's studio apartment in Astoria for an hour before Kamal had been picked up by Omar's men in a Honda minivan. With OMNI watching Kamal from above, Hicks could afford to hang back in traffic as he watched them drive him out to the Midwood section of Brooklyn.

Judging by the audio from Kamal's phone, the drive

to Brooklyn was a quiet one. After offering the tradi-
tional greetings and blessings as he got in the van, the
OMNI translator picked up what Kamal said next.

KAMAL: Where are you from, my brothers?

SUBJECT 1 and SUBJECT 2: Somalia

The men answered at the same time, but OMNI
had picked up two distinct voices. Kamal was slick.
He'd gotten them to speak so whoever was listening
would know how many men were in the van with him.
Neither voice belonged to Omar.

As he followed the white van, Hicks toggled
between the satellite view and traffic cameras along
their way. The Honda minivan's license plates were
clear but were registered to a gray minivan registered to
Elaine Finnegan in Rego Park. Hicks was fairly certain
that Elaine wasn't driving a group of terrorists all over
Brooklyn. They'd probably swapped plates at some
time the night before and Elaine hadn't noticed yet.
Most cops wouldn't notice, either. The description was
close enough to let it slide until she reported them
stolen. Another smart move on Omar's part.

Hicks had OMNI enhance the images of the driver,
but to no avail. The windshield was tinted darker than
the law allowed, so it was impossible to see him with
standard equipment. And OMNI didn't have the right
angle to get a picture of the driver. Thermal scans
confirmed there were only three men in the van.

Hicks wondered where they were going as he

followed the van through Midwood. Omar was a strange one. He sounded desperate on the phone but was cautious with bringing Kamal to the meeting spot. He'd risked giving away his location every time he touched a phone but took precautions to reroute the signal across three states. It was as if there were two sides of Omar. A cautious, dedicated side that didn't fit with the panicking side.

And as he tracked the van through Brooklyn, Hicks began to think if Omar wasn't the only one running the show.

His train of thought was derailed when OMNI alerted him that Kamal had stopped moving. Hicks was only a block away and pulled over into a bus stop as he toggled the screen to only reveal the satellite feed from above.

The minivan had parked in front of a mattress store and they were walking inside. He toggled the screen to the camera in Kamal's phone. It showed a Somali open a door for him as he entered a showroom full of mattresses.

The audio picked up his drivers asking him to follow them as they walked to the back of the store. The image from Kamal's phone confirmed this.

Hicks had OMNI run a thermal scan of the building, but the snow on the roof made for a difficult reading. There appeared to be five men in a lower level, but Hicks couldn't be sure.

He tasked the network with finding any internal cameras inside the mattress store, but OMNI found nothing. Hicks could see old cameras inside the store through Kamal's phone and figured they must be the old-fashioned kind that were directly wired into a bank of monitors somewhere.

The audio from Kamal's phone quickly became muddled as Kamal reached a staircase and several men began speaking in Arabic at once. OMNI broke the translation windows into six lines of dialogue. Five for the men downstairs and one for Kamal. They were offering each other standard Arabic blessings and greetings.

Thermal imaging confirmed the two drivers remained upstairs. Omar was smart. He compartmentalized. The Dean would've approved.

The translator window delivered the best news Hicks had seen in a while. It had identified Omar as one of the men in the room.

Hicks gripped the wheel tighter. *Bingo.*

OMAR: We know you have traveled far, my friend, and we welcome you to this sinful land. We wish you every comfort while you are among us. Part of that comfort requires us to live in the ways of our ancestors. In the ways of the Prophet, may peace be upon him. As is often the case, the old ways are best.

KAMAL: Meaning?

SUBJECT 3: Your phone, brother. We must ask you to give us your phone before we become more acquainted with each other. Our enemies are many and have many devious methods at their disposal. They can easily turn such harmless conveniences against us, so we must be careful.

Hicks had been expecting that. He heard Kamal politely argue while Hicks pulled out of the bus stop and drove to a quieter side street near the mattress store. He found a spot near a ballfield two blocks away. The audio feed from Kamal's cellphone went dead. They must've put it in a metal box or even an old coffee can. Either was a low-tech way to render a high-tech device useless.

Hicks watched the thermal display of the store take up the entire screen as the fuzzy thermal images penetrated the snow. Fortunately, Hicks had already prepared for that eventuality.

He checked his mirrors to make sure no one was around before he popped his Buick's trunk. The hydraulics the Varsity boys had added made sure the trunk lid opened completely. He tapped the Surveillance option on his dashboard screen and linked the four-propellered drone in his trunk to OMNI's location of Kamal.

The propellers began to spin and the device, which was roughly the size and weight of a large hardcover novel, gradually rose high into the air. The Buick's trunk shut tight as the drone took flight. Its onboard sensors linked with OMNI as it scanned the environment and automatically charted the best, straightest flight path toward the mattress store's roof.

Hicks tapped the wheel nervously as he waited for the drone to land. He could be losing valuable parts of conversation and cursed himself for not launching the drone sooner. The only saving factor was that Omar and his friends liked to talk and rarely got to the point quickly. He only hoped the drone reached its target before he missed too much. He didn't like the idea of having to solely rely on Kamal's honesty.

OMNI showed the drone had landed safely on the roof of the mattress store. No threats or recognition events had occurred in flight. The drone's optics and flight capabilities went dormant as it dedicated all on-board power to generating pulses that would allow it to hear through two levels to the basement below.

Hicks' eyes narrowed when he saw the pulses were having a difficult time penetrating the mattresses that covered the floor below it. Enemies in the Middle East had used similar tactics to weaken older models of the drone. Later versions rendered such efforts useless.

But Hicks knew Omar hadn't been in the Middle East when the technology had been introduced there. Perhaps meeting at a mattress store in Brooklyn had been a coincidence. But Hicks didn't believe in coincidence.

Maybe there were more than simply two sides to Omar.

Maybe Omar was more than just one man. Maybe he was working for someone else.

As he watched the drone's pulses reach the basement, the OMNI translator began working again.

The drone didn't identify voices but sounds. The creak of a door. Metal chair legs scraping on hardwood.

He checked the thermal scan. They had moved into another room.

Now they were getting down to business.

Omar began speaking in Arabic, but Kamal politely shut him down.

"My apologies, my brothers." Hicks thought the Nigerian accent on his English was perfect. "Arabic is not my native tongue, so now that precautions have been taken, I ask that we speak in English or even French if you prefer."

Omar chose French and the OMNI translator easily kept up with the change. The dashboard screen window read:

OMAR: Then let us speak of why we have invited you here in the language of the lesser white devil.

KAMAL: Thank you, my brother. Now, our wise and generous uncle has asked me to understand the difficulties you are having.

OMAR: Before we discuss such matters, your wounds trouble me. The cuts and swelling on your face.

Hicks gripped the wheel tighter. He hadn't counted on him having wounds after their run-in at the parking lot. He shouldn't have hit him, but he'd needed to make a point.

He only hoped Kamal's bruises didn't throw him off their game plan. *Stick to the script I gave you.*

KAMAL: These are the marks of the Great Prophet, peace be upon him, for I received them during questioning from the Nigerian Special Police in the airport before I came here. But don't think of them as wounds, my brother. I think of them as honors won in our ongoing struggle against the infidels and all those who aid them. A struggle our generous uncle believes you are willing to assist.

Hicks was impressed with Kamal's poise under pressure. And his French was pretty good, too.

OMAR: Do you need care, my brother?

KAMAL: Perhaps later, but for now, my uncle's interest in your request must take priority. He has asked me to assist you in any way I can, but I must know more before I can advise him how he might help

Hicks adjusted himself in his seat. *Here we go.*

OMAR: Beyond just his concern, I hope we might also have his support?

KAMAL: If the enterprise is worthy enough, he may wish to support it entirely. Which

192 / TERRENCE MCCAULEY

brings us back to my original point. I must know more before I can advise him.

Hicks wasn't surprised that Omar was being stubborn.

OMAR: We appreciate his intentions and his prayers, but we were hoping for something more tangible.

OMNI identified a canvas bag being slid across wood. Kamal was giving them the money.

KAMAL: Which is why he hopes you will accept this token of his praise of your noble efforts.

Hicks clapped his hand against the wheel. *That's it. Hook him and reel him in.* Hicks wasn't sure how much Kamal had decided to give him and didn't really care. At this point, he'd be able to track Omar from the mattress store to a location where a Varsity Squad could hit him.

But first he needed to know more about what Omar was planning. He hoped the money Kamal gave him would be enough to make him talk.

OMNI identified scuffling sounds as the three other men in the room looked in the bag. A translator window opened when Omar began to speak.

OMAR: It is a most generous. His faith in us is humbling.

OMNI didn't pick up on the disappointed tone in Omar's voice, but Hicks did.

KAMAL: This is but a small token of his esteem for your efforts. His support will be boundless once we know more.

OMAR: Our uncle's concern is both appreciated and justified. As you will soon see, his support will be vital to the success of our cause.

KAMAL: And when will I see such things?

Hicks listened through the silence that followed. The time for talking around things was over. He'd shown them the money. Now he wanted to see what they were planning. Kamal was good and smart.

OMAR: You will see evidence of this and more this very day, my brother. And I am sure you will agree to tell our uncle that our efforts will bring great glory to our cause. Our plans are grand in scope but humble in their execution.

It was Kamal's turn to be quiet.

KAMAL: I have given you his support and you have given me nothing but words in return. Our uncle is anxious to know what you wish to do, as am I. He is waiting to hear from me, and he is not a patient man.

OMAR: His patience will be rewarded. Come. Let us show you our plans.

Hicks knew they were on the move. He selected the Options window for the drone and selected the FOLLOW KAMAL option. When given a list of proximity choices, he selected BIRDSEYE VIEW.

While OMNI's thermal imaging showed five men leaving the basement through the loading bay at the back of the store, the drone's propellers began to spin before it quickly rose to a height of five hundred feet, approximately fifty stories in the air. It was low enough to avoid being detected by radar but high enough to be mistaken for a bird from the ground. The drone had been modified for a battery life of two hours. He also had another drone in the trunk to take its place while it recharged should it be necessary, allowing him constant audio surveillance of Kamar and whoever was with him.

OMNI switched from thermal imaging to its regular lens as Kamal, Omar and the three other men left the loading bay and climbed into a gray Hyundai SUV.

Omar was a slight man. Bone skinny and bug-eyed. The few teeth he still had were small and crooked. His black skin was marked with lighter patches and pockmarked from acne. He bore the haunted, hunted look of a man who'd been held down most of his life. Hicks knew that look was well earned.

In Somalia, Omar had been an orphan who'd grown up in the gutters of Mogadishu.The only friends he had were the gangs of orphans he ran with. He didn't have any any formal education, either. Somehow, he'd managed to scrape together enough money to leave his country and head to America. He'd started his own cab company and now wanted to be a major player in the *jihad* against the West.

Men like Omar scared Hicks because they had nothing to keep them going except hatred. That hatred gave him strength, motivation, and purpose. What he'd lost in life he found in the afterlife and lived only to secure his spot in heaven. People like that couldn't be reasoned with. They couldn't be educated to see the error of their ways.

The only way to stop them was a bullet to the brain, which Hicks would be glad to supply. After he found out what he was planning, of course.

Omar got behind the wheel as OMNI automatically locked on the faces of the three strangers and began running them through its facial recognition database.

Hicks turned on the ignition and the transplanted V-12 engine roared to life. He waited until Omar's SUV pulled out of the lot before he began following it.

A quick rundown of the SUV showed it was leased

to Omar's cab company. Nothing interesting there. It was even legal.

A bus drifted from the left lane into the center lane without signaling. Horns blared and tires screeched. Hicks floored it and easily shot past the whole mess. Sometimes, a big engine came in handy, even in the city.

Hicks tapped the dashboard screen and changed it to the standard GPS view. Omar's SUV became an icon on the maze of Brooklyn streets.

Hicks followed at a safe distance.

He wasn't hearing anything from the drone, which automatically reduced the chatter it picked up from other cars beneath it and focused only on the SUV. He ran a diagnostic to make sure the drone was working, which it was. Omar was rolling quiet. Smart man.

Kamal spoke to him in French and the OMNI translator kicked in.

KAMAL: Why so quiet, brother? You seem pensive.

OMAR: Not pensive, brother. Just cautious. Our enemies have ways of listening to us while remaining unseen. I find it best to speak less when we are outside the comfort of our surroundings. I ask you to do the same. Ours is a short journey and a pleasant one, I assure you.

Now Hicks knew there had to be another player in all this. Omar was a chatterbox. He never shut up in the cab office. He either teased his men or launched into anti-American tirades. Something had changed in him. Or someone had told him to be smarter about when and where he talked.

The evidence was racking up fast that Omar had friends. He hoped Jonathan was listening in and drawing the same conclusions.

Hicks followed the SUV from several car lengths away as they drove to a building near the Barclays Center and pulled into a parking lot.

Hicks coasted past their position, took a left onto a side street, and parked on the street. He killed the engine and switched the dashboard image from GPS to a live shot from the drone still trailing them from five hundred feet above.

OMNI identified the building as a former warehouse that had been converted into a modern self-storage facility.

Omar obviously had something to show Kamal. Something that had to be kept away from where they'd just met. Something that needed to be protected under constant lock and key.

He checked the facial recognition window, but the search hadn't yielded anything yet. The men with Omar were not in any database, including any immigration databases.

That confirmed Omar was simply a cog in a much larger wheel.

Hicks toggled back to the satellite and scanned for radiological signs from the building. He knew NYPD and Homeland Security kept a close watch of such things through their own resources, but he wanted to be certain. OMNI only detected acceptable, natural radiation levels.

That didn't mean Omar couldn't have something in a lead container in one of the units. It just meant that if it was radiological, it was well protected.

He ordered the drone to land on the roof of the storage facility as Kamal, Omar and the others went inside.

Hicks directed OMNI to access the building's security cameras. It was fairly new and was bound to have modern, wireless security coverage.

He had the satellite switch back to a thermal scan of the building's structure. The floors appeared to be solid concrete, so the satellite would have a difficult time giving him a definitive lock on their position now that they were inside.

The drone pinged away as it tried to hear what was going on inside the building. But the drone's sensors detected a thick sheet of ice from the blizzard had formed on the roof, making it difficult for the signal to penetrate. The cavernous interior of the structure further deflected the signal, resulting in tremendous feedback the software couldn't isolate.

He could've moved the drone to hover outside the windows at each floor but decided against it. Omar or one of his men might have spotted it, or worse, a civilian might call the police and the whole game would be up.

He checked OMNI's progress on hacking the cameras. A network was present, but the cameras had been taken offline.

That meant whoever ran the building was in on Omar's plans, or at least had been paid well enough to make sure no one could see what they were doing.

He knew it wouldn't yield much, but he set OMNI to search the storage facility's records to obtain a list of who rented units and where. It gave him something to do while he waited.

In the meantime, Hicks set the drone to idle mode to conserve the battery. So much for technology.

It looked like he'd have to rely on Kamal's honesty. That wasn't an option.

Hicks watched the satellite feed for twenty minutes when he began to wonder if he was being too cute by half. He had Omar and his men secured in one location. Maybe he should order a Varsity Team to hit the building, grab them up and have Roger go to work on them. Interrogations were always risky, but Roger was the best at what he did.

Hicks decided to let it play out. Since it appeared more likely that Omar was not the shot-caller in whatever was being planned, it might be best to continue to keep an eye on him. Gather intelligence and wait for him to wait for something bigger. The storage facility wasn't going anywhere, and neither was whatever was inside of it. While he waited, he ordered OMNI to put the building under passive surveillance. From now on, everything that happened inside would be under the watchful, unblinking eye of the network.

As time dragged on, Hicks noticed no other vehicles had pulled into the lot the entire time. No moving vans. No foot traffic. No little old ladies stopping by to check on their prized Hummel collections. OMNI had detected five hundred customers who used the building to store their goods and not one of them had come by.

It was as if everyone knew enough to stay away. Perhaps they did. This storage facility was growing more interesting by the minute.

Hicks perked up when the satellite picked up Kamal, Omar, and the others as they walked out of the building.

He didn't need OMNI to tell him that Omar and his friends had changed their appearance. All of them were now dressed identically to Kamal. They wore white skull caps and loose-fitting *ihrams* or robes.

"Why'd you go and do a thing like that?" Hicks asked the screen. "What are you up to?"

Kamal looked to be unharmed, and it was impossible to know what they had shown him based on his facial expression. It was also impossible to see if they were carrying anything under their billowing robes.

Omar was toying with something in his left hand. It looked like it might've been the key fob for his car.

Hicks toggled the satellite view back to the thermal scan to see if they were hiding anything different under their new clothes. The scan came back normal, so Hicks clicked back to the regular satellite feed.

Once again, Omar climbed in behind the wheel while the others got inside. Kamal rode shotgun. Omar started up the SUV and pulled away.

Hicks knew OMNI was tracking them, so he was in no hurry to follow.

Whatever Omar had been holding in his hand still bothered Hicks.

He tapped the dashboard screen and rewound the OMNI footage to focus on what Omar had been holding when he left the storage facility. Hicks stopped the playback at the point where Omar and Kamal had first left the building, then zoomed in on Omar's hands.

OMNI revealed it was a set of keys. But as he zoomed in closer, Hicks saw one key had the Hyundai logo on it.

But the other was a storage locker key. And the small label on the face of it read '338'.

"Bingo," he heard himself say. "Got you, you son of a bitch."

Hicks grabbed his handheld and was about to look up who owned unit 338 when his handheld began to buzz. He knew either the Dean or Jonathan had been watching the feed and saw what he'd been analyzing. He hoped it was the Dean. Unfortunately, it was Jonathan.

"This is Professor Warren," Hicks answered via Bluetooth, telling him it was safe to talk.

Jonathan's voice filled the interior of the Buick. "Excellent work, James. It appears Omar has taken our friend into his confidence."

Hicks knew he was looking for a pat on the back for picking Kamal, but he wouldn't give him the satisfaction. "Ten grand in cash helps buy a lot of confidence with a rookie like Omar, but we won't know what he told Kamal until we debrief him. The drone couldn't get a lock on what they said in there."

"We're still tracking them," Jonathan said, "and now we know which storage unit is Omar's. I know you were about to access the facility's records, but I've already reviewed them. It's a large unit registered to a John Smith of 505 Fifth Avenue in New York. The bill is paid in person in cash each month."

Hicks wasn't surprised by the phony record. "Something stinks about this place. The cameras were deactivated, and no one came in or out the entire time Omar was there. Who owns the facility?"

"A shell corporation out of the Caymans," Jonathan said. "That's not unheard of, though it's of mild interest. In the meantime, I want you to stay on Omar. I have a Varsity Team on the way to examine Omar's storage unit and see what they find."

"Call them off," Hicks said. "No one goes near that unit until I get the chance to debrief Kamal after Omar drops him off. Something's not right about that building and if you send in a wrecking crew, it'll tip off Omar that someone's on to him. Let OMNI watch and do its job."

"Scott's men aren't a bunch of cowboys," Jonathan said. "I think they can safely figure out if the storage unit presents a threat."

"I know they can because I trained half of them," Hicks reminded him. "But a proper infiltration will take planning. Let's see what Kamal has to report first before we risk tipping our hand."

Hicks could hear the disappointment in Jonathan's voice. This was where his lack of field experience came into play. "Very well. When will you debrief Kamal?"

"As soon as he's free of Omar." He checked the dashboard screen and saw Omar was heading back toward Queens. He probably wanted to drop off Kamal himself. Maybe see where the man was staying to make sure it wasn't too expensive and appropriately humble. "In the meantime, did the Dean have any more luck getting an ID on the image the British embargoed?"

"Yes," Jonathan allowed, "but we can talk about it after you debrief Kamal."

"We can talk about it right now," Hicks countered. "From what I've been able to put together, Omar's role in this seems to get smaller by the minute. I think someone's running him, not the other way around. And I think whoever is important enough for the British to protect might be part of it."

Jonathan remained silent.

And Hicks grew frustrated. "Come on, Ace. This guy can't be that important, can he? We would've had something on him ourselves if he was that big."

"We don't know for certain and that's the problem," Jonathan admitted. "The Dean reached out to our British cousins who admitted they'd embargoed the identification but they're refusing to say why. Whoever this man is, he's very important to Her Majesty's government."

Hicks swore as he put his head back against the headrest. He'd been hoping the French had embargoed the image. They were usually inclined to share information after a fair amount of posturing. They enjoyed reminding fellow intelligence agencies that they still had extensive networks in Africa and the Middle East.

But the British were different. Movies and espionage books liked to show the British intelligence forces as inferior to their American counterparts. Like a handsome, oblivious older brother who'd fallen to drink and now depended on his younger brother for support.

Hicks knew that wasn't the case now and never really had been. While America's intelligence services had gotten bogged down fighting Communist expansion in Korea, Vietnam and elsewhere around the globe,

Britain had quietly protected its networks and more than held its own in the intelligence community. Their empire may have crumbled after the war, but their intelligence capabilities grew stronger. American might dominate the world stage, but British resolve was still every bit as formidable as it had ever been.

Which meant there must be a damned good reason why they were protecting that image even after the Dean's involvement.

"Does the Dean think he can wear them down?"

"No," Jonathan said. "He's willing to call in a lot of favors if we need him to, but only as a last resort and he'll need convincing that it is, indeed, the last resort."

It was looking more like Kamal's honesty would be more important than Hicks would've liked. "I'll be in touch as soon as I debrief Kamal."

"See to it that you are." Jonathan killed the connection.

Hicks looked at the blank screen of his handheld. "Last word freak."

But his conversation with Jonathan had served a purpose. It helped solidify his thinking. Omar was looking like a much smaller player than Hicks had thought. That meant whatever was important enough in the storage facility to show Kamal must be important to the larger plan.

There were too many variables at play to rely on the good will of a professional liar like Kamal. Like Reagan said, 'trust, but verify'. And he'd need plenty of verification before he debriefed him.

After scanning the area for pedestrians, Hicks opened his trunk and recalled the drone from the storage facility's roof. Once the drone landed safely in his trunk and the lid closed, he grabbed a dark baseball cap from the glove compartment and put it on.

Investigating the storage facility was too dangerous for the Varsity Team, but one man might get by.

Hicks got out of his car, intent on testing his theory.

CHAPTER 17

THE BACK DOOR of the storage facility was little more than window dressing. His handheld showed the security cameras were still off-line, so he wasn't worried about being spotted.

The door was a heavy-duty fire door, but the lock had been damaged and repaired several times. Picking it was a piece of cake.

The door led to the fire stairs, and he took them two at a time on his way up to the third floor. The body of a large rat was slowly decomposing against the wall of the second landing.

The storage area of each floor, however, was brand new with sparkling linoleum floors and florescent lights bright enough to perform surgery under. A smoked globe was set into the ceiling panels above every storage unit. A quick check of his handheld showed they were still off-line. He hoped they stayed that way until he was done.

He reached the third level and had no problem finding 338. Omar's storage unit was bigger than some

Manhattan apartments. A steel roll-down barred entry. The lock was set on the right-hand side.

He took a casual glance around, then pulled out his pick set again and worked on the lock. It was more challenging than the back door had been, but not challenging enough to keep Hicks from opening it.

He popped the lock and set it on the floor. He grabbed the handle at the bottom and slowly pulled the door up. Other than making a big racket, nothing happened.

The inside was a large, dark space. He gripped the handle of the Ruger on his belt and turned on the light switch on his right.

It was empty.

No furniture. No desk. No filing cabinet or anything that would justify renting such a large unit. Just a dusty unit as empty as the day it had been built. Even the metal shelving built into the wall was empty.

He remembered the long flowing robes the men had changed into and wondered if OMNI's scan had missed something. Not even the clothes they'd changed out of were inside.

Hicks sank against the wall and lowered himself to the ground.

His mind had been spinning since Central Park. He felt like he wasn't seeing everything at once. Only bits and pieces and glimpses of things in his race to hunt down Omar.

He shut his eyes tight and tried to slow it all down. He took what he knew bit by bit and worked his brain. OMNI couldn't help him here. *OMNI is just a tool, remember?*

Technology had taken him as far as it could. He was

hunting a human being and he had to use his humanity to find him.

He concentrated on his breathing and forced his mind blank. As blank as the metal shelving across from him. He needed to concentrate before...

His eyes sprang open, and he got to his feet.

The metal shelving was empty of everything except for a thick layer of dust that had formed on the shelves. And as he approached it, he saw one square, clean outline in the dust on the bottom shelf.

Hicks took a knee and examined it closer. It was big enough to be a box or square container. The rest of the shelves had a fair amount of dust on them, so it wasn't a fluke. Something had been there, and recently.

But it hadn't been a box. None of the men he'd watched leave the facility had been carrying one. That meant they must've taken it out of the container and left it behind.

That meant whatever the container had been, it was still close by.

Hicks took another look around the unit, but there was no sign of anything except more dust.

He left the storage unit open and went into the hallway. He spotted a large trash bin at the end of the hall and looked inside. The bin was filled with torn papers, plastic bags, and other trash, but one thing stood out. It was an oversized padded envelope at the top of the pile.

Hicks slid on his tactical gloves from his jacket pocket and pulled the envelope from the trash. It had been slit open at the top but was still sealed at the lip.

Good. Any DNA on the seal would be intact.

He turned it over and saw a label had been ripped

off except for something that looked like part of a circular logo of a mailing label.

Hicks knew if there was any way to glean any information from the envelope, the University technicians would get it. The envelope didn't feel like much, but he knew it was more than he'd had when he'd walked in there.

He took the envelope with him as he went back and locked up Omar's storage unit before taking the back stairs down to his car.

No one had paid any attention to him. Then again, most people didn't.

———

As soon as he got back to his car, Hicks laid the envelope flat on the passenger seat, scanned it with his handheld – including the postmark – and uploaded it to OMNI for analysis.

Then he put the envelope in one of the evidence bags he kept rolled up in the glove compartment. He'd bring it to the University lab in Manhattan for a more rugged analysis after he checked the whereabouts of Kamal and Omar.

OMNI showed that Omar had taken Kamal on a tour of the city. They'd driven through various parts of Brooklyn and Queens where Muslim extremists had set up congregations and prayed for death to America. Was he showing Kamal his network or just showing him off to his friends? Was it a test of some kind to see how Kamal reacted?

Hicks didn't know, but each stop on Omar's tour had just been added to OMNI's ever-growing list of institutions and people to observe, if they weren't on the list already.

Judging by the leisurely pace they were taking throughout Queens, Hicks imagined Kamal wasn't in any immediate danger. This was all a dog-and-pony show for his benefit and, ultimately, for the benefit of the man Kamal was supposed to be working for.

Hicks started up the Buick and took his time heading back to Astoria. Friday traffic was heavy, so he was glad he wasn't in a hurry.

He watched OMNI's live feed of Omar and Kamal's movements. Everywhere they stopped to get out of the SUV, Omar and Kamal got the rock star treatment. People from Nairobi and Nigeria, Kenya, and Senegal flocked to give them warm greetings. The men who had come along for the ride served as bodyguards to keep the people back.

At least now Hicks knew the reason for the outfit change. They needed to be ready to meet their public. But he hadn't found their clothes in the storage unit. Were they still wearing them under their white robes?

Hicks remembered that OMNI had tracked Omar to these locations before, but as a citizen. He'd never drawn this much attention or adoration before. Something had changed. Omar had become a man to know and admire by the faithful.

He had OMNI scan the SUV for mobile devices, but none of them were carrying so much as a beeper on their belt.

But the people they met at each stop had phones, of course and OMNI accessed them so it could listen in on what happened as they greeted Omar and Kamal.

Their digital footprints would be followed by OMNI for the rest of their lives.

The translator program found one word common among the many dialects of the faithful who sought to touch Omar's robes and greet Kamal. A word directed at Omar.

Al Mabeuth. The Messenger.

Hicks was glad traffic back to Queens was moving at a crawl. He might've swerved otherwise.

Omar had acquired a formal title. Colin hadn't known that. OMNI, either. Omar was being called The Messenger. The messenger of what? For whom?

While he waited in traffic, he had OMNI open a new search for 'Al Mabeuth' in any message, emails or calls referring to Omar by this honorific. Hicks no longer thought Omar was coming up in the world. Now he had proof of it.

Hicks kept driving toward Astoria and kept watching the OMNI satellite feed. Omar's Hyundai SUV pulled into a gas station in Queens, where the van that had picked up Kamal at his apartment was waiting for them. Omar and his bodyguards got out and embraced him before parting ways. Omar and his body-guards drove away while Kamal got into the van with the others. The tour was obviously over. OMNI's surveillance was not. It would continue to track Omar's SUV and Kamal's van at the same time.

OMNI detected Kamal's cellphone was back online and Kamal was already typing. Hicks hoped it was a text message to him.

His handheld buzzed and a text message from Kamal appeared on his screen.

They took my phone. Not much to report. All is well.

Hicks was glad he'd kept it cryptic. Omar's goons might check his phone before they dropped him off at the apartment.

Now that the phone was on, OMNI picked up on the Arabic dialogue inside the van.

KAMAL: Fear not, my brothers. I was only telling our uncle that I am safe and have much good news to tell him tonight.

SUBJECT 1: What you saw today was what The Messenger wanted you to see. What happened was between you and him only, not us. But we are glad you found it pleasing, brother.

Hicks dictated his reply in French and kept it equally terse.

Good news. Talk later.

IT WAS six o'clock and already dark when Omar's men dropped Kamal at the apartment. They'd taken a winding route from the gas station back to Kamal's apartment, undoubtedly looking to see if they were being followed. They were too busy watching their mirrors to be concerned about the satellite they couldn't see. This was not the Middle East or Africa. They felt secure in the absence of drones.

Hicks was already parked one block away and watched the satellite feed as the van pulled up in front of Kamal's building.

The dialogue picked up again after the passenger got out and slid open the van door for Kamal.

SUBJECT 1: After you have refreshed yourself and have spoken to our generous uncle, The Messenger asks that you contact the first number you called last night. He will be most anxious to hear what you have to say.

Hicks watched the satellite feed as Kamal stepped out of the van.

KAMAL: I am certain he will be happy with what I will tell him.

They parted with the usual blessings. The passenger closed the van door, got back into the van and they drove away. Kamal walked into the building.

Hicks watched the van drive down the street, only to slow down next to a car parked on the other side of the street before driving away.

Hicks zoomed in on the parked car and switched to thermal. The engine was hot and running. Probably keeping the heater on against the cold.

The scan showed two men in the car, but just like the men in the van, no cellphone activity was detected. The car was leased to Omar's cab company.

OMNI began scanning the men's faces, but nothing

immediate came up. They were ghosts, just like the men in the van.

Omar had gotten smart. He wasn't taking chances since losing two men in Central Park.

Hicks listened to Kamal's labored breath as he walked up the four flights to his studio apartment. Prison life had clearly eroded the big man's stamina.

Hicks used the lull to switch over to the visual feed from the apartment. Alert windows had filled the screen. Footage from the television showed the same two men in the car had searched Kamal's apartment. They'd checked his laptop but didn't try to get past the password. He supposed they were happy they didn't see the FBI shield on the home screen.

They'd found the money in the closet and brought it over to the couch to count it. Now they knew exactly how much they could expect from Kamal. If he offered the whole hundred grand, they'd know he was pleased.

If he offered less, they'd know they'd have work to do.

The footage showed they'd put the bag back in the closet and left. They didn't seem to leave any listening devices or cameras behind.

Hicks waited until Kamal was in the apartment before he dictated a text to him.

They searched your room. You're being watched by a car across the street. Stay away from the windows. Let me know what you find.

Hicks switched to the live feed from the television

and watched Kamal begin to search the room. The audio from the phone in his pocket was muffled. After a few moments, Hicks saw Kamal sit on the bed and begin to type on his phone. His text read:

Place has been searched. No devices detected. Money's still there but it's been searched. They could still be listening. Don't come up. I saw someone is in the alley behind the building.

Hicks switched to the satellite view and went to thermal. No one was back there. He ran back the footage to when Kamal had entered the building. No one had been back there then, either.

Kamal didn't know he had satellite surveillance. Was Kamal just being cautious or was he putting him off?

Hicks dictated a response:

No one in the alley. I'm coming up for the debrief.

Kamal's response:

Nothing much to tell you yet. Not enough to risk being spotted. Tomorrow is the big show. We'll know more then.

Every instinct Hicks had told him Kamal was lying. Normally, Hicks let his Field Assistants call the shots on live operations. They were on the ground. They were in the thick of it. He had to trust their training and instincts.

But trust was earned, and Kamal hadn't earned it yet. He wasn't a normal Field Assistant. He was a convicted felon known for looking out for himself instead of his mission. He'd gone rogue before. He was going rogue now.

Hicks dictated his final response:

Good call. Good work today. Talk tomorrow.

He watched Kamal read the response via the television camera. The man laughed and tossed the phone on the couch. He continued laughing as he walked out of frame and went into the bathroom. The phone's audio picked up the sound of water running.

Time to move.

CHAPTER 18

HICKS HAD USED Kamal's studio as a safe house before. He already had an entry plan scoped out.

He entered the back door of the apartment building next door and took the stairs two at a time up to the roof. The chicken wire that stretched between the two buildings was rusty and sagging from the snow that had accumulated on top of it. He easily stepped over it and popped the lock to the stairwell.

He drew his Ruger and held it close to his leg as he walked down the stairs to Kamal's floor. If Omar had people outside the building, he might have someone watching the stairwell. Hicks made it to the apartment without incident.

He pressed his ear to the door as he took the key from his pocket. The shower was still running, and he could hear Kamal singing.

Hicks let himself in and quietly closed the door behind him. He relocked it without making a sound.

He took a seat at the kitchenette table and aimed the Ruger at the bathroom door. Omar could've slipped him a weapon at any point during their time together, so it paid to be cautious. Caution was why he had come to Kamal's apartment.

Hicks heard the water shut off and the shower curtain pulled aside. A great plume of steam billowed out the open door. Hicks imagined it had been a long time since Kamal had enjoyed the luxury of a long, hot shower.

Kamal was still singing as he toweled himself off and stepped out of the bathroom. He had just finished toweling off his bald head when he noticed Hicks sitting at the kitchen table.

And the Ruger that was aimed at him.

Kamal smiled as he finished drying himself off. "You're a persistent bastard, aren't you?"

"Let's just say you don't get to tell me no." He kicked the other chair toward him. "Grab a seat. We have a lot to talk about."

Kamal began toweling off his chest. "Can I at least get dressed first?"

Hicks shook his head. "Wrap the towel around you and sit down. But make sure you grab your phone first. You've got a call to make."

Kamal wrapped the towel around him as he walked over to get his phone from the bed. Hicks' Ruger tracked him every step of the way until he brought it back to the table and sat down.

"Where's the trust, boss man?" Kamal asked. "I thought we were on the same team."

"So did I until you lied to me."

"And when did I do that?"

"When you didn't tell me about the call you had to

make." He gestured toward the phone. "Best get busy. Omar is waiting."

Kamal grinned as he picked up the phone and began dialing. "I figured you were following me. You're pretty good. Omar was looking for a tail all day and never found one. How'd you do it? Alternating cars? Satellite?"

"You have your secrets and I have mine," Hicks told him. "Now, make your call just like you did last night. Don't forget I speak Arabic and French."

Kamal hit the send button and raised the phone to his ear. "You're just full of surprises, ain't you, boss man?"

Hicks remained quiet as he heard the call go through to the intermediary. This second conversation was identical to the one from the night before, with a promise that Omar would call him back in a moment.

Kamal set the phone on the table and crossed his arms across his chest. "See that, boss man? I'm doing everything you tell me."

Hicks kept the Ruger level. "We'll see."

Kamal's phone began to vibrate, and he let it ring for a while before answering it. Hicks could tell it was Omar. He mouthed, 'In French' to him as they spoke.

Kamal played his part well. "I have good news, my brother. Our uncle is impressed with your dedication. He is willing to offer his support..."

Kamal kept talking while Hicks felt his handheld vibrate in his jacket pocket. He pulled it out and saw Jonathan was calling. Hicks declined the call and texted him instead.

***With Field Assistant now. Change in lesson
plan.***

He knew Jonathan hated vague texts, but the situation called for it.

Kamal listened as Omar gushed his gratitude. Kamal waited until he was finished to add, "Let us talk tomorrow about the particulars, my brother. You showed me much today and I wish to get some sleep."

They ended the conversation with the usual blessings and fond wishes before Kamal ended the call. He tossed the phone on the table and glared at Hicks. "Happy?"

"Hardly. What angle are you playing?" An idea came to him. "You're going to squeeze me, aren't you? Hold out for something more based on what you saw today."

"Well, now you've just gone and lost me, boss man. I don't have the first damned clue what you're talking about. And I don't think you do, either."

"Prove me wrong," Hicks said. "Tell me what he showed you today. And if you lie, I'll get insulted."

"They ran me all over Brooklyn and Queens," Kamal told him. "First to a mattress store where he introduced me to some of his friends. No names were exchanged on either side. They were big on talk, but not on details. They told me they had a plan to strike at the heart of the infidels in a way they couldn't stop or detect. I waited for details, but they didn't provide them. I didn't feel like I was in a position to push."

"You're their money man," Hicks reminded him. "It's your job to push." But he'd get to that later. "Then what?"

"Then we got into Omar's ride, and he took me around to meet some people. He wanted to show me off to some people to prove he's a big shot now. They kept calling him The Messenger or some shit everywhere we went. I asked him why, but he told me everything would be clear tomorrow once our uncle showed his support."

"That's it?" Hicks asked. "Just a dog-and-pony show for the money man?"

"No," Kamal said. "We made a pitstop at a storage unit. But you know that already, don't you?"

"This isn't about what I know, Ace. It's about what you know. Why didn't you mention it until I brought it up?"

Kamal laughed again. "Damn, man. You've gone field crazy, you know that? Seeing boogie men and bad guys at every turn. You need help and a shitload of serious R and R."

"What was in the storage unit?"

"Nothing. He showed it to me because it's where they plan on stashing whatever's part of this big plan of his. I guess they were trying to get me interested because it's a big container." He looked around the apartment. "Almost as big as this dump from the looks of it."

Now Hicks knew he was up to something. "Nothing was in there. Not even an envelope?"

Kamal laughed and clapped his hands. "You went in there after us, didn't you? Man, whoever you're working for sure has some moves."

Hicks didn't laugh. "What was in the envelope, Kamal?"

Kamal sat back in his chair. "Well, I guess you

might say we've reached the heart of the matter, boss man. Because that information is important and real expensive. You see, with all your tech and gizmos, you boys still have absolutely no idea what Omar and his friends are cooking up. I do."

Hicks thumbed back the hammer of the Ruger. "Don't make me ask you again."

Kamal didn't flinch. "Put that thing away, *Ace*. We both know it doesn't scare me and you're not going to shoot me. Not until you know what I know. And I'm not going to tell you until I get what I want."

He stretched and laced his fingers behind his head. "I've had a lot of time to think since our trip to the storage unit, so I think five million is a fair number."

Hicks smirked. "In dollars or Euros?"

"Dollars, of course. After all, I'm a patriot. And after you pay me my money and I tell you what Omar's cooking up, you'll realize it's worth every penny. That boy and his friends are clever. His plan will blow your mind."

"Five million," Hicks repeated.

Kamal wagged a finger at him. "Don't go trying to haggle with me, now, or the price will go up. I had a damned nice nest egg in Afghanistan when those bastards took me down, so I'd say five million ought to be enough to make me whole. Cash, of course."

"Of course."

"Oh," Kamal added, "and I'll need you to throw in clemency as part of the bargain. A clean record might come in handy somewhere down the line. None of that's what you might call unreasonable, is it?"

"Not really," Hicks allowed. "Of course, I could just

bring you in and have the information dragged out of you for free."

Kamal shook his head. "I've been through all that in training, my friend. None of that Guantanamo jazz ever worked on me."

"Ace, my people have facilities that make Guantanamo look like a summer camp. And methods way beyond waterboarding. More effective, too."

"I don't doubt it," Kamal said, "but that kind of thing takes time, boss man. And time is something you and whoever you're working for don't have. Omar's scheme is so simple, it's perfect. It's golden and it's ready to pop. You won't even know what's happening until it's already too late. Not unless I tell you all about it, which I'm willing to do, provided I get what I need to make me whole."

"You're going to have to prove you've got something worth selling first." Hicks decided to show one of the cards he was holding. "Tell me about Saudi Arabia."

"Hot," Kamal said. "Spent some good times there."

"The envelope I took from the storage container had post markings that say it had been shipped to a distributor in Saudi Arabia."

Kamal shook his head. "Damn, you guys are good. Who the hell are you people anyway?"

"Right now, one of us is a guy with a gun to your belly. And you're the guy who's going to tell me what was in the envelope."

"I'll be glad to tell you everything you want to know as soon as you meet my price."

"Omar told you a lot, didn't he?"

Kamal nodded. "Your hundred grand put me in real good with him. Spilled most of the operation to me, but not everything. Give me what I want, and I'll go on playing spy for you." He nodded to the clock on the kitchenette wall. *"Tempus fugit,* boss man. So, do we have a deal or not?"

"That clock's busted," Hicks said, "and so are you."

Kamal lurched for him as Hicks fired twice. Both flat-head rounds from the Ruger punched through the left side of Kamal's chest, burying themselves in the wall behind him.

Kamal fell back into the chair before tipping backward and onto the floor.

Hicks got up and stood over Kamal as he gasped his final breath. "I told you it cored a charging bear, remember?"

Kamal's head hit the linoleum just as his eyes went vacant.

Hicks holstered his Ruger and pulled on his gloves. He went into the bathroom and found the robe he had been wearing all day. A .9mm Glock was tucked in one of the deep pockets of the shroud.

"Looks like Omar handed out tchotchkes on his tour." He put the pistol in his coat pocket. He'd have the University lab analyze it later. "Lot of good it did you."

Hicks grabbed the robe off the hook and brought it back into the kitchen. He toed Kamal's corpse onto its side and doubled it up before placing it beneath his wounds. It should be enough to sop up some of the blood before Hicks moved him.

There was already significant blood splatter in the kitchen, but nothing that the bleach he kept under the kitchen sink couldn't remove. It wouldn't fool a crime lab tech, but it should be enough to fool Omar's boys if they searched the apartment again.

Hicks noticed the two holes in the plaster wall were just below the religious calendar Kamal had hated so. He took the thumbtack and calendar from where it hung and lowered it to cover the holes.

He pulled out his handheld and called Jonathan as he took the bleach and rags from beneath the kitchen sink.

Jonathan answered on the first ring.

"This is Professor Warren," Hicks said, giving him the code that he was fine and able to speak freely.

"What happened in there?" Jonathan asked. "Is he dead?"

Hicks opened the bleach and poured it on one of the rags. "What do you think?"

Jonathan stifled a curse. "I hope he told you something before you killed him."

"He made the call to set up the money exchange." Hicks spoke as he began to wipe down the area. "He also told me more than he thought he did. Whatever Omar's working on is low tech, which explains why we haven't been able to hack it or track it. If it was radiological, the other agencies would've been all over it by now. That means it's probably biological. We might know more when the lab gets results on the envelope I took from the storage unit."

"I'll send a Varsity Team to help with the cleanup," Jonathan offered. "They can also run the envelope over to the lab."

"No." Hicks finished wiping down the wall and was moving to clean Kamal's kitchen chair. "Omar has people watching the building. We can't risk letting them see what happened here. They might've heard the shots and could be on their way up here. I'll drop it off at the lab after I clean up here."

"But what are you going to do with the body?"

Hicks tossed the rag he'd been using on Kamal's corpse and went to the kitchen sink to soak another one with more bleach. "Don't worry, Ace. I've got a plan."

"It's my job to worry," Jonathan said. "Did you place the isotope with the money?"

"I did that before I gave it to Kamal two days ago," Hicks said. Unless Omar's men ran the money through a Geiger counter, they'd never know the bills had been marked. "But Kamal's death changes things. The Dean's going to have to lean on his financier friend. Tomorrow, he needs to follow Kamal's protocols and reach out to Omar directly. Tell him Kamal had to tend to other business and already left the city, but that his men can pick up the money Kamal left behind. I'll make sure everything is cleaned up and cleared out within the hour."

"They're watching the building," Jonathan reminded him. "They saw Kamal enter, but they won't see him leave. How will he explain that?"

Hicks dropped another bleach-soaked rag on the floor beside Kamal and went to get a bedspread he kept in the closet. "He went out the back door or something. Omar doesn't care about Kamal. He wants the money and the financier's ongoing support. Kamal said they're on a tight timeframe to pull off whatever they're planning. They won't worry too much about some stranger they met yesterday."

"I hope you're right," Jonathan said, "but I still don't

like the idea of letting them leave with the money. I don't like what they might use it for."

Hicks laid out the bedspread on the floor and rolled Kamal onto it. The robe had absorbed a fair amount of blood, but not all of it. He pulled the robe onto the bedspread and began to roll it up.

He didn't have time to give Jonathan a crash course in spy craft. "OMNI's tracking everyone and everything now. Were we able to track Omar to his hide out?"

"OMNI tracked him to a home in Midwood," Jonathan said. "I've got a Varsity squad nearby and ready to take him at a moment's notice."

Hicks knew that could be dangerous, depending on which squad it was. "Who's leading the team?"

"Scott. He and his men have been fully briefed and have been watching the building from a converted truck from a parking lot three blocks away for the past hour or so. A few people have gone in and out of the building, but none of them Omar. OMNI says the house registers at least thirty heat signatures, so it may be the staging area of whatever they're planning."

Hicks finished wrapping Kamal's body in the bedspread and began using the rag to clean up the rest of the blood. "I'll be in touch after I'm done here. I've got some work to do."

CHAPTER 19

AFTER HICKS HAULED Kamal's corpse up to the roof and stashed it where a Varsity crew could pick it up later, he retraced his steps across to the other building, down the stairs and reached the Buick.

Traffic was light on the drive back to Manhattan and he made it to the University's lab in good time.

At some point in the 1970s—for reasons lost to history— the University had acquired a dilapidated three-story townhouse in Alphabet City. None of Hicks' predecessors had used it for anything more than a temporary hideout for Field Assistants and Faculty Members in need of a place to lie low for a couple of days.

The building had long been deemed an eyesore in the community and for good reason. Layers of graffiti marred the building's masonry. The doors and windows had been boarded up for years. It had served as a squatters den for the homeless, a shooting gallery for junkies, a flop house for runaways, and a den where crack whores brought their johns.

But when Hicks became head of the New York Office, he decided to put the building to a better use.

Knowing any activity in front of the building would only bring unwanted attention, he purchased the old tenement building behind it and had University-approved contractors enter through a common basement both buildings shared. This way, improvements could be made inside the original dilapidated building without drawing unwanted neighborhood attention.

The contractors had worked around the clock for two months to transform the interior of the building into a solid steel structure independent of the façade. All windows and doors were blocked by walls of plating. The building was impervious to scans from the outside save for OMNI signals, of course.

Cameras and motion detectors were subtly installed around the perimeter of both buildings to monitor the area.

Hicks opened the gate and parked in the narrow alley of the old tenement building behind the safe house. He took the envelope from the storage facility with him as he descended a set of stairs that led to the sub-basement of the tenement. He walked into an intentionally dark, uninviting space that had once served as the building's coal room.

When he grabbed hold of the old coal bin's handle, biometric sensors hidden throughout the basement thoroughly scanned his identity. Once cleared, a section of the wall popped in and slid aside, leading to the access tunnel that led into the old townhouse. The wall automatically slid closed behind him as soon as he was clear.

Neighborhood activists periodically called for the

old building to be revitalized or turned into a homeless shelter or school or torn down alltogether to make way for a community garden. Hicks saw to it they were subtly convinced to turn their attention elsewhere.

In the revitalization effort that currently took over the city, several developers had tried to buy the property but were told the owner had no intention of selling. Few had taken no for an answer. Hicks hadn't been as subtle in changing their minds.

Junkies and drug dealers and homeless people occasionally tried to gain entrance to the building. They were dealt with in a far more permanent manner.

The interior of the old townhouse was as modern as its façade was decrepit. He walked through the basement of the structure, which served as a bunk area where Field Assistants or Faculty Members could sleep in relative comfort. All the modern technological features were available, via OMNI, of course.

The first floor of the building served as a base of operations for the Varsity Team. The second floor was the lab for the New York Office while the third level was used for office and storage space.

Since he'd had his fill of stairs for one night, he took the elevator up to the second floor. He stepped out into a lab complex that would have made other agencies envious. The lab could do everything the finest criminal labs in the country could do and perhaps more. The two scientists assigned to work there had separate quarters and were on call every day, no matter the hour.

He found Dr. Jaqueline Carter at her computer, scrolling through a series of data that populated the three screens in front of her.

"You sure look busy," Hicks said as he approached her.

"Never too busy to help out the boss." She had lost a bit of her Jamaican accent since coming to work for him two years before, but her long dreadlocks reminded everyone of her proud heritage.

She looked down at the envelope he was holding in the evidence bag. "I take it that's for me?"

"Be careful with it," he said as he handed it to her. "We might be looking at biological agent here. It's not lethal or otherwise I wouldn't still be standing here, but there could be traces of whatever it was used to transport inside."

"You always give me the most thoughtful gifts." She carried it over to a plastic cube at the far end of the room. "I should have some answers for you in about an hour or so. Do yourself a favor and grab a cup of coffee in the meantime. This won't go any faster if you just stand around here looking over my shoulder."

No matter what he had endured before walking into the lab, Dr. Jackie always had a way of making him feel better. "I'll grab a desk upstairs. Let me know what you find."

Hicks took the stairs up to the third level and sat down at one of the desktop computers set up around the sparse room. He fired off a text to Jonathan that Kamal was on the roof and ready for pick up once Omar's men stopped watching the building. He also said he would be at the safe house until the analysis on the envelope had been completed.

Hicks accessed the desktop and began analyzing OMNI's reports on all the people Omar had introduced to Kamal earlier that day. Kamal had probably been telling the truth about Omar simply showing him off to his friends, but not why. What made these people so important that Omar needed to impress them? And why had they called him The Messenger? That hadn't been one of Omar's known titles and it gave Hicks a bad feeling.

He was surprised to find that most of the people Kamal had met throughout the day were already in the system.They were African emigrees who'd come into the country legally and held regular jobs. A few were clerics who had peaceful congregations. None of them had any warrants or raised any red flags except now through their association with Omar. They were all regular people who'd come to the U.S. for a better life. Legally, too.

What use could Omar have for them?

Hicks ordered OMNI to track their digital footprints anyway. They would be monitored for the rest of their lives.

Hicks felt his handheld begin to buzz in his pocket. He took it out and saw the Dean was calling. That couldn't be good.

He accepted the call. Since he must know he was already in the safe house, Hicks dispensed with the normal protocol greeting. "Evening, sir."

"I see you've been busy," the Dean's electronically-altered voice said. "Bad day or good day?"

Hicks hadn't thought about it. "I've lost two Field Assistants this week, sir. Not my finest hour."

"One wasn't your fault, and the other was practically begging for it," the Dean said. "That damned fool should've known you'd have no choice but to kill him for pulling a stunt like that."

"At least we got some actionable intelligence out of him first," Hicks said.

"But?"

"But Omar's tour around Brooklyn and Queens is troubling, sir. They were all just regular people. Omar's never been public before. I don't know what makes him so popular now. And there's something about this 'Messenger' business that scares the hell out of me."

He knew the Dean didn't like profanity but was glad he didn't make note of it. "I think it's time to pick up Omar, James. But I'd like to hear your thoughts on the matter before I make it an order."

Hicks had been expecting that. "I think that might be premature at the moment, sir. We've got him buttoned down tight. I'd like to wait until he grabs the money tomorrow so we can find out the extent of his network. Did Jonathan pass along my request about reaching out to the financier?"

"He did. Do you really think a few hours will make the difference? If we grab him now, we might be able to stop whatever he's planning."

"We might," Hicks allowed, "but I don't think Omar's running this show and never was. Letting him take the money can only help us find the extent of his network. None of the men he had with him today are on file. Neither were the two men he sent to the park with Colin. That means we're looking at a lot of question marks. Grabbing Omar now might send them underground before we know who they are. We'd delay what they're planning, but I'd prefer to stop them so they can't try again later."

The Dean grew quiet. "It's risky, James. Very risky. I'm inclined to grab him now. Our scans say he's got thirty people in his home in Midwood as we speak. If he's planning some kind of major assault, I want to get them now while they're all in one location."

Hicks couldn't argue with his logic. His gut told him the Dean was right. But his head told him to wait for the scans on the envelope to come back first in case it gave them a better picture of what they were facing.

The Dean had always encouraged his people to speak freely, so that's what he was about to do.

"James."

He turned to see Dr. Carter standing on the stairs behind him. And, judging by the look on her face, it wasn't good news.

He went back to the Dean. "Sir, Dr. Carter has some results on the envelope. Please delay the go-order until I understand what she found. A few minutes either way won't make much of a difference."

He heard the Dean sigh heavily. "You've got thirty minutes, James. Make them count."

He killed the connection and followed Jacqueline down the stairs. Judging by the way she was gripping the banister; he knew it wasn't good news.

HICKS FOLLOWED her over to the cube that held the envelope.

"Where did you find this?" she asked him.

"In the garbage of a storage facility in Brooklyn," he told her. "Why?"

She ignored the question. "How long ago?"

The whole day had blurred together, and he couldn't recall the exact time. "I don't know. Five, maybe six hours. It's been in the evidence bag practically since I found it."

"Define practically."

Hicks didn't like where this was going. "I pulled it out of the trash, brought it down to my car, scanned it up to OMNI and put it in the evidence bag where it's been ever since. Why?"

Jackie waved him off. "Did you open the envelope? Run your hand inside it? Anything like that?"

Hicks had to think about it. "No. I just saw that it was empty, but I didn't touch the inside."

Before he could ask her why, she grabbed one of the largest syringes he had ever seen. "Roll up your sleeve. No questions. Just do it!"

He took off his jacket and rolled up his sleeve. She plunged the needle deep into his arm, causing him to wince. "What is that stuff?"

She tossed the empty syringe into a metal container and picked up another one. "Pull up your shirt."

He knew better than to argue with her and watched her jab the needle into his liver. This time, he cried out as she pulled the needle free.

Sweat broke out across his forehead, possibly from the pain. Possibly from whatever she'd pumped into him.

She grabbed him by the arm and sat him down in one of the chairs around the lab. "I'm sorry for that, James, but this was for your own good."

He looked at the letter in the cube. He didn't need to be a scientist to know it was the reason for the injections. "What the hell was in that thing?"

She grabbed an infrared thermometer and aimed it at the middle of his head before squeezing the trigger.

She closed her eyes and hung her head with relief. "Your temperature is normal. Thank God."

He felt his senses grow intense as sweat popped along his back. He knew an adrenaline rush when he got one. "What did you pump me with?"

"A cocktail of antibiotics, vitamins and adrenaline to help it carry through your system faster," she told him. "The shot in the arm should do the trick, but I gave you one to the liver just in case."

He waited for her to set the thermometer down and tell him what she had to say in her own good time. She looked as worked up as he was beginning to feel.

"I found traces of several viruses on the inside of the envelope, James."

So, Omar was working on something biological. Just as he'd feared. "Like what?"

"SARS, MERS and Ebola were most prevalent," she told him. "But influenza and coronavirus were also present." She pointed at the cube. "To put it in layman's terms, that little envelope was holding some pretty bad shit."

It took a second for the information to settle in his mind. Severe Acute Respiratory Syndrome (SARS) and Middle Eastern Respiratory Syndrome (MERS) were deadly diseases that had threatened to turn into pandemics for years but hadn't. Ebola was difficult to catch, but equally deadly when someone caught it.

There'd always been rumors of scientists in the Middle East and elsewhere who'd tried to weaponize these diseases but failed.

But from what Dr. Carter was telling him, there was a good chance someone might've finally figured it out.

And Omar was in the middle of it.

Dr. Carter went on. "They were only trace amounts in the envelope, and your exposure was limited, so I think you're okay. The injections I just gave you should help in case I'm wrong. But you're not the problem. The fact that this stuff was being stored in Brooklyn is the problem."

"The container was empty except for the envelope," Hicks told her.

"I don't know your world," Jacqueline admitted, "but I'd say these are samples of something some pretty bad people were cooking up. Each of those diseases are highly transmittable and lethal if they aren't treated right away. Somebody's up to no good, James. No good at all."

He pushed himself out of the chair before Jackie could stop him and pulled the handheld from his jacket pocket.

He called the Dean and asked Jackie to repeat everything she'd just told him.

Hicks asked her to step away while he got back on the line with the Dean. "I know it's bad, sir, but we have to wait."

"For what?" the Dean asked. "For people to start dropping dead in the street? I'm ordering Scott and his men to take Omar down right now."

"Please, sir!" Hicks shouted. "Whatever they're planning is still in a holding pattern until they get the money. We still don't know how deep this goes. It might not just be New York." He remembered something that had seemed so important yesterday but had slipped through the cracks until now. "That embargoed image the British have, sir. We need to know who it is, and we need to know now. If he's important enough for them to hide, he's got to be part of this somehow. If we find him, we might know the full scope of what we're dealing with here."

Despite the electronic alteration, Hicks could hear the Dean's breathing change. He'd been ready to pull the trigger and take down Omar. But now he was considering something else in mid-thrust. Something that made sense.

"Hold the line, James."

Hicks took the towel Jackie offered him and began to wipe down his face as he waited for the Dean. He hadn't felt this amped up in years.

Hicks hadn't realized he'd been holding his breath until the Dean came back on the line. "The British have agreed to lift the embargo, but only for us. None of our other agencies can know about this. They were emphatic on that point."

Hicks sagged against the counter. "Good. That's good. Are they sending us the information?"

"No," the Dean told him. "Nothing transmittable, not even over encrypted lines. But your counterpart in New York will meet you to give you the information personally. I'm texting you the information now. Bleecker and Sixth. One hour. Don't be late. The British are sticklers for punctuality. And James? I want to be notified the moment you have the information in hand. Do I make myself clear?"

Hicks already had on his jacket. "Perfectly, sir. I'm on my way."

CHAPTER 20

HICKS LEFT his Buick in the alley and took a taxi to the meeting spot in the West Village. Parking was always a nightmare in that part of town. Taking a cab just made sense.

Although most cabs had cameras that recorded passengers, Hicks knew his handheld would generate enough interference to render the image unclear throughout his trip. Chances of the cab driver noting the interference was slim.

Hicks looked out the cab window as he rode across town from the gentrified Alphabet City to the gentrified West Village. It was Friday night, and the streets were filled with young people bundled up against the cold on their way to celebrating surviving another week in Manhattan.

He found himself wanting to admire their blissful ignorance. That delightful agony of youth when waiting for the person you liked to text you back or going on a first date was everything. Saturday afternoons spent sharing a beer with your friends while you watched the game. Nursing a mild hangover while reading a good book in a coffee shop on a quiet Sunday afternoon.

But Hicks didn't admire them. He'd never been that young, not even before he was James Hicks. He'd always had responsibilities to fulfill and orders to carry out. People had been depending on him his entire life, just like these strangers he passed in a crosstown cab were depending on him now. They would never know if he had stopped Omar's plot, just like they didn't know how many times he and people like him had saved their lives countless times in the past. He received neither credit nor blame for his victories or defeats. He'd never be a talking head on a news channel, and he'd never write a book about his career. His was a life spent in the shadows cast by the light of regular people doing regular things every day. And Hicks wouldn't have it any other way.

He pulled out his handheld and looked at the fleshy face of his British counterpart in New York. The British referred to their version of the University as The Club. It maintained an informal relationship with their more well-known counterparts while the University avoided their sister agencies at all costs. The feeling was mutual.

The British rotated Club assignments to the New York Office every couple of years or so. They viewed the posting as a reward to agents in good standing who were close to retirement and looking to run out the clock on their careers. They were men and women who'd been put out to pasture in the concrete jungle. The Club allowed them to enjoy the Big Apple while doing a bit of spying for queen and country before hanging up the old cloak and dagger for good. The Club served a purpose, but Hicks didn't understand why such an organization would be trusted with information on one of the most guarded identities on earth.

Hicks took the cab as far as Bleecker and Thompson before he decided to get out and walk the rest of the way. He never liked to go directly to a meeting without getting a feel for his surroundings. It also gave OMNI a chance to scan the area for any familiar, troubling faces.

He dodged packs of people walking along Bleecker to any number of the bars and restaurants that lined the famous street. The smell of pot mingled with the smell of coffee houses along the way. He wondered if any of them sold Roger's civet coffee.

He made it to Bleecker and Sixth and was glad his counterpart had picked this location. It had plenty of benches around spits of parks where old people sat during the day. At night and when the weather was warm, the predators came out to claim their spots. Low level dealers peddling grass. Criminals looking for a law to break. Drunk kids who needed a place to sit for a while but passed out until the sun or a cop woke them up.

The blizzard had driven them all inside, save for a heavy man sitting beneath a barren tree. Hicks glanced at his handheld and OMNI confirmed this was his contact. A man known to the system simply as Clarke.

The snow hadn't shown any signs of melting and there were still large piles of it clumped on one side. The Brit had only cleared off enough snow on the bench for himself to sit while he ate falafel wrapped in tinfoil.

Clarke filled the entire side of the bench meant for two people. He wasn't simply big. He was incredibly obese. The fleshy rolls of his body were evident beneath his green parka. Its zipper's teeth were strained to the limit. Tufts of unruly reddish gray hair tucked out from beneath a faded green ski cap. His fleshy face may have been reddened a bit from the cold wind but Hicks would have bet ruddy was his usual color.

Watching Clarke eat almost turned Hicks' stomach. Bits of lettuce and meat had fallen on to his parka and he made no effort to push them off. They were cleared by a sharp wind which blew up Sixth Avenue.

The fat man glanced at Hicks from head to toe before going back to his falafel. "You the Yank?"

Hicks nodded at the snow next to him. "Thanks for saving me a seat."

Clarke spoke through a mouthful of food. "I'm not your butler, Yank. Clear it off yourself and have a seat. Standing up talking only draws attention."

Hicks pulled his tactical gloves tighter and shoved a mound of snow off the other section of the bench.

"You're not what I expected," Hicks said as he settled on the damp bench.

Clarke grunted as he took another bite out of his falafel. "You were expecting some poofter in a tuxedo, sipping a martini." More bits of meat and lettuce fell on his parka as he spoke. "You bastards really make me laugh sometimes."

"I was actually expecting a professional who knew enough to pick in a better location than this."

"What's wrong with here?" Clarke swallowed his food. "A park bench in the middle of the night just after a snowstorm? No one around to pay us any mind. Who's going to bother with a couple of dodgy looking bastards like us? Besides, if you're as good as you're supposed to be, this won't take long. You'll be sipping hot cocoa in a coffee house in no time."

Hicks knew he was being tested and tried not to let the fat man get to him. He made sure no one was listening before he got down to business. "You embargoed information on someone I'm looking for. I want to know why."

"Sure you do," Clarke said, wiping his mouth with the back of his hand, then folding the tinfoil over the rest of his falafel. "Damned good, this. The fuckers might not be able to govern themselves, but their food is right tasty."

"The man in the photo," Hicks repeated. "Tell me about him."

"Drop the imperious attitude, Yank. We taught it to you, remember?" Clarke found a way to stuff the falafel into the pocket of his parka. "I'm not telling you anything until you tell me why he's important to you."

Hicks kept it vague to see how far it got him. "We need him for questioning on a matter that's come up."

"Oh, fuck off," Clarke spat. "Your Dean called my minister less than an hour ago, demanding this meeting. That wouldn't happen if you were just looking to talk to him. Now, you play nice and tell me why you care about this man or I'm leaving."

Hicks had never heard of Clarke before. He didn't know who he was or where he'd worked. He had no idea if he was capable or if he was just another fat man with a big mouth. He also didn't have any choice but to trust him.

"We think he's involved in some kind of event that'll happen in here in New York in the next few days."

"Not good enough." Clarke began to get up, but Hicks grabbed his arm.

"A small time Somali hack named Omar turned two of my agents and it looks like they're planning something big."

Clarke remained sitting. "How big?"

"Probably biological," Hicks said.

Clarke's eyes narrowed. "What do you mean 'probably'?"

Hicks had no choice but to tell him. "We found traces of MERS, SARS and Ebola on the inside of an envelope we know was in Omar's possession. We think they might be samples of something Omar's people are working on, but that's just a guess at this point."

Clarke pulled his arm free from Hicks' grip. "Did you find anything else in the envelope?"

Hicks hadn't thought it was important. "Influenza and coronavirus, but in much smaller amounts. The postmark on the envelope proves it had been shipped to Saudi Arabia."

"Medina," Clarke muttered more to himself than to Hicks. "Those lying bastards."

Hicks knew about the Saudi Arabian city. "What about it?"

Clarke ran his hand over his cap. "I think you've found more than you know, Yank. More than any of us thought you had."

"So cut the shit and tell me why you guys embargoed the picture I sent for analysis."

"Because the man in the image you found is an Algerian national named Rachid Djebar. We call him 'The Moroccan'. He's a nasty bit of business we've lost track of and want very much to find again." He looked at Hicks. "Sounds like you've found him."

Hicks had made it a point to know the names of the most wanted people in the world. This name meant nothing to him. "What does Djebar have to do with Medina?"

"If you'd asked me that same question three minutes ago, I would've said he had nothing to do with it. But when I put it together with your envelope and his disappearance, I think he may be the link between the two. And that is very bad news for all of us, believe me."

Hicks waited for him to keep talking, but he didn't. He simply sat there, going from ruddy to pale despite a steady cold wind.

Hicks didn't push Clarke. He might be in a hurry, but some things couldn't be rushed.

He knew the fat man was deciding what we should say as he looked out at the traffic mulling up Sixth Avenue instead.

Despite the snow and the slush, bicycles darted alongside cabs and cars. Trucks and buses. Several deep puddles had formed in potholes and at crosswalks, sending dirty water into the air every time a car or bike drove through one. It was a bland scene on a bland night that should've been forgotten as soon as it happened.

But judging by Clarke's reaction, Hicks had a feeling this was a moment he'd remember for a long time to come.

Clarke pitched to the left side and pulled out a file in a plastic bag from beneath him. He held it out to Hicks but didn't let go. "Anything I tell you stays between us, yeah? I'm talking about operational detail. We don't like seeing our dirty laundry on CNN like you lot."

"All I care about is Djebar."

Clarke let him take the file. "Rachid Djebar is a Moroccan national who burned all of our assets in Tangier during a joint operation with the French six months ago. A lot of good people died that night, some who'd been working with us for years. We've been hunting him ever since. The bastard has been completely off the grid until your picture hit the system and set off all sorts of bells."

Despite where Clarke had been hiding it, he tucked the file into his coat. "Who is he?"

"Grew up as a common street peddler from Rabat, then somehow became a Legionnaire. Started in mercenary work after that. Got himself a job with an Iranian front organization and acquired a host of nasty contacts. He'll sell anything he can get his hands on. Arms, information, state secrets, drugs, contracts on people's lives. Even dabbled in the slave trade a few years back. Anyone who crosses him or gets in his way meets a violent and ugly end. Lately, he's transitioned into peddling what he calls 'relationships'. He puts two particularly nasty fuckers together so they can do whatever their black hearts desire. Weapons and munitions mostly. He gets a finder's fee for introducing them and brokering the deal, then goes on his way."

Hicks knew the type. "Those guys usually aren't ideologues."

"Neither is he," Clarke said. "He'd have to be human first. The only god he worships is money and he'll work with anyone willing to pay his fee. Mexican cartels looking for arms. Drug dealers looking for new outlets. That sort of thing. No product for him to worry about and it's very profitable. Little risk for a lot of reward."

Hicks realized he may have seen the name mentioned in a few intelligence reports over the years, but not specific details. If he'd been tied to a threat on American soil, he would've remembered.

"What the hell is a money man like Djebar doing with a low-level Somali punk like Omar?"

"Haven't you been listening?" Clarke frowned. "I just told you he's a matchmaker now. If he's working with your man Omar, then there's two things you'd do well to consider and none of them pleasant."

Clarke held up a round finger. "The first is that this Omar isn't the punk you believe him to be. Djebar doesn't come out of his hole for less than a hundred grand, plus a small percentage of whatever the action is. Since he was on your man's camera phone, that means Omar must have money."

Hicks had seen Omar's travel activity. He'd gauged his spending and his contributions and he had a fair assessment of how much he raised at the cab stand. He could've raised that much if he squeezed the drivers and ran a little credit card fraud on the side. Drunks wouldn't notice an extra couple of miles on the odometer until the next morning, if then.

The Djebar connection would also explain how Omar had gotten the numbers for the financiers he'd contacted. He'd must've spent every cent he'd been able to scrape together on whatever meeting Djebar had arranged for him. The question was who else was in that meeting.

"What's the second thing?" Hicks asked.

"Given that you found an envelope with trace amounts of diseases inside it means Djebar helped Omar acquire them. There's not really much of a commission in that sort of arrangement."

"So?"

"So, it means your friend Omar really is planning something major. Because Djebar has always said his biggest regret in life was that he wasn't connected enough to help Osama and his friends fund their grand show." He nodded his fleshy face down Sixth Avenue toward One World Trade. "Right down there."

Hicks didn't have time to think about past attacks. He was too focused on stopping the next one. "You said something about Medina before."

"You may have read that there's been a rash of small, but rather nasty outbreaks of MERS, SARS and Ebola in small villages throughout the Middle East for the past few years. The Saudis, being good neighbors, have taken the lead on studying the outbreaks and have their laboratories searching for ways to treat and cure these diseases. One of those labs is in Medina."

All the pieces were falling into place and revealing a nasty picture. "Go on."

"The Saudis believed these outbreaks were suspicious and so did we," Clarke explained. "We helped them track down who might be behind the outbreaks and traced them back to three scientists in the Saudi lab in Medina. Two of them were French and one of them was American. None of them were Muslim and all of them had passed extensive background checks before being employed at the lab. They'd apparently been contacted by some ruthless bastards who'd paid them well to look into ways to weaponize the viruses they were studying. The outbreaks were trial runs."

Hicks knew there'd been several attempts to figure out how to turn these viruses into biological weapons for years, but none had been successful. Yet. "Why haven't I heard any of this before?"

"Because the Saudis were embarrassed by the whole thing happening at one of their labs and moved in to quickly arrest all three scientists. All three were said to have been killed while resisting arrest. Forces fired upon their car, which conveniently exploded as it ran off the road. Bodies were burned beyond all recognition but authorities assured us they'd killed all three men. That was two months ago. They assured us all samples of all the viruses were present and accounted for. Since they're our allies and prickly about having their honor questioned, we took their word for it. Given this business with the envelope in Omar's possession, I'd say they either lied or got the wrong men."

Hicks felt his hand begin to shake and not from the cold. "If we'd known about all of this, we could've been on the lookout for something like this. Maybe even prevented it."

Clarke shrugged. "I'm sorry, old boy, but American secrets have a habit of winding up on the front page of the New York Times."

"The University is different and you know it."

"So you say. Well, that's all in the past now. Little we can do about it now except put a lid on Djebar and Omar. I trust you're tracking Omar?"

"We've got a team sitting on his residence right now, but I need Djebar first."

Clarke's eyes narrowed. "Why? Omar's the more

immediate threat. Grab him right now and stop what he's doing."

"Because Omar's just a tool in all this," Hicks said. "If we grab him, Djebar goes underground. He'll sell Omar's plans to the highest bidder. But if I have Djebar, Omar's cut off and alone."

Hicks didn't wait for Clarke's approval. He didn't need it and he didn't want it. He patted his jacket and the file beneath it. "Thanks for this. I'll let you know what we find, but you might want to stay out of public areas for a couple of days. If this is a biological attack, nowhere is safe."

Clarke grabbed Hicks' arm before he got up. "That file isn't free. We get Djebar after you're done with him. He won't be easy to break, but you have to agree to not kill him or hurt him to the point where he's useless to us. You honor your end of the bargain, and my office works with yours in the future. You don't, I never answer your phone calls again. Not even if your president calls the Queen."

"Fine," Hicks said. "But we have to get Djebar first, don't we?"

Clarke held out a gloved hand to him. "Do we have a deal?"

Hicks shook it. "We have a deal. But he's not going to be pretty when you get him back."

Clarke smiled. "I wouldn't expect him to be."

CHAPTER 21

As soon as he got back to Twenty-third Street, Hicks gave the Dean a summary of what Clarke had told him. He agreed to focus on finding Djebar first, if possible, but Omar remained the prime target.

He gave Hicks an hour to find what he could on The Moroccan before he took down Omar.

Hicks scanned in the latest image of Djebar from Clarke's file and put OMNI to work. It was much clearer than the blurred shot they'd gotten from the phone.

OMNI began comparing it to millions of images taken in the New York area in the past week. Airport security cameras, traffic cameras and social media pictures. Even cell phone pictures from all over the New York area were examined.

Within five minutes, OMNI had discovered fifty incidences of where Djebar had been before and after Colin's murder. More hits on more images came in each second.

The first viable hit came off a security camera at

JFK airport a week before. It was a picture of Djebar as he stepped off a plane from Mumbai. Hicks made a note to tell his friends at the Indian Intelligence Bureau that he'd been in their country for a time.

Hicks noted the resemblance on Djebar's forged passport to the blurred image they'd gotten from the phone, only this one was much clearer.

Djebar had a thin face and now sported a pencil thin mustache. He had deep set eyes and a light tan that probably helped him pass for Latin, Turkish, Mediterranean, Arabian or even Persian if he'd wanted. Ambiguity was invaluable in the shadows.

The next hit came from a traffic cam in Long Island City. The image showed a clear image of Djebar and Omar in the back seat of an Escalade. Two men in the front were stocky black men and looked like hired security. They must've been Djebar's men.

The Escalade's license plate was clearly visible and showed it was registered to Shabazz Security in midtown Manhattan. Another search for the car's black box showed it was currently parked over at the Millennium Hotel in Times Square. That didn't necessarily mean Djebar was there, too, but it was worth looking into.

Hicks accessed and checked the Millennium's lodging information to see if Djebar was registered under his own name or any of the aliases the British had provided.

When all aliases came up negative, Hicks went old school and put OMNI to work searching the hotel's security cameras for matches of Djebar's likeness.

He had a hit from two nights before at the check-in desk. Hicks matched the time on the image to the entries made in the hotel's system and found that a Francois Andabe of Zaire had checked in at that exact moment.

And he was scheduled to check out the day after tomorrow.

Hicks' mind flooded with questions. If Omar had the money to bring a man like Djebar to New York, then why the hell had he made panicked calls for funding? It didn't make any sense.

Not yet, anyway. He hoped Djebar could tell him why.

Omar still needed Kamal's hundred grand. He didn't know why, and he didn't care just then. He'd be in a holding pattern until the financier told him to pick up the money in Kamal's apartment. A Varsity Squad was ready to take him at a moment's notice.

Djebar had been the wild card in all of this from the beginning. He had all the answers. He was now the priority.

Hicks called the Dean and laid out his position. The Dean reluctantly agreed and gave the order to grab Djebar but break him fast. It was already two o'clock in the morning. The financier would call Omar at eight and tell him to pick up the money in Kamal's apartment. Any longer would make Omar suspicious and they needed to keep him steady.

Hicks told the Dean he understood. Then Hicks called Roger and told him to get ready.

IT WAS JUST past three in the morning when Hicks walked through the pulsing neon heart of Times

Square. Tourists and teens mugged for selfies.
Costumed characters hustled for spare change. Homeless people nodded wherever a free seat was to be had.
Two cops stifled yawns and stood in a doorway out of
the cold. Large screens and blinking signs hawked prod-
ucts and services, oblivious to the misery going on just
below them.

Hicks checked his handheld to get an exact lock on
Djebar's location. He was still in his room. Hotel
records showed the door hadn't been opened in hours.

Djebar's security detail's Escalade was still parked
on the street next to the hotel and hadn't been moved
since Hicks had first located it. A high roller like Djebar
was above taking cabs or subways. He'd prefer to roll
deep with an armed posse and a fancy car to take him
where he wanted to go.

The tricky part was the hour. Hotel security
ramped up at this time of night. They worked to keep
the drunks and the homeless from roaming the halls
while their guests slept. They threw out boozers who
resented last call in the hotel's bars and restaurants.

Fortunately, Hicks had a plan.

The lobby of the Millennium Hotel was too
crowded with guests saying their last goodbyes for
anyone to notice Hicks duck into an elevator. It was
locked and could only be activated by a guest tapping
their key to a sensor.

Hicks tapped his handheld against it and OMNI
got him access in seconds. He punched the number for
Djebar's floor and rode up alone.

Knowing his handheld was distorting the elevator
camera, Hicks made a final check of his gear. He'd
reloaded the Ruger on his hip and hoped he wouldn't

have to use it. He pulled his tactical gloves tighter and hoped they'd be enough to take down the guards with one punch.

His black pants, baseball cap and jacket would make him forgettable to anyone who saw him after.

Everything that could be done had been done. All he had to do was grab one of the most wanted men in the world and hand him over to Roger Cobb.

The screen in the elevator told him it was already three-twenty in the morning. Only a few precious hours before the financier called Omar about the money.

Hicks closed his eyes and breathed in deep. He focused on the task at hand.

The doors opened on Djebar's floor and Hicks stepped out. He spotted one of the security men seated on a chair at the end of the hall. He was the bigger and balder of the two men he'd seen in the traffic footage of the Escalade.

If he shot him, the entire floor would wake up and call the desk. The cops manning Times Square would be on him in five minutes. He'd have to do this the old-fashioned way.

Hicks weaved a bit as if he'd had a few too many while he quickly walked toward him. "Hey! Are you guys here with Miles? I've got a bone to pick with him. He can't just fire me like that. He owes me money!"

The guard got off the chair and began walking toward him and motioned for him to be quiet. "Not so loud, my man. People are trying to sleep. There's no Miles here."

Hicks kept walking toward him. "Don't give me that crap. Don't you know who I am?" Ten feet away now.

"The talent I signed? I made the money that pays for that suite, damn it."

The guard squared up to block Hicks' path. Three feet away. "I told you once to be quiet and I'm not gonna tell you again. I don't know..."

Hicks fired a straight right hand. The hardened polymer knuckles shattered the bigger man's nose and rocked his head back. Hicks grabbed him by the collar and slammed his head against the wall. He was dazed but still conscious, so Hicks slammed his head into the opposite wall as he fell. A final kick to the head made sure he was out cold.

Hicks took a knee beside the man and searched him. He pulled a nine-millimeter Glock from the holster on the guard's belt. As he patted him down for other weapons, he found a hotel room key card.

Hicks left him on the floor and walked toward the suite at the end of the hallway. He paused to listen at the door. A television set was playing low. The other guard was trying to be considerate of his boss.

Hicks stepped back and checked his handheld a final time. The thermal scan of the room was fuzzy, but there appeared to be only two people inside. He hoped one of them was Djebar.

Hicks put the handheld in one pocket and the Glock in the other. He didn't want to leave it in the hall in case the guard wasn't as unconscious as he should be.

He tapped the key card against the sensor and the lock opened. Hicks found himself in a dark room with only a flat screen television providing any light.

One of the guards was sitting on a couch with his back to the door. "Man, you've got to piss again? You'd better get that checked out or..."

Hicks smashed the butt of the Glock across the back of the guard's head. He sagged to his left but wasn't out cold until Hicks hit him again.

Hicks stood and listened for any sign that Djebar had heard them. All he heard over the low sound of the television was a light snoring coming from the bedroom.

Hicks approached the door and stopped once again to listen. The rhythm of the snoring hadn't changed.

Since the OMNI scan had been fuzzy, he decided not to take any chances. He stood to the side of the doorway, turned the knob, and pushed the door in.

The door was only halfway opened when a gunshot rang out from the darkness.

The snoring stopped and a woman began to scream.

Hicks bolted into the room and charged the spot where he'd seen the flash.

The woman kept screaming as Hick barreled into the man in the dark. He grabbed hold of the gun and slammed the man against a wall. He heard the gun hit the carpet amid the woman's screams.

Pinned against the wall, Djebar tried to bring a knee up into Hicks' groin. Hicks blocked it with his own knee and headbutted Djebar in the face. The blow made him go slack as Hicks kept hold of his right hand and threw him down on the bed. He wrenched Djebar's right arm to his back and made the man scream. "Don't move or I'll break your arm."

Hicks heard a muffled whimpering in the darkness and knew Djebar had company. "You. Turn on the light."

A lamp beside the bed came on, revealing a naked brunette on the floor next to the bed.

Hicks could tell by the smeared makeup and wild hair that she wasn't Djebar's wife. "You working?"

The woman nodded quickly. "He paid for the whole night."

"Hope he paid in advance. Just keep quiet. I'm here for him, not you."

"You damned fool!" Djebar cursed him despite a face full of mattress. "You'll die for this."

Hicks grabbed a handful of dark hair and pulled his head back from the mattress. "You first."

He let go of Djebar's hair and brought his left hand behind him. He produced a plastic slip cuff and secured the terrorist's hands behind him. He kept a knee on his back as he reached for a pillow. As he pulled the pillow from the pillowcase, he saw the hooker's red panties in the bed. He grabbed them and stuffed it in his mouth as a gag before slipping the pillowcase over his head and tying it around his neck.

"You're blind and bound," he said to Djebar. You try anything, you're dead. You do anything except what I tell you, you're dead."

He reached into his pocket and tapped the hand-held to connect with Roger. "You ready?"

"I'm at the loading bay," Roger said. "All clear."

Hicks pulled Djebar off the bed and realized he was just in his boxers. It didn't matter for where they were going.

As he pushed Djebar out of the bedroom, he told the working girl, "This never happened, and you never saw me. If you tell anyone, I'll know and I'll find you. You wouldn't like that."

She shook her head as she crawled back up to the

bed without looking at him. "I don't want that. I didn't see anything, I swear."

"Good. And get some sleep. It's a nice bed. Might as well enjoy it."

Djebar tried to speak through his gag as Hicks steered him out of the bedroom, into the living room and out the door into the hallway.

He struggled to keep the terrorist still as he grabbed his handheld and tapped the sensor that led to the service elevator. When they elevator arrived, it was empty, and he took it all the way down to the basement.

Djebar continued to mutter through his gag, but Hicks pulled the pillowcase tighter. "I'll choke you out and carry you out of here if I have to."

The service elevator didn't stop until it reached the basement. When the doors opened, Hicks pushed Djebar out and steered him right. The door to the outside was only twenty feet away.

A guard booth was forty feet away, but the guard has his head down. He was awake but he was reading or writing something.

Djebar let his legs go limp and Hicks tightened his grip on the pillowcase as he kept him upright. He pushed the man through the door leading to the street and heard the guard call after him.

Roger already had the sliding door open, and Hicks practically dove into it, landing on top of Djebar. The terrorist cried out in pain as Roger hit the gas and sped away. The van door slid shut on its own.

Roger kept his eyes on the street as he said, "There's a syringe back there to settle him down. I suggest you use it."

Hicks found the syringe in the medical bag and

injected it in Djebar's neck through the pillowcase. The man struggled briefly before going completely slack.

Hicks dropped the syringe back in the bag. "Thanks."

"Looks like you've had a successful evening," Roger said as he sped along the quiet, dark street.

Hicks pulled Djebar into the sitting position. "That's up to you now."

CHAPTER 22

IN THE WAITING room of an old dentist's office in the West Village, Hicks checked his watch while Roger prepped Djebar for questioning.

It was four-fifteen in the morning. In less than four hours, Omar would have his money and his plan would begin its final stage. Roger might be the best interrogator he had ever worked with, but now he needed him to be the fastest.

Hicks watched Roger prepare Djebar via the television set he'd set up in the waiting room for such sessions. Roger referred to the interrogation chamber as his studio.

The ancient couch creaked as Hicks struggled to find a spot where a spring didn't hit his back. The years of abandonment hadn't dulled the smell of desperation and fear most dental offices tended to have. Roger's usage of it in the years since had only added to it.

The office was still outfitted with late seventies furniture, complete with a glassed-in receptionist's area where patients could make their payments. An old sticker on the window still read 'MasterCharge The Interbank Card Accepted' and 'Your BankAmericard Welcome Here'.

But Roger's patients didn't make payments in cash, check or credit card. They didn't have to present proof of health insurance either. They paid by telling Roger the truth. And if truth was currency, then Roger Cobb was often well compensated.

Hicks saw that Roger had strapped Djebar's arms and legs to a dentist's chair. The chair had been re-covered in soft rubber to make for easier clean up after a session.

A drain had been installed in the center of the floor and florescent lights powerful enough for surgery hung down from the ceiling. The small dentist's tray had long since been removed in favor of a proper surgery table that held scalpels and clamps and cutting tools. Steel bone saws and rib spreaders that hung on the wall sparkled in the strong light. A car battery and cables completed the look.

Many of Roger's patients often laughed when they saw the setup, trying to convince themselves it was all just for show. After all, this was America. Torture wasn't allowed here.

But Roger was too willing to prove to them that he did not see himself as an American. He was a citizen of the world and the Constitution stopped at the threshold of his studio. By the end of their session, they'd learned that Roger never wasted time on theatrics and, quite often, put many of the tools at his disposal to effective use.

Through the old television in the waiting room, Hicks watched Roger slip the heavy rubber coroner's apron over his head before he injected something into Djebar's vein.

Djebar snapped awake just as Roger pulled the needle from his neck, his eyes instantly bright and alive.

Hicks watched Roger pull up a stool and sat next to his subject. He smiled down at the Moroccan. "Welcome back, my friend. How was your sleep? Restful, I trust?"

Djebar squinted at the light and tried to look away but couldn't turn his head. It was secured in a vice that Roger had attached to the chair's headrest long ago.

"Where is this place?" Djebar asked.

Roger reached up and dimmed the light just enough to stop it from shining into his eyes. "That's an interesting question. I like to think of this as a spa of sorts. A place for renewal. Of new beginnings and new truth. Where precious few people have enjoyed the rarest of opportunities."

"O-o-opportunities?" Djebar repeated.

Roger nodded. "Opportunities to shed the burdens of their old lives and embrace a rebirth. To become something clean and pure."

Hicks watched Djebar struggle against his bonds as he tried to look anywhere but at the light. He managed to move his head just enough to get a glimpse of the bone cutter glinting on the wall on his left.

The sight of it seemed to allow him to compose himself. "I see you have a flair for the dramatic."

"There's no drama here, Mr. Djebar. Everything in here has its purpose. Its use." He ran the side of his gloved hand along Djebar's cheek. "Even you, as you will soon see."

Djebar worked up a sneer. "Do you think this is the

first time I've been interrogated by Americans? I know what you can and cannot do. And nothing you do will make me talk."

"That's where you're wrong, my friend. You see, I don't view myself as an American. I think of myself as a citizen of the world, so awkward things like the Constitution and the Geneva Convention simply don't apply to me. But we'll get to that, don't you worry. It's all part of the process."

Hicks tapped his foot as he willed Roger to pick up the pace. Time was wasting and he needed answers now.

He watched Djebar tense as Roger ran his gloved hands over his body. It was only then that the prisoner realized he was naked.

Hicks saw Djebar's eyes go wide. "I don't care what you do to me. I won't tell you anything but lies."

Roger placed a finger lightly to Djebar's lips. "Of course, you'll lie. At least at first. Then, when we're deeper into the process, you'll tell me anything at all, especially whatever you think I want to hear. But I'm afraid that won't be good enough for our purposes because I don't want you to tell me just anything, Djebar. I want you to tell me everything. Eventually, you'll even tell me the truth. The pure, unadulterated truth about your friend Omar and why you're here and what you were hired to do for him."

Djebar began to speak in a panicked jumble of English and Arabic and French, but Roger hushed him. "Everything's going to be fine, Djebar, because the truth isn't just a mere assemblage of facts. It's a process of self-discovery that can't be rushed. Anything you tell me now will only be a hint of what I really want to know, but I want to know everything about everything. About Omar. About why you're here and about all your other dealings all over the world. Together, you and I will help you remember things you thought you forgot. Things you never thought you knew."

He took the terrorist's face in his hands. Djebar's eyes were wide as he knew he was at the mercy of a madman.

But Roger's expression was as tender as his prisoner's was terrified. "But you won't be alone. We'll take this journey of discovery together, my friend. A journey that has been oh so long in coming."

"No," Djebar whispered. "No, please. We can deal. That's what I do. I make deals. We..."

"It's too late for all of that, my friend. Our destination on this journey is already set and it leads to the purest truth we can know. You and I will arrive at that glorious plateau together very soon."

Hicks watched Djebar dry swallow. The prisoner began to tremble in his restraints as he saw Roger tie a thick rubber surgical mask under his nose.

"Why are you doing this?" Djebar whispered. "I told you I'll tell you anything. You don't have to do this to me! I can pay you. I have money. You know who I am."

Hicks watched Roger reach for his rubber gloves. "But this isn't about me, or you or who you are now. It's about who you're about to become through the exquisite beauty of pain."

Through the old speakers of the television set, Hicks could hear Djebar begin to whimper and pray in Arabic as Roger snapped on the rubber gauntlets that came up to his elbows.

Hicks saw Djebar's surprise when Roger joined him word for word in his chant of a passage from the Quran. In Arabic. It was a passage Hicks had heard prayed in other interrogations many times before. In English, it meant:

"The righteous shall return to a blessed retreat: the gardens of Eden, whose gates shall open wide to receive them. Reclining there with bashful virgins for companions, they will call for abundant fruit and drink."

Roger spoke to Djebar from behind his rubber mask. "Such a beautiful sentiment in a sacred book used by such ugly people with horrible intent. People like you who want to exterminate people like me."

Djebar shut his eyes and whimpered when Roger stroked the side of his cheek with the cold rubber glove. "In pain, there is truth and beauty to be found, Djebar. And by the time you and I are done here today, you will be the purest, most magnificent man alive."

Hicks watched Roger pick up a scalpel and let Djebar watch the light dance along its sharpened edge. "Let us begin our journey to paradise together."

Hicks got up and turned off the television as Roger brought the scalpel down on Djebar's belly.

He could still hear the gurgled screams though the thin walls. It was, after all, an old building.

Hicks had burned through a Churchill before the examination room door opened.

Djebar had screamed until he went hoarse. A heavy silence followed, then gasping whispers and tears and muffled words. He thought he'd even heard laughter at one point but had tried to block it out.

Roger had already removed his rubber surgical mask and gauntlets when he walked into the waiting area. Except for the rubber apron, he looked as refreshed as someone who'd just woken up from a long afternoon nap.

"My," he sighed as he sat in an ancient metal and pleather chair across from Hicks. "That was *quite* a session. Glad I had the recorders rolling for that one. We made tremendous progress. Broke down a lot of barriers."

"I only care about one barrier in particular." Then, Hicks noticed a sliver of something bright pink on the belly of Roger's apron and quickly looked away. "Jesus, Roger."

Roger noticed it and laughed as he plucked it up with two fingers. "Sorry about that. A pound of flesh, as it were, only this one was just a couple of ounces."

Hicks was no stranger to blood and carnage, but Roger's interrogations were always something more than that. He didn't just break the body. He broke the soul. Hicks had never believed in things like souls until he'd seen the results of Roger's work.

Hicks swallowed down the bile rising in his throat. "What did he tell you about Omar?"

"Quite a bit. Your friend Clarke was right about our Djebar, you know? He's been exceptionally well trained to hide information. He's spent a lifetime hiding behind several walls in his mind. Selective memory, disassociation and the like. He's far more complex than your typical run of the mill matchmaker and now I can see why he's so well paid."

"I'm glad you're impressed," Hicks said. "What did he tell you about Omar?"

Roger took the piece of tissue and tossed it in a small trash can between the tables. It made a wet smack off the side and a small puff of dust rose as the flesh struck the bottom. "Omar had hired Debar to put him in touch with some scientists who've been working on weaponizing SARS and MERS and Ebola in a lab in Saudi Arabia. The Saudis told their allies that all the scientists were killed. They weren't. In fact, they all got away. Their deaths are just a cover story the Saudis are using to cover their mistakes."

Hicks hadn't told Roger about the envelope because he didn't want him to lead Djebar in that direction. As good as Roger was, he was still human and humans are prone to being influenced. "You said there were three scientists. Which of them did Djebar put in touch with Omar?"

"He mentioned something about a Samuelson who'd been working at the lab. By then, Djebar was a little tired, so the details were foggy. He mentioned something about shipments and samples and keeping everyone on program, whatever that means. He said there were three scientists, but didn't tell me anything about the other two, only Samuelson."

"Did he tell you how much of the viruses this Samuelson had given Omar?"

"One thousand vials," Roger said.

"A thousand?" Hicks couldn't believe it. "How did they get so many into the country?"

"Over the Mexican border, bit by bit," Roger explained. "It took months, but they used undocumented Africans who were looking to come to America.

They had a small lab set up in a storage facility in Brooklyn where some of their scientists made more. He doesn't know how many and, believe me, he would've told me if he did. Before he passed out, he kept confusing phrases. Instead of payment, he kept referring to 'his people' and 'us' and his 'reward'. I thought you said he worked alone."

"I thought he did," Hicks said. Then again, he'd once thought Omar was just a cab driver with a big mouth and no network. The rest of what Djebar had said could've been babble or it could be everything.

Hicks pulled out his handheld. "I've got to let the Dean know about this. You said the session was uploaded to OMNI?"

"Yes, but wait." Roger put his hand over the handheld. "He also said something about an antidote. Said only a few doses were made and shipped separately. It doesn't cure the carriers, but it prevents the poison from consuming them. They're still capable of spreading the diseases."

Now Hicks knew why Omar had taken Kamal on a tour of the neighborhoods in Brooklyn and Queens. He wasn't just showing off Kamal. He was infecting them with the sickness. Legal, working people who no one had a reason to expect.

Hicks dialed the Dean. "Did Djebar say why Omar needs the money?"

"The first batch was impure, but this Samuelson was in the U.S. and arranging for vials of a more refined contagion to arrive today or tomorrow. He didn't know where or when. Omar worked that part out. When they give Samuelson his money, he'll tell them where they can find the new batch."

Hicks called the Dean, who answered on the second ring. "OMNI is already analyzing everything he got out of Djebar. Tell Roger he hit the mother lode with this bastard."

Normally, Hicks would've been happy that the Dean was pleased, but he didn't have that kind of time. "We need to pour everything into finding Samuelson and the other two scientists from the lab. We need to know where he's been since the Saudi raid. Where he is now. We need to find out where that new batch is headed, and we'd better find out fast."

"We're already working on it," the Dean assured him. "In the meantime, Dr. Carter has already sent a batch of the cocktail she injected you with to Scott's Varsity team. They're being inoculated as we speak. They're outfitted with ballistic masks that should filter out the infection. They're ready to hit Omar's facility at any time."

Hicks got up from his chair and headed out the door. "Tell them to sit tight until I get there."

"I figured as much. There's a mask ready for you, too. According to Scott, no one has moved from the building all day. No one in, no one out, so maybe they're waiting for word on the delivery you mentioned."

Hicks checked his watch as he ran out of the building and hit the street. It was five-thirty, and the sun was about to rise.

"Sir, you have to tell the financier to hold off on making that call about the money. We have to do everything we can to make sure they stay put."

The Dean grew quiet on the other end of the phone. "James, since we're dealing with a biological agent, I think we should play it safe and have a drone level the whole building right now. We can claim it was a gas leak or a meth lab that blew up."

Hicks knew that was a bad idea. "That'll kill Omar and the existing samples, but it won't help us find out where the next batch of samples are. These guys have managed to stay off the grid for this long. Anything we get out of him will have to be through interrogation."

"I'm scrambling a drone anyway," the Dean said. "I'll also alert the CDC of a possible contamination in the area. But I want to wait until you hit the building first. Once we involve outside agencies, this gets public real fast."

"Understood, sir. On my way to Midwood now." He flagged down a cab to take him over to the safehouse where he'd parked his car. "I'll let Scott know I'm en route."

"Happy hunting," the Dean said. "And, for what it's worth, you were right all along."

Hicks didn't care about praise. "I'll be in touch, sir."

He killed the connection and climbed into the back of the cab. He told the driver to take him to the address in Alphabet City.

He'd just finished tapping out a text to Scott, telling him to wait when a text popped up from Roger.

You left before I could ask. Can I keep him? Just for a little while. Please?

Hicks closed his eyes. With everything else going on, he still had that crazy bastard to deal with.

A crazy bastard who might've just saved countless lives.

Hicks replied:

Just don't kill him. Our cousins want him back.

Roger's reply was immediate.

It'll be my pleasure.

Hicks didn't know what to say to that, so he simply deleted the message.

CHAPTER 23

Hicks pulled up next to the Varsity observation van in a Midwood lot. It was an old Mercedes Sprinter with the faded signage of a fruit vendor on the side. The white paint on the cab was peeling and gray, showing the rusting metal underneath. Graffiti covered most of the exterior. The truck looked like it belonged in a junk-yard instead of playing a role as a forward observation post, which was the general idea.

Hicks got out of the car and pounded on the back door twice. One of the doors opened, and he climbed in, shutting it behind him.

The inside of the cargo area had been outfitted as a cramped forward observation post. It had four bunk beds for operatives to sleep in while two others monitored the equipment. Everything was hooked up to OMNI via the network, making the whole set up a mobile version of his Twenty-third Street facility. A state-of-the-art ventilation system made the truck cool in the summer and warm in the winter, but the air still smelled like stale coffee.

"Nice to have a Faculty member finally join us," Scott said Hicks. "What happened, professor? Lecture ran long?"

"Anatomy class, actually."

Hicks didn't mind the jab. He'd worked with Scott at various postings all over the world. He had close cropped gray hair, deep set eyes and a square jaw. He looked like he'd just stepped off a Marine recruiting poster, which was accurate since he'd been in Marine Recon before enrolling in the University. It made him bad for field work, but he was born for tactical situations like this.

"You boys take your shots?" Hicks asked the men.

The five men nodded. Scott was their leader and he spoke for them. "Heard there might be some nasty shit going on behind that door."

He was glad to see they had their gas masks and helmets ready. The bulletproof armor was a given.

"The injections you took should help keep us from getting infected," Hicks explained. "The masks will help, too. I know they already sent you a mission package, and the man we want to avoid killing is Omar. Burn his face into your memory. We have reason to believe this threat goes beyond just Midwood. Maybe even beyond the city. If we keep him alive, we have a good chance of finding out for certain."

"And if he doesn't give us that option?" Scott asked.

"Then put a bullet in his brain." He let the men see the resolve in his eyes before adding, "This is nothing you men haven't done before. And with Scott's permission, let's suit up and go to work."

Scott gave the order, and the men began to put on their masks and helmets, then checked their weapons.

Each of them was carrying an M4 Commando rifle, used by special operators and S.W.A.T. teams all over the world. Extra ammo clips bulged from their ballistic vests.

Scott handed Hicks a helmet and mask and a vest. Hicks only took the head gear. "My jacket's Kevlar. I'm fine."

While his men ran through final comms and weapons checks, Scott moved through the cramped quarters to crouch beside Hicks.

"The Dean said he's scrambling a drone."

"That's Plan B." Hicks pulled on his mask and fit the helmet on his head. "If it comes to that, we'll already be dead."

"Copy that."

Scott went to the computer and brought up a three-dimensional rendering of the building from the OMNI satellite. "When the second team arrives, we'll have a twelve-man force, so this will be a classic containment-and-breach scenario. The second unit will cover us with two men in the front, two in the back and one sniper stationed at the front of the building and one at the back. With the front door covered, we'll breach through the back door where they're least expecting it."

He switched screens to a thermal read of the build-ing. "We're looking at a three-story structure that has been modified several times recently. Scans show thirty people moving freely through the building and base-ment since yesterday. About six of them have been on the top floor and appear to be in bed. Judging by what we've been able to see through thermals, they're all running fevers and they might be sick."

"Or infected," Hicks observed.

"You catch on fast," Scott said. "If Omar is still inside – and we've got no reason to think he's anywhere else - that means they all know him and are probably part of his plan. We go in assuming there are no innocents in that building. Everyone is a legitimate target."

"Except for Omar," Hicks reminded him. "We need him alive if possible."

"If possible," Scott repeated. "But what makes you think you can get him to talk?"

Hicks flashed back to the sounds and smells he'd just left at Roger's studio. The piece of Djebar he'd thrown in the garbage. "Don't worry. He'll talk."

One of the men pointed at the screen. "Boss, it looks like something's going on."

———

Hicks looked at the OMNI thermal feed on the monitor. Inside the building, he saw several heat signatures blurring into one as they massed in the hallway by the front door.

"Damn it," Hicks said. "They're getting ready to come out."

"Then we're going in." Scott pushed past the men and climbed into the driver's seat. Hicks moved behind him and rode shotgun.

One of Scott's men put his hand up to his earpiece and repeated, "Sir. The second team is a block out."

"Good. Tell them we're moving in and to back our play."

Scott turned on the ignition and the van's motor roared to life. He threw the van into reverse and pealed out of the lot backwards. He threw it back into gear and floored it.

Omar's house was dead ahead, and they were closing fast.

But not before ten men streamed out of Omar's house and piled into five cars that had been parked on the street in front of the building.

"Shit," Scott cursed as he slammed on the breaks and slid the van to a halt on Omar's lawn. "Brian, tell Team Two we've got five tangos in the wind. Pursue as necessary.

Brian repeated Scott's orders as Hicks and the others spilled from the van and closed in on the house.

Someone inside had spotted them and began yelling.

Scott signaled two of his men to peel off and head toward the back.

Hicks pulled his Ruger and blasted the lock with one shot. Scott raced forward and kicked the door all the way in.

The narrow hallway was crammed with people trying to get away but couldn't. Scott yelled over them to get on the floor and keep their hands raised.

Hicks broke left and entered the living room. Two of Scott's men followed, sweeping the room with their rifles.

The room was overloaded with furniture. Sofas and chairs were crammed in everywhere.

And on them lay sick people coughing, too weak to move. Some of them had sores on their faces. Screaming from the hall died down as people began to obey Scott's orders.

Hicks pushed people out of the way as he went into the kitchen. He found the door to the basement, but didn't barge in. He moved to the left of it and both of Scott's men stacked up behind it.

He pointed at the last man, telling him he was covering the door. Hicks reached out and turned the knob, pushing the door open.

Scott's man dropped to a crouch as the door banged against the wall.

AK-47 fire raked the ceiling as someone fired from the bottom of the stairs.

Scott's man closed in and took him down with a short burst, then proceeded to move down the stairs. Hicks and the remaining man followed.

The stairs were flimsy and creaked beneath their weight as they descended.

The first man turned right to cover the basement as they climbed down and stopped at the base of the stairs to cover the room.

Hicks could hear sobs and coughs rise from the basement.

The landing at the base of the stairs was dark and the windows had been boarded over. Hicks passed the cover man and saw the only immediate light came from the broken wooden walls on his right.

The OMNI scans of the building were accurate. The basement had been sectioned off into rooms some time ago. But now, the plaster was cracked and all of the walls had gaping holes.

Hicks took cover behind a fractured wall and looked through the holes at what was happening in the center of the room.

Despite the chaos happening in the rest of the house, he saw Omar holding a syringe as he stood in front of five men lined up in a row. All three men were black and short and painfully thin; probably Somali. Their clothes were faded t-shirts and cheap jeans that didn't fit them right. Not baggy in a fashionable gang-banger way, but in a poverty way. Like a missionary handed out a garbage bag full of clothes from the back of a truck in a village a long time ago.

One of the men moved off to the side, rubbing his right arm. The other three held their right arms, veins-side out, waiting for Omar to inject them.

Hicks braced himself against the wall. The son of a bitch was injecting them with the virus. Making them carriers. Signing their death warrant and the death warrants of anyone who came in contact with them.

Two of Scott's men began clearing the other rooms while Hicks watched Omar inject another willing victim.

Through the cracked wall, Hicks scanned the room for guns or guards. Seeing neither, he stepped around the wall and into the light behind the others. He brought up the Ruger and aimed it at Omar's chest.

"Put it down, you son of a bitch."

Omar looked up at him as calmly as if he'd been asked the time. The needle and vial were still in his hand.

The rest of the men turned to face him and slowly backed away.

"Don't do anything stupid, Omar," Hicks said. "Just set it down on the table, nice and easy and we can all walk out of here alive."

Omar gave him that crooked, gaping smile Hicks had seen in countless surveillance images, but had never seen in real life. "Walk out of here? And walk into what? A cell? Guantanamo? One of your black sites?"

"I'm not with the CIA and neither was Halaam," Hicks said, using Colin's cover name. "No Guantanamo and no jail cell. Just the two of us working this out as soon as you put that shit on the table and step away."

"And what if I don't? You'll shoot me?" Omar surprised him by laughing. "You think I'm doing this because I fear death?" He picked up something from the table with his left hand.

A device with a blinking red light that Hicks had not seen until then.

But Omar wasn't smiling any more. His eyes were flat. Committed. "I do not fear death for I am the Messenger of Death!"

Omar's thumb moved.

Hicks fired. The flat head round obliterated his left shoulder. He bounced off the wall and slowly slid to the floor.

The device skidded away from him as he fell.

As Omar cried out in agony, one of the infected, a man who was taller than most of the others, looked at the device, then back at Hicks.

Hicks took a step closer, aware that the infected in the room could rush him at any moment. "Don't. Just don't."

The man reached for it as others stepped in to block him.

Hicks fired three times down at the man through

those who had tried to protect him as two of Scott's team rushed into the room.

Hicks remained in position as the other infected threw up their hands and knelt on the floor. His gun still aimed down at where he had seen the device fall.

All three of his shots had punched through the men and struck the infected man as he reached for the switch. His outstretched fingers were less than an inch away from it.

Scott's men swept their rifles over the infected as they yelled for them to remain still. Omar's screams made it difficult for them to be heard.

Hicks stepped between them and gently picked up the switch. It looked like a modified garage door opener, but he knew it was probably something much deadlier. Garage door openers didn't have blinking red lights.

Hicks asked Scott's men, "Either of you boys carrying any QuikClot on you?"

Both men answered in the affirmative and Hicks pointed down at Omar. "Use it on him. See if it'll do any good. I'll cover you."

One of the men knelt beside Omar and administered the silicon anti-coagulant designed to stop wounded soldiers from bleeding out on the battlefield.

Hicks looked up when he heard rumbling on the floorboards, followed by shouting from upstairs. Scott was barking orders for someone to halt.

He heard the unmistakable sound of an M4 opening up, which brought a new wave of screams and cries from the people in the hallway above.

Scott's voice came over his earpiece. "Hicks. Report."

"We've got several infected covered and Omar is

badly wounded. He made a play for some kind of switch, so the building may be rigged to blow. Tell your men to be careful."

"Copy that," Scott said. "Five infected just ran down the stairs and tried to make a break for it. Virus was contained but is now airborne."

"Copy," Hicks told him. "Report to Jonathan and stand by for a coordinated response."

Scott signed off and Hicks turned his attention to the man treating Omar. "He alive?"

"Took two doses of QuikClot to stop the bleeding, but it seems to be holding, sir. His left arm's hanging on by a thread, so his fiddling days are over."

"Let's just hope he can still sing." Hicks motioned for the man to resume his position as Hicks knelt beside Omar.

The man had lost a lot of blood, but the hate in his eyes was still strong. He spat at Hicks, but the gas mask prevented it from finding its mark. "You might as well kill me. I'll never tell you anything, do you understand? Never!"

"We'll see about that." Hicks snatched him by the collar and pulled him up on his feet. To Scott's men, he said, "You boys clear the rest of those rooms down here?"

"All clear," the men answered in unison.

Hicks half dragged Omar into a room across the hall. It looked like an original part of the house, for it still had a cast iron radiator on the floor. "You can rest up right here."

He threw Omar into the room, causing the man to cry out again. He grabbed hold of his right arm, pulled out one of his plastic slip ties and secured him to the radiator.

Omar struggled against the tie but had nowhere to go. "I'll tell you nothing," he shouted at Hicks as he left. "Nothing!"

Hicks left him alone to scream with his useless arm and his rage.

CHAPTER 24

HICKS FOUND Scott in the van monitoring Team Two's chase of the five escaped vehicles. He may have led the raid on the house, but he still had men in harm's way.

"You'd better get the Dean on the line to run interference for us, Hicks. The scanner's picking up a lot of units inbound, and I don't want my men in a firefight because some flatfoot got spooked."

The Dean surprised them by coming over their earpieces. "No need to worry, gentlemen. They've been advised it was a federal operation and will act accordingly. HAZMAT teams are en route and will help secure the sick and dying."

Scott was glued to the OMNI stream of the car chase. The Dean told him he would switch off to a private conversation with Hicks.

"I've got Jonathan on the line with us," the Dean told him. "Is Omar still alive?"

"Barely," Hicks reported. "His left arm's hanging by a thread but the boys used QuikClot to stop the bleeding. It'll hold until a real doctor gets here. Advise everyone approaching the scene that the house may be rigged to blow. I got Omar before he could reach some kind of device."

"Scott tells us there are at least thirty infected in the house with room for thirty more," Jonathan said.

Hicks was glad the van had air scrubbers so he could finally take off his gas mask. "I think that was his plan, sir. He was still injecting people with the disease when we hit the house like nothing was wrong. That was his plan. To infect people and send them out into the open to mingle with the population."

"Super spreaders," Jonathan said. "God only knows how many might be infected."

"Everyone Omar and Kamal met the other day should be treated as infected," Hicks told him. "Right now, Scott's men are in pursuit of the ten we know who escaped. Once we neutralize them, we can worry about the others."

Jonathan said, "You have to get Omar to tell us about where the remaining doses are located. Or at least for him to tell us where we can find this scientist who knows. Samuelson, I think his name is."

"I'll work on him in a bit," Hicks said, "once the cavalry arrives. For now, let's focus on the ten we know we've got in the wind."

"Understood," Jonathan said. "Switching over to tactical now."

Hicks muted his earbud to avoid feedback from Scott as he directed the chase from the van.

"Viper Two this is Viper One," Scott said. "I have visual."

Hicks saw they were heading east through Brooklyn toward the on ramp to the Belt Parkway.

"Copy, Viper One," the commander said. "All five cars are still moving in a loose formation. We have eyes on the targets and are trailing at a fair distance. OMNI feed is live and working."

Hicks pulled up the live OMNI feed on his hand-held. He saw the five cars moving along in the center and left-hand lanes. None of them were moving particularly fast or particularly slow. They were driving slightly over the speed limit, but probably not enough to garner any attention from the cops.

Hicks wondered aloud, "Why the hell were they heading east onto the Belt Parkway? Manhattan is west. What the hell was east of the city? Where..."

Hicks and Scott traded glances before Scott zoomed out from their current location. Heading east on the Belt Parkway would lead Omar's men to one of two locations. And Hicks bet they were going to both.

So did Scott. "Viper Two, please be advised that tangos may be en route to JFK Airport and LaGuardia Airport."

After Viper Two acknowledged, Scott muted his feed. "You think they're picking up the samples at the airport?"

"No," Hicks said. "I think they're infected and going to spread the disease to as many people they can."

Scott opened the channel again. "Viper Two, you must intercept those tangos before they split up. I repeat. You must not allow them to split. You don't have the wheels to hunt both."

"Copy, Viper One. We're on it. Will advise."

Scott switched back to the tactical line where Jonathan and the Dean were patched in. "What's the status of that drone you scrambled?"

"Still an hour out," Jonathan said. "And it's only equipped with one Hellfire missile. We were looking to hit a building, not several moving targets. Calling in a different asset will take a lot longer than an hour."

"Then it's up to my men," Scott said. "Don't worry. They're up to it."

Hicks thought of something. "Have the NYPD Traffic unit slow up traffic between their location and the airports. Viper Two can take them that way."

"It'll take some explaining," Jonathan said, "but I'll do it. Stand by."

Scott celebrated by pounding Hicks in the chest. "Good thinking, Professor. I knew we kept you around for a reason."

He went back to the tactical feed. "Viper Two, be advised that traffic will begin to slow shortly. Keep a sharp eye on tangos and eliminate when possible."

"Copy, Viper One. We stand ready."

Scott muted his feed again. "Now all we have to do is hope Jonathan can get the NYPD to play ball."

Hicks knew that was instrumental to the operation. "Hope they're not stuck in traffic."

Scott and Hicks watched the OMNI feed silently as the five marked vehicles rolled along the Brooklyn-Queens Expressway. None of them made any sudden moves or switched lanes. They knew where they were going and no hurry to get there.

Both Hicks and Scott tensed when they saw break lights begin to appear on the screen. A few moments later, traffic came to a complete halt.

Scott zoomed out and saw two NYPD Traffic cars had forced traffic into a single lane.

Scott focused back in on the five cars around Viper

Two's position. They were ten car-lengths away from the last of Omar's men. The first was about twenty cars ahead.

"A lot of ground to cover," Hicks said. "A lot of innocents in the way."

"A lot more innocents at the airport," Scott said. He opened a channel to his men. "Viper Two, you are clear to engage. Again, you are clear to engage."

"Copy, Viper One. Stand by."

JUST BEFORE THE doors of Viper Two's Trailblazer opened, a call went out over every NYPD radio in the area that a preventative Federal action was taking place on the BQE with information to follow.

Hicks watched as the six men from Viper Two slipped out of the SUV in full ballistic armor and gas masks as they moved through the packed cars at a crouch. Their M4s lead the way.

Hicks watched one Varsity man move toward the rear car and fire a short burst through the back of the windshield.

"Two down," Viper Two said as horns and yelling erupted all around him. "Eight to go."

The four Somalis in the next two cars got out of their vehicles and began to aim pistols at Viper Two.

They didn't notice the Varsity men moving on either side of their lane. Several quick bursts from the M4s cut them down amid a shower of broken glass from their open doors.

"Six tangos down," Viper Two reported as the six-man team continued moving between cars to the lead men.

Hicks saw some panicked civilians tried to open their doors to escape, but quickly ducked back inside when they saw the men in battle gear and rifles approaching their cars.

By then, the drivers of the lead cars knew what was happening behind them and began to work the wheel to get free. But with nowhere to go and no shoulder to speak of, they had nowhere to go.

The driver of the second car jerked the wheel to the right and rammed the car next to him before throwing it in reverse, which moved his car at a broader angle.

Scott pounded the console. "The son of a bitch is trying to make a firing line for the others."

The men in the lead car got out of their vehicles and ran back toward the barrier their friends had just created. The passenger of the car got out on his side as the driver tried to crawl across the console to join him.

One of the Varsity men cut loose with a short burst into the car, killing the driver as he fled.

The passenger reached the trunk of the car and managed to get off a couple of shots before another Varsity man brought him down.

"Eight tangos down," Viper Two reported. "Two on foot."

Hicks saw the last two men forget about returning fire and took off running in the opposite direction.

Four of the Viper Team cleared the blocking car, giving measured chase while the last two climbed on top of the stopped vehicle. One on the trunk. One on the hood.

One of Omar's men made it all the way over to the

left lane, crouching as he ran along the cars. He made the mistake of stopping to turn around between cars to see if anyone was behind him.

The Viper on the hood of the car brought him down with a head shot.

"Nine tangos down," Viper Two reported. "One on foot."

Hicks and Scott watched the last infected man forget about looking behind him as he ran flat out along the right lane.

The lead Viper member took a knee, took careful aim, and fired. The runner's body jerked wildly as each of the bullets hit home. He stumbled forward and skidded to the asphalt.

Hicks felt like he'd just watched the Giants score the winning touchdown in the Super Bowl.

But he took his lead from Scott, who remained cool as the final report came over their earpieces.

"Viper One, this is Viper Two. All tangos eliminated. Awaiting further instructions."

"Copy that, Viper Two. Return to your vehicle and button up tight. Stand by for further instructions. We'll find a way to get you out of there as soon as possible."

Hicks watched as the men returned to their Trailblazer and closed the doors. Just another SUV in BQE traffic. Except that they had just killed ten dangerous men.

Scott switched back to the tactical channel. "My boys did their job, now you do yours. Find a way to get that traffic moving again and fast. They're sitting ducks out there if any civilians decide to join in the fun."

"I'm on it," Jonathan said. "Nice work, Scott."

"Stow the compliments," Scott said, "and help me get my men home."

Scott killed the connection and looked at Hicks. "Just another day at the office."

Hicks looked out the van's front window and saw every kind of emergency vehicle the City of New York had at its disposal.

"Stay here and let Jonathan coordinate with the cops and firemen. I'll make sure your men get out of the house unharmed."

"Where are you going?"

Hicks opened the van door and climbed down. "To get some answers."

CHAPTER 25

HICKS PULLED on his gas mask and helmet as he
walked back to the house. The front yard was full of
personnel in full Haz-Mat gear. A crew was erecting a
large containment tent in the street. The five men and
women Scott had cut down had already been zipped up
in red bags.

One of Scott's men approached Hicks as he entered
the house. "What do you want us to do now that the
civilians are here?"

"Check in with your boss," Hicks said as he passed
him. "They know you're the good guys, so no one
should hassle you."

Most of the people in the hall had spread out into
other parts of the house. He heard wet, gagging
coughing of the people around him. Most of them
women and children.

He made the mistake of looking in the living room
before he entered the kitchen. He saw a young girl of
about two weakly tugging at her dead mother, a filthy
doll on her lap.

Hicks felt something catch in his throat and looked away. He found two of Scott's men guarding the back door in the kitchen. More sick and dying had found their way in there, too.

"Anyone go downstairs?"

Both men shook their heads. One said, "Just our boys covering the infected down there."

Hicks walked downstairs, slowly this time, not worrying about making noise. He took out the Ruger and held it at his side; just in case.

But when he got to the bottom of the stairs, two of Scott's men were still keeping the infected on the floor.

Hicks broke toward the room on the left and found Omar still slip-tied to the radiator pipe.

The QuikClot had kept his shoulder from bleeding any further, but his dead right arm was beginning to turn in color.

Omar struggled to lift his head when saw Hicks standing over him. His thin face was slick with perspiration. But he still managed a sneer.

"Ah, it is you, American. You came back to finish what you started. I knew you wouldn't just walk away. You're wasting your time. I won't tell you anything."

Hicks kept the Ruger at his side. "Your men are dead."

"Which men? The men in this house? The men I sent to Central Park with the traitor? His curiosity got him killed, you know? I wasn't sure he was a traitor until he mentioned you."

Hicks flinched at the mention of Colin. "What did he see?"

"It's what he heard," Omar said. "One of the new men called me 'The Messenger' in front of him. He asked some of the others why and they told me. I don't like questions."

Hicks grinned through the gas mask. At least he finally knew why Colin died. "What was that you said about never answering my questions?"

The terrorist looked away. "I refuse to say another word without my lawyer."

"That's too bad for you because you're the last one still alive," Hicks said. "We're going to be asking you all sorts of things in all sorts of ways. You remember those ten assholes who sped out of here just before we kicked in the door? The men you sent to infect people at the airport. They didn't make it. They're just ten blood-stains on the BQE now. You and your men have accomplished nothing."

"They accomplished everything," Omar spat. "So, they didn't make it to the airport. Do you think your first responders will know they are infected? Do you think they'll believe they are infected?" He slowly shook his head. "Americans are so gullible. So ready to believe the best of every situation. My men will take lives, even in death, if it pleases Allah."

Hicks reared back and kicked the radiator, missing Omar's head by inches. "Allah's got nothing to do with this. Nothing! Tell me where the next shipment is supposed to land."

Omar's eyes widened for a second. He hadn't expected Hicks to know about that. "I want to speak to my lawyer."

"You don't get a lawyer," Hicks said.

"Of course, I get a lawyer," Omar laughed. "This is America. Everyone gets a lawyer. It's the law."

"Sure is." Hicks lifted his Ruger and opened the

cylinder. "Only trouble is, you're not under arrest and I'm not a cop."

"Cop, FBI, CIA, NSA," Omar sneered. "What difference does it make? There are rules about how you can treat me. So get out of here and bring me a lawyer. You don't scare me."

Hicks picked out the spent rounds from the Ruger and began tossing them at Omar's head. They plinked off the radiator as he said, "No cops. No lawyers. No laws. No judges. No Guantanamo Bay. No one's coming to get you because no one knows you're here. Just me and my men."

He chucked the last spent bullet at him and held up a live one for Omar to see. "It's just you and me and Mr. Ruger here in a filthy basement in Brooklyn." He slid the live round into the cylinder, gave it a spin and flicked it shut.

Omar eyed the pistol. "You don't scare me. I'll tell you nothing."

"Sure, you will. Djebar did."

Omar's eyes sparked with fear and denial. "You lie."

"Got no reason to lie, Ace. We broke your friend inside of fifteen minutes and he's a hell of a lot tougher than you. Better trained to hold up against that kind of thing. He told us where to find you and what you were planning. He told us about the viruses. He told us Samuelson is expecting another shipment of a purer toxin today or tomorrow. Now, I know you don't know where the shipment's landing, but you know where Samuelson is."

"You lie!" Omar yelled. "You play games!"

"Djebar led us here to you." Hicks aimed the Ruger

down at him. "What makes you think you won't talk, too?"

"Djebar is loyal," Omar panted. "You lie about what he said."

He flinched when Hicks cocked the Ruger and aimed it at Omar's left foot. "You saw what this did to your shoulder. Imagine what it'll do to your foot. You're already a one-armed man. How'd you like to be a cripple, too?"

Omar cursed Hicks as he cocked the pistol. He screamed when Hicks squeezed the trigger, and the chamber was empty.

"Your luck's running out, Omar." He shifted his aim toward his knees. "Tell me where I can find Samuelson."

Omar cut loose with a string of curses in Arabic.

Hicks looked down at him from behind the pistol. "You sure you want those to be your last words?"

Omar began to shake as Hicks thumbed back the hammer.

When he squeezed the trigger, Omar's bladder went.

CHAPTER 26

THE NEIGHBORHOOD around Omar's house was under siege by personnel in Haz-Mat gear and equipment.

As he stepped out of Omar's house, Hicks was met by a technician who sprayed him down from head to toe and back to front. He tossed his helmet and mask into lined bin for hazardous materials before walking back to his car.

He felt the handheld buzz in his jacket pocket but didn't bother to answer it. It could be Jonathan. It could be the Dean.

Hicks didn't care. He had what he'd come for. That's all that mattered.

He'd decided he'd taken enough orders for one day. It was time he to go on offense for a change.

He got behind the wheel and turned on the ignition, but nothing happened.

His dashboard screen came alive and showed a text from Jonathan.

***I've remotely locked your vehicle until you
talk to me.***

Hicks answered Jonathan's call. "Don't you ever
deactivate my vehicle again. Turn it on. Now."

"Fine."

Hicks hit the ignition and the engine roared to
life. But he kept the car in park. He needed to set a
few things straight before he acted on Omar's
information.

"Did you question Omar?" Jonathan asked.

"I did. We were right about his plans to spread the
virus. The good news is that his version of the virus is
unstable. It burns through the host quicker than it
should. It doesn't make them any less contagious, but it
makes them too sick to move. The newer version
Samuelson is supposed to deliver has a longer incuba-
tion period."

"Good God," Jonathan said. "We're working with
the appropriate authorities on containment procedures
and contaminated populations in Brooklyn and
Queens. Our preliminary models say the disease may
have spread well beyond the city. It may be as far north
as Toronto and as far south as Washington, D.C. I'm
afraid many people will die, but not as many as would
have without your efforts. You should be proud of yourself, James."

Hicks was in no mood for compliments. "I've got
to go."

"Did he tell you about where you could find
Samuelson?" Jonathan asked. "And the larger batch of
toxin scheduled to be delivered?"

"No," he lied.

Jonathan paused. "Are you sure? OMNI shows you're being deceptive and so do I."

Hicks raised a middle finger to the dashboard screen. "OMNI show you that, too?"

Jonathan ignored the vulgarity. "What are you up to, James? I'm not going to try to stop you or threaten you, but I'd like to know. This is more than about you here. It's about more than any one of us. You must remember that."

Hicks shut his eyes and drew in a deep breath. His mind had been going around in circles for days. He finally had a straight line on a problem and wanted to handle it. His way. "Omar told me where Samuelson is and I'm going to get him, and I don't want to argue about it."

Jonathan surprised him by asking, "What do you need me to do?"

Hicks shifted the Buick into drive. "Stay tuned and out of my way. I'll be in touch when it's over."

As HICKS DROVE toward New Jersey, he knew Jonathan would be tracking him via OMNI. There wasn't much he could do about that.

There wasn't much that Jonathan could do about him going alone, either. Two out of the three Varsity teams in the New York Office were occupied in Brooklyn. The third team was at the Alphabet City safe house and could be called upon if needed.

Hicks didn't think he'd need them to handle one lousy scientist. He wanted to bring him in on his own. New York was his Office. He would protect it his way.

Because the scientist had put all of this in motion. Omar wouldn't have had a reason to kill Colin if Samuelson hadn't weaponized diseases. People wouldn't be dying right now all over the city if Samuelson hadn't created the toxin.

Samuelson would have to pay.

As traffic into Manhattan slowed to a crawl, Hicks had OMNI conduct a search for Dr. John Samuelson. He'd been an American biologist working in Saudi Arabia. He'd first been sent to the region by UNESCO as a biologist specializing in the study and treatment of infectious diseases. The Saudi government offered him more money to work for them and he took the job. Everything was above board.

Hicks saw nothing in Samuelson's background to explain why he'd decided to conspire with his fellow scientists to steal the viruses and sell them on the black market. He didn't have any known religious or political affiliations. He'd never even registered to vote. He didn't have a family or outstanding debts or expensive habits that made him need the money.

By all accounts, Dr. John Samuelson was a bland man of fifty with bad teeth and thinning hair. There was no reason in the world why anyone would think him capable of breaking the law, much less helping to create a lethal toxin. He'd crossed the line and threatened to turn the world upside down.

He was that bolt from the blue that institutions like the University feared. The actor you couldn't predict. The man who shot up a playground one day just because he felt like it.

Only Samuelson hadn't used a gun. He used a test

tube and a petri dish to create a monster and turned it over to some very nasty people.

There'd be plenty of time for Hicks to ask him why. But he had to get him first.

OMNI had scanned every public security camera in the city and saw Samuelson had boarded a bus for Philadelphia at the Port Authority Bus Terminal on Forty-second Street. OMNI had found footage of him at the Philadelphia Bus Terminal on Filbert Street. He didn't look different from anyone else. Just a poor traveler dragging his bag behind him one cold Philly night.

Why Philadelphia? Hicks didn't know. But he was going to find out.

Security cameras tracked him through the terminal and out to the street and all the way to a Hilton Garden Inn a block or so away from the bus station. That had been three nights ago. He'd paid in advance for five nights and a scan of the hotel's system said he was still there, waiting for a phone call for his money.

He'd be receiving a different kind of call very soon.

It was half-past noon by the time Hicks pulled into the hotel's parking lot. He parked in the fire lane next to the fire door stairs that were closest to Samuelson's room. It would make it easier to get out of there fast when the time came.

He pulled his Ruger and fed fresh rounds into it from the glove compartment. He still had the Glock he'd pulled off one of Djebar's guards. He decided to leave it in the glove box. He'd need stopping power, not fire power. He pocketed an extra speed loader for the Ruger, just in case.

He used OMNI to access the security footage of the stairway and Samuelson's floor. Both were empty. Nothing moved. He recorded a thirty-second loop and uploaded it to the hotel's system. It would continue to play until the system was rebooted.

Hicks holstered his pistol and got out of the Buick. The fire door didn't have a lock to pick or a handle to open, so he walked through the lobby as though he was a guest. He even waved at the desk clerk, but the pimple-faced kid was too enraptured by the glow from his iPad to notice.

Hicks entered the elevator and pressed five. No keycard-controlled elevators here.

He took the elevator up to the fifth floor and walked down the hall to room 505. Samuelson's room. He paused outside the door and listened. The TV was on, so he figured Samuelson must be inside, waiting for his call and wondering why it hadn't come yet. He had no idea if he'd thrown the security latch or not and the OMNI satellite wasn't in range to scan the room. He'd have to try his key and take his chances.

Hicks pulled his Ruger and tapped his handheld against the sensor lock. OMNI found the frequency and the door unlocked. He pushed in the door, his pistol ready.

From the doorway, Hicks could see the bathroom light was off, and the bed was unmade. The room was empty. No sign of Samuelson.

Hicks shut the door behind him and began searching the room. His suitcase was on the floor and open. He turned it over and dumped the contents on the rug. He sifted through it but found nothing unusual. No vials of toxins.

A quick search of the nightstand and bureau was equally unfruitful. Nothing in the drawers and nothing taped under or behind them, either. A check of the mattress revealed nothing but a few dead bedbugs.

He hit the bathroom next, but only found the usual men's toiletries. He checked the shaving cream can in case it was hollow, but it was genuine.

Hicks found a mini-safe in the closet. And it was locked.

Luckily, it was an older model that could only be opened by entering the right code. The cleaning staff could reset it if they had to, but he couldn't involve them.

He activated the camera on his phone and took a picture of the keypad. He kept the phone still as it flashed a series of different lights on the keypad.

Several images of the keypad filled his screen as OMNI scanned them for a possible four-digit combination. The black light flash revealed latent prints on the numbers and more recent prints.

When the system combined the prints with Samuelson's record, it registered an eighty-percent likelihood that the combination was zero-four-one-eight. His mother's birthday.

Hicks punched in the code, and the door opened. Samuelson's messenger bag was stuffed inside.

Hicks tucked his Ruger back in the holster and slowly eased the bag out of the safe. It was heavier than he thought it would be.

Hicks laid the bag on the bed and undid the leather straps. He found a metal case roughly the size of a cigar humidor and slid it out of the bag. He opened the metal catches and slowly opened it.

Inside were fifty plastic vials held upright in foam padding.

Fifty vials not of the toxin, but of the antidote. Just like Omar had said.

Hicks didn't know why Samuelson wanted the hundred grand. Maybe he needed it to pay someone off at the airport or docks where the toxin was from?

Hicks knew he was looking at Samuelson's end game. This would be how he'd get rich. Once the outbreak turned into a full-blown pandemic and people started dying in the streets, people of means would pay anything for the antidote.

Hicks heard the gentle ping of the elevator in the hall. He shut the case and gently slid it and the bag under the bed. He didn't expect Samuelson to be armed, but he didn't know if he'd be alone.

Hicks took cover behind the bed and aimed his Ruger at the door.

He watched the door open as Samuelson and another man walked into the room. A tall, dark-skinned man. Painfully thin. Bald with a wiry beard.

They hadn't noticed Hicks until the door was closed. "Don't move. Either of you."

Both men put up their hands without being told to do it. Samuelson grew even paler than he already was, but the dark-skinned man looked calm and cool. "I don't know what you're doing here," he said, a hint of a French accent, "but you have made a terrible mistake. It will cost you your life."

"I've heard that before." Hicks stood up and stepped out from behind the bed.

To Samuelson, he said, "Throw the latch on that door nice and slow. Don't do anything stupid."

Samuelson did as he was told. "We don't want trouble, mister. If it's money you want, I've got money right here in my jacket. It's yours if you just get out of here and leave us alone."

"I didn't come here for money, Samuelson," Hicks said. "I came here for you." He looked at the tall man. "Who's your friend? One of Omar's buddies?"

The tall man's eyes narrowed. "You know of Omar. You must be the man he fears."

"I don't know about that," Hicks said. "I'm a pretty nice guy once you get to know me. As long as you're not trying to kill millions of people, that is."

He pulled some of the plastic cuffs from his back pocket and tossed them on the bed. "Put those on. Pull them tight with your teeth."

Samuelson looked up at the tall man, then back at Hicks. "Look, you seem to know who I am and what I do, okay? We can make a deal, here, man. Let's talk."

"You're going to be doing a lot of talking." Hicks looked up at the tall man and decided to take a gamble. "Just like Omar. And Djebar."

The man didn't say anything, but his eyes said plenty. He knew exactly who Djebar was.

And suddenly, a lot of loose ends began to tie together.

Hicks spoke to the tall man in French. "Who are you working for?"

The tall man finally smiled. "I work for Allah. His will protects me."

"We'll see about that." Hicks shifted the Ruger from

306 / TERRENCE MCCAULEY

Samuelson to him. In English, he said, "Put the ties on. Now."

The man took one of the ties and handed one to Samuelson. "Let us do as he says, doctor. My men will free us when we get outside."

Samuelson watched how the tall man put the ties on his own wrists and did the same. "He's not kidding, man. He's got five real mean looking bastards downstairs."

"We'll see." Hicks didn't let it rattle him. "Turn around and put your hands against the wall."

Samuelson pled his case while Hicks patted them down. "This is bigger than you think it is, man. You don't need this kind of trouble. You CIA boys cut deals all the time, right? We can cut one here, believe me. You could walk away a wealthy man."

Samuelson's pockets came up clean except for a wallet, a hundred in cash and two condoms. Hicks tossed them all on the bed. "I'm not CIA."

As Hicks began patting down the tall man, the man said, "Don't waste your time trying to bargain with him, doctor. He'll be dead in a few moments anyway, so save your breath."

Hicks finished patting down the man's leg and brought his fist up into the man's balls. The man's knees buckled and he fell forward into the wall. Hicks grabbed the tie that bound his hands and pulled it back until his hands were behind his neck and his head was flush against the wall. The man screamed.

"That's the second time you've threatened my life in the last five minutes, asshole. I don't like that. Maybe you've got guys outside and maybe you don't. Anyone shoots at me; you get it in the back."

Hicks let the tall man fall to the floor. He went back to put the metal case back in the bag and pulled it over his shoulder. Then he pulled out his handheld and had OMNI scan the area for security cameras. Anything that could tell him what might be waiting for him outside.

From the floor, the man said, "Are you calling the police? They'll never get here in time and my men will kill them when they do. Unlike you, we do not believe in leaving witnesses behind. Like you did with Djebar's men."

Hicks looked up from the handheld.

The man said, "That's right. Those two guards you left alive were dead fifteen minutes after Djebar failed to check in with us. You have no idea how far we can reach, but soon you will. And by then, it will already be too late."

Hicks went back to the handheld. He couldn't let himself get sidetracked by talk of what may have happened. He had to focus on what was happening now and that meant getting a look at what was waiting for him outside.

OMNI picked up a wireless camera feed from a security camera across the street. Hicks selected it and image came up of a security camera from the building across the street. It was focused on the lot in front of its own building, but Hicks was able to readjust the focus to center on the hotel lot. He saw his Buick right where he'd parked it.

And a red SUV just inside the entrance to the lot. It hadn't been there before, and the motor was running. It didn't look like it planned on staying there long.

Hicks put the handheld away and adjusted the

messenger bag's shoulder strap over his shoulder. "Time to go, boys and girls." He pulled Samuelson off the wall and told the tall man to get up.

He rolled over onto his knees and stood. "If you are a religious man, you should make your peace with your God now because you will not have time when we get downstairs."

Hicks shoved him toward the door. In Arabic Hicks said, "To Him we belong and to Him we shall return."

HICKS PRODDED the tall man and Samuelson down the hallway faster than they would've liked to go. He kept them side by side, making sure they provided him with cover if anyone got off the elevator.

Halfway down the hall, the elevator began to move downstairs.

The tall man said over his shoulder, "Your time is running short. My friends are coming to check on me."

Maybe they were and maybe they weren't. Hicks didn't care. He planned on taking them down the fire stairs anyway.

He dug another tie out of his pocket. "Stop moving." They followed his orders, and he slipped a tie through both their belts and pulled each loop tight. "Now you two are literally tied at the hip. Move to your right and head down the stairs."

"You can't expect us to go downstairs tied like this," Samuelson said as Hicks pushed them into the stair-well. "What happens if one of us trips and falls?"

"Then you either get up, or I put a bullet in both of you." He shoved the tall man by the back of the head.

"Keep that in mind before you pull any shit. You'll get your virgins, but you'll be screaming a long time before you get there."

The two prisoners remained quiet as Hicks urged them down the stairs one step at a time.

As the stairwell door closed, he heard the whir of the elevator starting up on the other side of the stairwell wall. Hicks saw the smirk on the tall man's face and prodded him forward with the barrel of the Ruger. "Keep moving."

They made decent time going down the stairs and made it to the bottom of the stairwell as the elevator reached Samuelson's floor.

There were two doors at the bottom of the stairs. One led to the lobby. The other was the fire door where Hicks' car was just outside.

Hicks pushed them both through it and squinted at the bright noonday sun.

He grabbed the tall man by the belt and pressed the Ruger hard into his back. "You make a sound, and you die. Move toward the Buick. Now!"

Hicks led them over to the sedan and got the back door open when he heard someone call out to them.

Hicks looked up and saw two men begin to get out of the SUV. He pegged them for Somali, too, but shorter and broader. And they'd already spotted their friend standing next to Samuelson, but not Hicks. He was crouched behind them.

The two men called out to the tall man in Arabic, but with Hicks' gun at his back, he didn't say a word.

The two men kept coming. They reached under their coats as they moved.

Hicks pushed his prisoners in the back seat with his left hand, raised his Ruger and fired.

His first shot hit the left gunman on the left center mass through the chest.

The second man broke to dive behind a car, but Hicks' next shot got him through the back before he made it. The man landed on his belly, yelling in Arabic.

Samuelson and the tall man had fallen halfway into the back seat and were trying to get to their feet. Hicks kicked them in the backsides until they crawled onto the back seat on their bellies.

Hicks looked up when he heard someone punch a window. It had come from Samuelson's room.

He'd been spotted and now more gunmen were on their way downstairs.

His troubles weren't over yet.

He shut the back door and ran around to the driver's side and got behind the wheel. He threw the car in reverse until the back bumper was flush against the firewall door.

A few seconds later, he heard banging and cursing from the other side of the door.

"You're dead!" the tall man yelled as best he could with the scientist on top of him. "You have no chance now. They will cut you to ribbons."

Hicks kept the Ruger on his lap as he watched the front door of the hotel. He knew they'd come out that way next.

He didn't have to wait long as two young Somali men of about nineteen or twenty ran out into the parking lot, their pistols drawn. Nine-millimeters, from what Hicks could see. A mean gun.

The tall man in the back cheered them on as they

raised their pistols and emptied them into the driver's side of the Buick. They didn't stop firing until their pistols clicked open and empty.

They had already begun to eject their clips as Hicks lowered the window and shot them both in the chest.

The tall man let out a long, mournful wail.

Hicks raised the window, put the Buick in drive and sped out of the lot before the cops arrived.

Over the tall man's sobbing, Hicks said, "Bullet proof glass and armored plating, Ace. Comes in handy sometimes."

A quarter of a mile away, he pulled into a strip mall parking lot and lowered the back windows. With the tall man and Sampson still piled on top of each other, he slid one plastic cuff through theirs, binding them together, and looped the other end through the inside door handle.

The wail of approaching sirens pierced the air as Hicks got back in the driver's seat and headed back north to Manhattan.

CHAPTER 27

THE CHEAP PLASTIC chair popped as Hicks stretched his legs. A rat scurried along the base of the wall only a few inches from his shoe. It looked well fed and didn't pay Hicks any mind.

He had no idea why Jonathan had insisted on meeting in a dump like this; an old pizza joint in the East Village that had gone out of business more than a year ago. The place looked as dirty and tired as the day they'd closed shop.

In fact, Hicks didn't know why Jonathan had insisted on meeting at all. He hated meetings. He hated the waiting. An emailed response to a report or video conference call was easier. Far more antiseptic. Even the harshest email was better than biting his tongue while someone yelled at him from across a table. And Hicks hadn't been yelled at in a long time.

He looked over at Roger, who was perched on an old bar stool against the wall. Hicks thought about starting up a conversation to pass the time, but Roger was busy tapping away at his phone; smiling and biting his lip at whatever image someone just sent him. Hicks had neither the urge nor the stomach to ask what he was looking at.

That's why he was surprised when he said, "I don't know why you're so worried. You're a hero now."

"Who said I'm worried?"

Roger looked up from his handheld. "Maybe worried is too strong a word. Tense is more accurate. Pensive, even. Either way, there's no reason for concern. Not with all the information you've given them. They're probably going to give you some kind of medal."

Hicks watched a rat descend on a cockroach struggling across the floor. "If they were giving me a medal, we wouldn't be meeting in a shithole like this."

Roger watched the rat begin to eat its catch. "I don't know. I think it has a certain charm to it."

"You would."

Jonathan came out of the kitchen and quietly beckoned them to follow him. He was wearing a charcoal gray suit and a dark red tie; looking very much the banker. That worried Hicks. Jonathan was a J. Crew boy at best and never one for formality. If he was wearing a suit, whoever they were meeting with was important enough to warrant the sartorial effort.

Four plastic chairs had been arranged around a high stainless steel preparation table in the middle of the pizzeria's kitchen. Three of the chairs were empty.

One of them was not.

The man sitting in the chair had his back to the door and didn't turn around when they walked in.

314 / TERRENCE MCCAULEY

He was a black man, maybe sixty years old; neither thin nor heavy. His hair was still mostly dark, but silver highlights had begun to creep in at the sides and back.

Jonathan motioned to Roger and Hicks to take the two chairs on the other side of the table, which they did.

As Hicks sat down, he saw the stranger's face wasn't as full as it should've been, and his brown eyes looked tired. Like the color had been washed out of them long ago.

His shirt used to fit him but looked big on him now. His hands were folded on the table, but Hicks still noticed a slight tremor in his left hand.

Hicks had never seen the man before, but he knew exactly who he was.

And that's why Hicks knew this was not just a regular meeting.

As soon as Jonathan sat down, the stranger began, "You know who I am, don't you?"

"I thought I did when I walked in," Hicks said, "but now that I've heard your voice, I'm sure of it. It's a pleasure to finally meet you, sir."

The Dean neither smiled nor nodded nor unfolded his hands. "Let me guess. I sounded taller on the phone, right?"

Hicks knew what he was implying, but didn't take the bait. "You always sounded and looked different on the phone. I never cared what you looked like, sir. I still don't."

"No, I suppose you wouldn't." He looked at Roger. "What about you?"

"Makes no difference to me either," Roger said, "though I always think men in your position should look like Donald Sutherland for some reason."

The Dean looked at Jonathan. "You were right about him."

Roger laughed. "No one's ever been right about me, sir. Not now. Not ever."

Hicks knew the banter was meant to break the ice. But it only served to make him more anxious.

The Dean's gaze returned to Hicks. "I know how much you hate these face-to-face meetings. You think they're a waste of time and energy. A voice on the phone or an email in an inbox is easier to deal with than flesh and blood. Anonymity in an anonymous world."

Hicks hated that he knew what he was thinking. He hated being easy to read, even by him. "You're very perceptive, sir."

The Dean's eyes narrowed just a bit. "How long have you been working for us?"

"Going on twenty years, sir."

"Eighteen years and four months to the day, to be precise," the Dean said. "One of the smartest hires I ever made. But in all that time we've never met, not even once. You never asked for a meeting and I never offered one. Why do you think we're meeting now?"

"Because something has changed."

"Correct. What do you think has changed?"

"British intelligence made a mistake," Hicks said. "Djebar isn't 'The Moroccan'. The tall man I grabbed in Samuelson's hotel is 'The Moroccan'. Djebar was just a matchmaker and Omar was just a pawn. The Moroccan was in charge the entire time."

"That's one reason," the Dean grinned. "I always get a particular jolt out of proving the British wrong. Don't ask me why. But the intelligence you two have gotten from Samuelson has proven invaluable.We seized the toxin shipment and prevented it from being distributed throughout the country. According to OMNI's estimates, you saved more than a million lives. Keep up the good work."

Hicks flinched as the echo of Samuelson's agony echoed in his ears. He'd never heard a human being make such a sound before. Roger had tried out some new techniques on him. "We will, sir. But that's still not the reason why you wanted to meet. Like I said, something has changed. And it's not just The Moroccan."

"You're a perceptive young man, James. What do you think it is? Speak freely."

Hicks looked at the Dean's skin. The size of his collar. His eyes. The sense he got from him. "You're dying."

Jonathan slapped the table. "Damn it, Hicks. You'll have some respect for..."

But the Dean held up his left hand. It didn't tremble much, but enough for Hicks to notice it better this time.

"You're right. I am dying."

Jonathan sat back in his chair, deflated. Hicks almost felt sorry for him. "What?"

"Cancer in my brain and damned near everywhere else it can go," the Dean told him. "I've fought it as best I could, but the end is near. It's only a matter of time."

"It's always a matter of time, sir," Hicks said. "Some just have a more finite deadline than others. It's what we do with the time we have that counts."

"That's true," the Dean said, "which is the real reason for this meeting. The University existed before me, and it will go on well after I'm dead. This institution has always been about much more than just one person and, it could be argued, it's never been needed more than it is right now. Not even during the Second World War."

Hicks' eyes narrowed. "Because of what we've pulled from Omar and the Moroccan."

The Dean motioned to Jonathan, who took it from there.

"The Moroccan – and I mean the actual Moroccan, may have had his fingerprints removed and undergone facial reconstructive surgery, but by process of elimination, OMNI has been able to determine his likely identity is Mehdi Bajjah. He's a thirty-five-year-old software engineer whose family moved to England when he was an infant. He was educated at Eton and later Trinity College before coming to the United States as a software engineer. Like Samuelson, he'd never been particularly religious and never demonstrated the slightest interest in politics. He married a nice Irish girl living in London and even had three children with her. He had the life any man in his right mind would envy until, one day six years ago, he simply disappeared."

"What do you mean disappeared?" Roger asked.

"Dropped completely off the grid," Jonathan said. "Walked away from his wife, his family, friends. Just went to work one morning in San Jose and never came back. No note, no contact of any kind with his family. His wife wound up on public assistance when the money ran out. She had to move back with her family in Ireland. They had him declared legally dead a year ago."

"He left no trace of Bajjah at all?" Hicks asked. "That's no ordinary software engineer."

Jonathan continued. "No one had seen him or

heard of him until he walked into that hotel room last week with Samuelson. We think the British intelligence on Djebar and Bajjah got jumbled together somewhere along the way and the Brits thought they were looking for one man. Now we know they were always separate. We have no idea where he's been or who he's been with for the past six years. But you're right that software engineers don't just disappear like that. That's why we think he was a sleeper. Someone activated him and he's been involved in some nasty business over the years."

The Dean asked, "Do either of you think there's much more we can get out of Samuelson? Can he help fill in some of Bajjah's missing timeline?"

Hicks deferred to Roger. "Samuelson's resolve isn't quite as firm as it used to be. In his more lucid moments, he's quite emphatic about not being a thief. That he was just doing what he was told." Roger threw open his hands. "I don't know what to make of it, though I don't think it's gibberish."

Jonathan looked down at his hands while the Dean let out a heavy breath.

Hicks knew that sound from their many conversations over the years. "What? What do you know?"

"Once I told our British cousins they were wrong about The Moroccan," the Dean said, "they began to look at the intelligence they had gathered in a new light. Certain facts that had been discarded suddenly became relevant again. A new picture has emerged."

Hicks locked on the Dean. "And what does it look like?"

"It looks like Samuelson is telling the truth. He didn't steal the viruses to sell them on the black market. He didn't steal them at all. The Saudis may have hired Samuelson and his colleagues to study diseases, but the man who controlled the lab ordered them to create the toxin instead. The man who subverted the lab was the same man who provided the funding for it."

"Djebar." Hicks dropped his head in his hands. He rubbed his fingers along his scalp and squeezed his head until his knuckles popped.

It was all so simple, so clear. "Djebar wasn't working for Omar. Omar was working for Djebar and Bajjah."

"In a way," the Dean allowed. "They're all working for someone else. They're part of a greater machinery we're only beginning to understand. We'll find out more in time, but it'll be slow going. Bajjah is proving more resilient than we thought."

Roger smiled. "Give him to me for the weekend and we'll see how tough he is."

"We want him functional," Jonathan said. "The British say you practically turned Djebar into a catatonic. He still screams when the lights are on."

Roger shrugged. "They're so dramatic. I gave him a local and an appendectomy. He thought it was a piece of intestine. I can't help it if he doesn't know basic anatomy."

Hicks' head was spinning. He'd been wrong about everything from the beginning and only saw it now. He'd had everything upside down. About Omar and Djebar and everything.

The Dean snapped him out of it, "Stop kicking yourself in the ass, James. We wouldn't have known any of this if it hadn't been for you and Colin. Christ knows how far those diseases could've spread if we hadn't gotten a lid on it as fast as we did. I think OMNI's predictions were low. You saved countless lives."

Hicks knew it was supposed to make him feel better, but it didn't. He'd helped them contain the outbreak. Over a thousand people had still died, but that was small compared to OMNI's projections.

"We got lucky."

"Luck happens when hard work meets opportunity," the Dean said. "You stopped the immediate threat. Your instincts led us to a wider operation no one knew existed and I mean no one. CIA, NSA, FBI or anyone overseas." He frowned. "But your success comes at a price."

Hicks didn't like the sound of that. "Meaning?"

"Meaning we no longer have the anonymity we once enjoyed," the Dean explained. "Every member of the alphabet soup of intelligence wrote us off as a joke for decades. Now they're all banging at our door with plenty of questions about what we do and how we do it."

Hicks had been expecting something like that. You can't stop a pandemic without drawing some attention. "What does that mean for the University, sir?"

"You've stopped the immediate threat here in New York and whatever Bajjah was planning to do. We think he was looking to start an outbreak in D.C. when Omar's New York operation fell apart, but that's just speculation at this point. What's clear is that Bajjah and Omar and Samuelson are part of a much larger network we didn't know existed. And I'm going to need you to go after them."

"In New York?" Hicks asked.

"Anywhere they are in the world," the Dean said.

"Samuelson's scientist colleagues are still out there. Whoever they're working for know they've been captured. And that shipment we intercepted proves they have a more lethal product now."

Hicks didn't doubt whoever was behind this would try again. "What do you want me to do, sir?"

"This enemy poses the greatest threat to our nation's security since the Cold War. Discovering it has put our autonomy at risk. I'm dying, so I can't hold off our enemies and allies for much longer. That means I need someone who can fight and fight smart. That's why we need you to take my place and become the new Dean of the University."

The words and their meaning landed heavily on him. He felt their impact. He knew their value.

He knew Roger, Jonathan and the Dean were looking at him when he said, "No, sir. My duties at the New York Office are too great and I don't have the experience for the job."

"That's bullshit and you know it," the Dean said. "You're more qualified now than I was when I took the job. But don't worry. I'm not handing you the keys to everything today. It'll be a gradual process. For now, your mission is simple. Find these people, learn everything you can from them and kill them. All of them, before they kill us."

He nodded to Jonathan. "He'll be managing the New York Office while you're hunting our new enemies. He's the only member of the University system who knows what's happening in New York as well as you. As for becoming Dean, I still have a few weeks left, hopefully months. I'll see to it that you grow into the job more each day. When the time comes, your elevation will be a seamless transition. Until then, your primary focus will be on rooting out these new enemies we've uncovered."

Hicks hoped that day would never come but saw no reason to discuss it now. "I'll need some resources for my new assignment, sir."

"I'll alert all the University Office Heads throughout the system that you have the authority to call on them whenever you need it," the Dean said. "But you're an industrious man, James. I'm sure you'll find a way to get what you need with or without my help. And I'm asking Roger here to serve as your Inquisitor in this effort, a role I know he'll appreciate."

Hicks saw Roger looked less than pleased. "I don't want to leave New York." He motioned to Jonathan. "And I sure as hell don't want to work with him."

"Just make sure your den of inequity continues to turn a profit," Jonathan said, "and our interactions will be limited."

To Hicks, Jonathan said, "We won't need you to move out of your Thirty-fourth Street facility yet, but I may have to move in at some point. We'll broach that subject later."

"I'm not going anywhere," Hicks said, "and it's not on Thirty-fourth Street."

The Dean seemed to enjoy the banter. "Happy hunting, James. For all of our sakes."

Neither of them offered to shake hands, so neither did Hicks. He and Roger simply stood up and walked out of the kitchen.

There was plenty of work to do.

Roger took a cab back to his club and offered to open a bottle of champagne to celebrate. He even offered to put the men in leather hoods in another room.

But Hicks declined. He wanted to walk for a bit. He needed to be alone with all that he had just learned.

He knew he should've been at least excited about his promotion but wasn't. Men like Jonathan had ambitions. Hicks had his work. His people. It had always been enough for him. He could see the results of his efforts in hours, not years. He didn't want to spend his life reading reports. He wanted to generate them.

But the University was changing. Everything about this coming fight was different and it meant Hicks would have to act different. He'd have to change, too, if he wanted to win. The battle ahead was one he couldn't afford to lose.

Not change, he decided. Adapt. Adjust. Find a way to win, just as he'd always done.

A light snow began to fall. Some of it had already begun to stick on the cars and sidewalk.

Another storm was rolling in.

Hicks zipped up his jacket. He was ready for it.

*A LOOK AT BOOK TWO: A MURDER
OF CROWS*
BY TERRENCE MCCAULEY

A FAST-PACED CONTEMPORARY THRILLER.

The crows are gathering. War is coming.

For years, every intelligence agency in the world has been chasing the elusive terrorist known only as The Moroccan. But when James Hicks and his clandestine group known as the University thwart a bio-terror attack against New York City and capture The Moroccan, they find themselves in the crosshairs of their own intelligence community.

The CIA, NSA, DIA and the Mossad are still hunting for The Moroccan and will stop at nothing to get him. Hicks must find a way to keep the other agencies at bay while he tries to break The terrorist and uncover what else he is planning.

When he ultimately surrenders information that leads to the most wanted terrorist in the world, Hicks and his team find themselves in a strange new world where allies become enemies, enemies become allies and the fate of the University - perhaps even the Western world - may hang in the balance.

"A fast-moving spy-vs-spy thriller." — **Kirkus Reviews**

COMING DECEMBER 2021

ABOUT THE AUTHOR

Terrence McCauley is an award-winning writer of Thrillers, Crime Fiction and Westerns. A proud native of The Bronx, NY, he currently lives in Dutchess County, NY where he is writing his next work of fiction.

Made in United States
North Haven, CT
03 October 2022

24940675R00200